The Cliff Hangers: The Quarterback

A Cliff Ford Mystery

TERRY TOLER

Cliff Hangers: The Quarterback
Published by: BeHoldings, LLC

Book Cover: BeHoldings Publishing
Editor: BeHoldings Publishing

For information email: terry@terrytoler.com.

Our books can be purchased in bulk for promotional, educational, and business use. Please contact your bookseller or the BeHoldings Publishing Sales department at: *sales@terrytoler.com*

For booking information email: booking@terrytoler.com.
First U.S. Edition: April 2022
Printed in the United States of America

ISBN 978-1-954710-11-5

OTHER BOOKS BY TERRY TOLER

Fiction

The Longest Day
The Reformation of Mars
The Late, Great Planet Jupiter
The Great Wall of Ven-Us
Saturn: The Eden Experiment
The Mercury Protocols
Save The Girls
The Ingenue
Saving Sara
Save The Queen
No Girl Left Behind
The Launch
The Blue Rose
Body Count
Save Me Twice
Cliff Hangers: Anna
Cliff Hangers: Mr. & Mrs. Platt

Non-Fiction

How to Make More Than a Million Dollars
The Heart Attacked
Seven Years of Promise
Mission Possible
Marriage Made in Heaven
21 Days to Physical Healing
21 Days to Spiritual Fitness
21 Days to Divine Health
21 Days to a Great Marriage
21 Days to Financial Freedom
21 Days to Sharing Your Faith
21 Days to Mission Possible
7 Days to Emotional Freedom
Uncommon Finances

Uncommon Health
Uncommon Marriage
The Jesus Diet
Suddenly Free
Feeling Free

For more information on these books and other resources visit terrytoler.com.

Thank you for purchasing this novel from best-selling author Terry Toler. As an additional thank you, Terry wants to give you a free gift.

Sign up for:

Updates
New Releases
Announcements

At terrytoler.com

We'll send you *The Book Club*, free of charge. A fun Cliff Ford Mystery adventure.

1

Champions Bar
Chicago, Illinois

Murders in Chicago were down ninety percent over the last four months. Homicide Detective Cliff Ford wasn't complaining. His workload had dropped proportionately. So much so that the Lieutenant had started assigning him cold cases.

"All because of a football team," Cliff said to his wife, Julia.

They were sitting in *Champions Bar* having a discussion. More about the Chicago Bears than the homicide rate, although they were related.

"I'm seeing the same thing at the women's shelter," Julia said. "We have available beds for the first time since, I don't remember when."

Julia ran a shelter for abused and battered women and young girls.

"It's amazing how a football team affects the mood of a city," Cliff said. "On a weekend when the Chicago Bears win, violent crimes decrease on Monday. When they lose, they increase."

"I guess that's human nature. People live vicariously through their professional sports teams. It's sad, but true."

"Fortunately, the Bears haven't lost a game this year," Cliff noted.

Julia raised her glass of soda. "Here's hoping they win two more."

The crowd in the bar let out a roar. It seemed like the cheer was in response to her toast but that was only a coincidence.

Champions Bar was hopping. The entire city of Chicago was abuzz with Chicago Bears football fever. Today was championship Sunday. The Bears were playing the New York Giants at four o'clock that afternoon, for the right to go to the Super Bowl.

Cliff and Julia were at the bar for brunch and to experience the excitement. More than a dozen televisions were tuned to the NFL pregame shows and a local sports talk station was set up on the dance floor talking about the big game.

Even though kickoff was still a few hours away, the bar was already full of standing room only patrons. Cliff and Julia had gotten there early to get a table. They'd ordered their food but weren't expecting it anytime soon.

The plan was to watch the game at a friend's house, along with a dozen other die-hard Bears fans. Thousands of similar parties were happening across the city. Chicago was basically at a standstill, as the Bears had captured the heart of a city, and all eyes would be on Soldier Field and the big game later that day.

Another reason murders were down. Even the bad guys were football fans and would be glued to a television somewhere.

"I can't believe the Bears are undefeated," Julia said.

Cliff strained to hear her over the din. Occasionally, the radio hosts would say something, and a deafening cheer would go up from the patrons.

"18-0," Cliff said. "That's their record. No NFL team since 1972 has gone undefeated."

"The Miami Dolphins," Julia said with a satisfied grin that she knew who it was.

"That's right," Cliff said. "They were 14-0 in the regular season and won all three playoff games to finish 17-0."

"I remember that."

"How could you remember it? You weren't even born yet," Cliff said jokingly.

Julia was born in Miami and raised by Cuban immigrant parents. Even though she moved to Chicago to go to college several years before, she still had those roots. And the Latin looks. Jet black hair. Mocha colored skin. Intense eyes with heavy dark eyebrows.

Still as gorgeous as the day Cliff met her. Today, she wore jeans and a Bears long sleeve T-shirt. They'd been married for several years, but she still sent a charge through him when she dressed like that.

Really, it didn't matter how she dressed. He always wanted her.

"I know I wasn't born when it happened, but I remember hearing about it," Julia said. "The city of Miami took pride in being the only city with an undefeated team. My dad told us stories about watching Larry Csonka play football."

Cliff nodded.

"Are you impressed that I know the name of the quarterback?" Julia asked with a smug smile.

"Larry Csonka was the running back."

"Darn." Julia frowned, then snapped her fingers in disappointment that she'd gotten that wrong.

"I'm still impressed by you. Especially by that sexy T-shirt you're wearing."

Julia flashed Cliff one of her patented seductive smiles.

Cliff noticed a couple of guys in the bar checking out his wife. He reached over and touched her hand and stroked it for their benefit. She had a wedding ring on her finger, but it didn't hurt to remind all the guys in the bar that she was with him. A public show of affection would do the trick.

Probably not, but he did it anyway.

Julia was oblivious to the other men ogling her.

"The Bears have actually surpassed the Dolphins mark," Cliff said as an afterthought. "The regular season is three games longer now and the Bears won last week's playoff game. So, technically, they've already won more games without a loss than the Dolphins did in 1972."

"It won't matter how many games they win if they don't win the Super Bowl."

"That's true. But don't worry. They'll win it all," Cliff said.

"I hope so."

"They're sixteen-point favorites today against the New York Giants. I don't see anyone beating them. Not with Cole Dillinger as their quarterback."

"He's amazing," Julia said. "And good looking."

She threw that in to tease Cliff.

Cole Dillinger was movie star handsome. Something Cliff was reminded of every day. The Bears quarterback's face was plastered all over Chicago on the side of all the buses. He saw at least a half dozen of those ads on the way to work each morning.

Dillinger had no shortage of endorsement opportunities. The league's MVP was only in his second year, but he'd already set the Bears' single season passing mark and was well on his way to staking a claim as the best NFL quarterback ever.

"At this pace, he'll be the GOAT," Cliff said.

"What do you mean by goat?" Julia asked.

"Greatest of all time, It's an acronym."

"I thought a goat was someone who messed up a play. Somebody who choked."

"You need to stay up with the times. The word has more than one meaning."

"I didn't know."

"Our language is constantly evolving. Stick with me and I'll keep you informed."

"I plan on sticking with you."

"That's good to know. There are a dozen men in this bar who'd love it if you dumped me."

"Only a dozen?" she quipped, and grinned so he'd know she was kidding. "I'd think it would be a lot more than that."

Cliff twisted his lips to the side in response to the snarky comment he deserved.

She changed the subject back to how words were twisted in their society. "You're right about the language. I heard someone at work talking about how *bad* Cole is. I started to argue with her and tell her he's really good. She agreed with me. It seems *bad* means good these days."

Cliff laughed after swallowing another gulp of his drink. He'd need it refilled soon.

"I heard someone on the radio say that Cole was *sick*. I thought they meant he was literally sick. It had me worried that he might miss the game. The Bears would lose for sure without him. Our backup quarterback is not that good."

"My young girls at the shelter use the word *sick* all the time. Sick means good. I think it's *sick* to change the meaning of words like that."

A picture of Cole Dillinger flashed on all the televisions at once.

"There's your man," Cliff said, pointing at the screens.

"You're my man," Julia corrected him, after she looked. "Besides, he's not my type. He's too good looking."

"Ouch."

She tilted her head to the side when Cliff frowned at her.

"I didn't mean to imply that you aren't good looking," she said. "What I meant to say is, that *you* are more my type. A strong, manly man. A man with a gun in his hand is way sexier than one holding a football."

She was trying hard to get out of the hole she had dug for herself.

This same conversation was probably happening all over Chicago. The handsome quarterback had single handedly increased the female viewership of NFL football games and Cliff knew for a fact that it made some husbands and boyfriends jealous.

A couple of months ago, in an upscale neighborhood in Chicago, a husband became upset at his wife for paying too much attention to a Bears game when she'd never watched them before. She made a comment about how sexy Cole Dillinger looked in tight football pants.

An argument ensued and she ended up dead.

Cliff decided now was the time to get the conversation off the quarterback's looks.

"They call Cole Dillinger the best gunslinger since John Dillinger," he said.

"I've heard that name, John Dillinger. Who's he?"

Sometimes Cliff forgot that Julia didn't know a lot about the history of Chicago. He was born and raised there so he had that advantage and would use it to educate her.

"John Dillinger was a gangster," Cliff explained.

Julia seemed interested, so he continued. If she got a faraway look and gave him a forced smile, he'd move on to another topic.

"He lived back in the 1920's and 30's. A mean son of a gun. He robbed banks and murdered hundreds of people. Maybe thousands. His band of killers were called the Dillinger Gang. They call the Bears offensive line, the Dillinger Gang."

"I'm not sure it's a good idea to compare our great quarterback and his offensive line to gangsters."

"I don't disagree with you. Especially since I deal with gangsters almost every day of the week at work."

Cliff faced down gunslingers for a living. He preferred that his entertainment not remind him of his job.

"There are a lot of gun references in football," Cliff said pensively. "The quarterback has a rifle of an arm, or a cannon. When he takes the snap, he's in the shotgun formation."

Julia feigned interest so he decided to shock her attention back to the conversation.

"Did you know the Bears backup quarterback tried to commit suicide?" he said, in his most serious tone.

She sat straight up in her chair.

"No! When did that happen?"

"It didn't work. The bullet was intercepted."

"That's a horrible joke!"

"He tried to kill himself a second time, but he fumbled the gun."

"Cliff Ford, you're terrible!"

Cliff laughed more than he should have at his corny jokes.

On the football field, it wasn't funny. The Bears backup quarterback was known to throw a lot of interceptions and fumble a lot.

A cheer went up in the bar, and Cliff pretended it was for him and his jokes.

After the decibels in the bar got back down to a dull roar, he continued telling her about Dillinger the gangster.

"John Dillinger was born in Indiana," Cliff said, "just across the state line. He wreaked a lot of havoc in Chicago and all through the Midwest."

"Interesting."

He could tell she didn't mean it, so he got to the juicier part.

"Dillinger was gunned down by FBI agents, not far from here. At the *Biograph Theater* on Lincoln Avenue."

"I've seen that place."

She sat forward in the chair and put her elbows on the table like she wanted to know more.

A clip of Cole Dillinger throwing a touchdown pass came on the screen. The crowd in the bar went wild. So, Cliff quit talking. He could barely hear himself think much less carry on a serious conversation. Between the crowd and the radio announcers, Cliff's voice was starting to get raspy anyway.

He took a swig of his soda to wet his dry throat. As he did, he felt a vibration on his hip meaning his phone was going off. He unhooked the cell phone from his belt and looked at the text alert.

His mouth flew open.

He couldn't believe what he was seeing.

"What is it?" Julia asked, reacting to the surprise that had to be written all over Cliff's face.

Cliff stared at the television screens. Lost in thought. Trying to consider all the ramifications of the words on his phone.

"We gotta go," he finally said.

"We haven't gotten our food yet," she replied.

Cliff signaled for a waitress. When he got her attention, he asked for a check.

"What's wrong?" Julia asked. "Why are we leaving without eating our food?"

"I'll tell you when we get outside."

Cliff paid the check and escorted his wife out of the bar.

"Will you tell me what's happening?" she demanded. "You're scaring me."

He didn't say anything. He took her by the arm and walked quickly to their car.

"Get in," he said.

Once inside the car, he didn't start it right away. He just sat there. Stunned.

"For the umpteenth time, what is it, Cliff?" Julia asked in a stern voice. "Tell me what happened."

"I got a text from the Lieutenant."

Cliff said the words slowly for effect.

"I figured it had to do with work," she said. "I thought you were off today."

"I'm supposed to be. But Cole Dillinger is dead. He was found murdered at his house this morning. About thirty minutes ago. The Lieutenant wants me there, A.S.A.P."

2

The drive to Cole Dillinger's house would take about twenty minutes. Enough time for Cliff to organize his thoughts and mentally open a murder book, but not enough time to wrap his head around all the ramifications involved in the starting quarterback of the Chicago Bears being murdered the day of the big game.

Cliff had risen through the ranks to senior detective. He was the one his Lieutenant turned to for the more difficult and high-profile cases. The murder of Cole Dillinger would be his case to solve.

It didn't get any higher profile than this.

The FBI might even be called in if Cliff requested it.

On the drive over, Cliff thought about any scenarios where he might want to get help from the Feds. Usually, they were only contacted when a federal interest was involved. Such as, if the murder occured on federal property, involved a federal employee like a judge, or there was some kind of hate crime or civil rights violation.

If organized crime or an international concern was behind the killing, they'd definitely be called in. If terrorism, it'd be their jurisdiction for sure. If it affected interstate commerce or the murderer traveled across state lines, there could also be a fight over jurisdiction. Even if the killer sent something through the US Mail or wired money through the federally regulated banking system, the FBI would need to be involved.

Too early to know if any of those applied.

Regardless, Cliff would be under intense pressure and scrutiny which he was starting to feel. His shoulders were tense. He moved his neck from side to side to try and release some of the tightness.

When his thoughts turned to the media, the tension increased two-fold. The national networks would report on this case. It'd be one of the priority news stories for the next few weeks. He'd never really had to deal with that before.

If he found the killer and it went to trial, he could imagine a media circus at the courthouse. The trial would be televised, if the judge permitted cameras in the courtroom. He'd have to testify. Justify the arrest. There'd be a lot of pressure on him and the DA to get a conviction.

If he didn't succeed, this could have a negative impact on his career. There was no upside other than maybe fifteen minutes of fame. The downside was enormous. He could be the goat. The one who botched the highest profile murder case since the days of John Dillinger. Or Jimmy Hoffa and the Chicago 8, which were more recent celebrity trials.

Local officials like the mayor and state officials including the governor would all be in his business, wanting constant updates. Second guessing his decisions. Strong arming him if they didn't like the decisions he made.

Cliff rubbed his eyes roughly with one hand while steering the car with the other.

He was getting way ahead of himself.

He should be thinking about the case and formulating a game plan. Instead, he was worrying about the periphery. The chatter that hadn't yet started.

He couldn't help but think that this case could be a blessing or a curse. A triumph or a nightmare. At the very least, it might cause him a lot of sleepless nights.

Julia knew enough to keep quiet when Cliff was deep in thought like this. She obviously could sense his angst and had probably already realized some of the same things he was thinking. About halfway to Cole Dillinger's house, she broke the silence.

"Do you think they'll cancel the game?" she asked.

He welcomed the interruption. His thoughts were getting out of control. Although, admittedly, he hadn't even thought about the game set to kick off in a few hours. A thousand complications were now screaming for attention in his head.

First and foremost, what would happen if the Bears lost the game?

They probably would.

The town would explode in riots. The murder rate would sky-rocket again.

An awkward silence filled the vehicle.

He took too long to answer Julia's question. He didn't want her to think he was ignoring her, so he stated an opinion.

"I wouldn't think they'd cancel it," Cliff said slowly and thoughtfully. "I mean, tickets are already sold. The game's televised. All the national media is in Chicago for the game. Millions of dollars are at stake. I think they have to play the game."

Truthfully, he didn't know what they'd do. He could only imagine what the owner and commissioner of the NFL would be going through once they learned about the murder. Whatever decision they made would be a difficult one.

Cliff thought about the coach. Imagine the shock he'd feel. The human tragedy for sure. The loss. He might also see the hopes of a Super Bowl Championship slipping out of his grasp.

What about the players?

Their worlds were about to be turned upside down. All the hard work could be for nothing. What a letdown that would be. Most players went through their whole careers never getting a chance to play in the Super Bowl. Cole Dillinger was their best chance. They could still win, but the odds were against them.

How would they have the emotional strength to go out and overcome the adversity? Would they even be in the right state of mind to win the game?

Of course, there was the personal tragedy to consider. Cole Dillinger had a family. The game was important, but probably the last thing on his mother and father's minds. They would be devastated.

Once again, Julia interrupted his thoughts. "Maybe they'll postpone it. Since the Bears will have to play the game with their backup quarterback."

"They'll have to play with their backup either way. Even if the game is postponed, Cole Dillinger will never play another down of football."

That thought brought a momentary sadness into his soul. He didn't tamp it down like some detectives. An emotional connection to the case helped him. He liked having sympathy for the victims. It made him remember why he did what he did. To solve the crimes. To put bad guys behind bars for the victim's sake. To make Chicago a safer place for everyone.

"It's such a tragedy," Julia said. "Cole was so young."

"A tragedy for the entire city."

"Who would do such a thing?"

Cliff hadn't even begun to think about possible suspects. He usually preferred to wait to see the crime scene. No use wasting mental energy coming up with possible scenarios in his mind when the clues at the murder scene might lead him in a totally different direction.

He didn't offer a response to Julia's question for that reason.

"I can think of a few suspects," Julia said. "Do you want to hear them?"

"Sure. Tell me your thoughts. This early in the investigation, everyone is a suspect."

Julia had incredible instincts when it came to murder investigations. He often ran things by her, especially when he was at a dead end in a case. She'd helped him solve more cases than he could remember. At least pointed him in the right direction on many occasions.

"Deuce Dixon was the first person I thought of," she said emphatically.

"The backup quarterback?"

"He has a motive. He's the starting quarterback now. With a chance to go to the Super Bowl."

Cliff didn't dismiss the thought out of hand. That was incredibly insightful on Julia's part. Unlikely. But a thread he'd have to pursue. It seemed like Dixon would have more to gain if the Bears went to the Super Bowl and they won. He'd get the Super Bowl bonus given to the players of the winning team. He'd also get the experience of being there.

He'd also get a coveted Super Bowl ring. Women would be impressed by the ring. A conversation piece at every bar in town. Most people wouldn't remember that he didn't play a down.

On the other hand, if Dixon led the Bears to a Super Bowl victory, he might be in line for a big contract with another team or an extension with the Bears. He'd be beloved by the city. Right now, he was the punch line for a lot of jokes. The least respected player on the team.

This was why Cliff didn't like to think about suspects this early on. His mind was processing scenarios that might be a waste of time. Deuce Dixon most likely had an alibi. He was almost certainly with the team when the murder occurred.

A burning question suddenly popped into Cliff's mind. Why wasn't Cole Dillinger with the team?

Cliff knew for a fact that the entire team stayed at a hotel the night before a game. Even a home game. That was an NFL rule.

One of the first questions he needed to ask the coach.

"The backup quarterback is certainly someone to look into," Cliff said, so Julia would know he appreciated the comment.

"What about gamblers?" she asked.

That thought had entered his mind when he saw the text at the bar. Millions of dollars were wagered on pro football. The betting line was sixteen points with the Bears as favorites. There's virtually no way they'd cover the spread now. A huge bet on the New York Giants would pay off big time.

The gambler would only place that bet after he knew Dillinger was dead. Cliff made a mental note to investigate large wagers that came in on the Giants that morning.

If the gamblers were from out of state, this was a scenario where the FBI might be called in.

Cliff thought of something along the same vein.

"What about a fan?" he asked. "There might not be a financial motive. Just an emotional one."

Julia laughed.

"That narrows it down. How many people live in New York? Twenty million?"

"Not all of them are Giants fans. The New York Jets play there as well. So that cuts the suspect list in half."

"So, you have to investigate ten million fans," Julia quipped. "That should make your job a lot easier."

Cliff sighed loud enough for her to hear it.

This job wasn't going to be easy, regardless. The worry was already raging inside of him.

A momentary pause ensued as they were both thinking. Since Julia had started him down the road of considering suspects, he couldn't help but think about it.

"It could be something simpler than that," Cliff said, as much for his benefit as Julia's. "You said so yourself. Back at the bar. Cole Dillinger is, er... was, a good-looking guy. He's probably had his share of hookups. Girls throw themselves at professional athletes. The Bears, I'm sure, have groupies. He might've gotten involved with the wrong girl."

He'd ask some team members if they saw Cole with a woman the night before. Maybe someone hanging around the hotel.

"Most murders are crimes of passion and are killed by someone they know," Julia said. "Am I right? A woman could be behind it. Maybe not a groupie. A girlfriend. Another woman's husband. He might've been having an affair."

"Yep. A famous rich football player like Cole Dillinger can have any woman he wants. Even married ones."

"He can't have me," Julia said. "I'm married."

She waved her wedding ring in the air.

"I stand corrected," Cliff said. "He can have any woman he wants, except you."

"He wouldn't want me."

"Are you kidding me? You'd be the first person he'd choose."

"He's not going to be dating anybody. Not anymore." She said it soberly, bringing the banter to a crashing halt.

"It's a real tragedy," Cliff said.

"You know there's going to be a lot of pressure on you to solve the case."

Was she asking a question or making a statement?

"I know."

"Cole Dillinger is a celebrity in Chicago," Julia continued. "He's as big as it gets. The Lieutenant is going to expect you to work this case 24/7. I may not see you much over the next few weeks."

Don't remind me.

"When I took this job," Cliff said, "I vowed to work just as hard on behalf of a poor kid in south Chicago as I did a rich businessman in Lincoln Park. That's what I intend to do. Cole Dillinger is just another murder victim in my mind."

He doubted the Lieutenant would see it the same way.

"That's what I love about you."

"I thought what you loved about me was my sense of humor."

"Yeah. That's it," she said sarcastically. "I'm sorry, Cliff. But you're not that funny."

Her hand was back on his head, lovingly stroking his hair, which sent a warmth through his heart.

15

"You're right, though," Cliff said. "A lot of people will be looking over my shoulder. If I can't solve it for some reason—"

Julia interrupted him. "Don't even speak it. You will solve it. I have faith in you."

The words were penetrating. A moment of self-doubt had crept in. Never a good thing this early in the investigation. Cliff had seen it many times. Especially with young detectives. When they feel pressured to solve a case, they make mistakes. Overlook clues. Get too focused on one thread and ignore the real ones.

"Let me put it this way," Julia said. "If this case *can* be solved, you *will* solve it. I can't imagine a better person to investigate it."

"I appreciate that. Sometimes a little luck helps as well. Maybe I'll catch a break early on."

About that time, they arrived at the guardhouse at the entrance of the gated subdivision. Cliff flashed his badge and was motioned through.

"Wow," Julia cried out. Her eyes were as wide as a receiver who'd just caught a touchdown pass as they drove by the massive houses in one of the wealthiest neighborhoods in Chicago.

Cliff had been in the subdivision before. Julia probably hadn't seen houses this big before today other than on television.

"I'd hate to have to clean that house," Julia said, pointing to one particularly large mansion.

"I doubt they clean it themselves. They can afford maids."

"I suppose."

Cliff came to a stop in front of Cole Dillinger's house where there was a flurry of activity. Forensics was already there. As was the coroner. Clearly, people didn't consider this a normal case. He sometimes had to wait hours for forensics and the coroner to show up at a crime scene.

Thankfully, Cliff didn't see a news truck. The media apparently hadn't gotten word of Cole's death. Knowing the Lieutenant, he was trying to keep it under wraps as long as possible. The first few hours of an investigation were usually the most important. It'd be complicated by a swarm of media.

In this case, the national media. Cliff could imagine that once word leaked out, the networks and cable channels would interrupt regular programing and talk about this murder nonstop for a while. The talking heads, the so-called experts, would be on every television and radio station postulating on what might've happened to Cole Dillinger and what the investigators were looking at.

This might be the biggest story to hit the news in a long time.

And Cliff was going to be right smack dab in the middle of it.

A jolt of nervousness came on him again. Usually, he got an adrenaline rush when he arrived at a murder scene. That same rush was there today but also accompanied by a weight. A burden. Pressing down on his chest.

A voice in his head asking why he hadn't solved the case already.

The self-doubt.

Another voice saying he was in over his head. That he'd never be able to solve this case.

Before he stepped out of the car, he looked over at Julia who smiled reassuringly. As if she sensed the inner turmoil.

That made him feel better. He asked her to come in with him. Having her near him would help calm his nerves. When they got inside the house, he was immediately met by the Lieutenant who acted like his hair was on fire.

He pulled Cliff to the side.

"The news just hit the airwaves," the Lieutenant said excitedly. "I held it off as long as I could. All hell is about to break loose. I don't have to tell you how important this case is. I want it solved. Find the killer. Sooner rather than later. Understood?"

The anxiety and self-doubt returned with a vengeance.

3

Ironically enough, Dick 'Buddy' Martin's biggest coaching break came when he was out of coaching. Five years before, he'd been fired by the Tampa Bay Buccaneers and was out of football altogether.

When the Chicago Bears lost their final game of the season three years ago to the Tampa Bay Buccaneers, another irony, they secured the first pick in the NFL draft and the Bucs the second. The Bears took Cole Dillinger, which was a no-brainer. The Bucs took a running back with the second pick, who blew out his knee in training camp and had yet to see the field.

The Chicago Bears hired Buddy Martin as their coach two weeks before the draft. He had an abysmal losing record as a head coach, but also had forty years of coaching experience as an assistant. The Bears wanted a stabilizing figure to work with their young upstart quarterback, Cole Dillinger.

Buddy's personality wasn't conducive for the role of head coach. He was abrasive and terse with the media. He was overly controlling and a micro manager. Because of that, his assistants didn't like him, and he had a hard time keeping them from leaving to greener pastures.

He was tough as nails as an old school, hard-nosed coach who borderline abused his players in practice. So most of the players hated him. Too many times, he'd get in a player's face and rip him a new one with colorful language that'd make a drunken sailor blush.

For all his faults, Buddy Martin was the right coach at the right time for the Chicago Bears. With Cole Dillinger at the helm, the Bears won six games the first year. A huge improvement.

The next year they won seventeen games in a row and Buddy, who was pushing seventy, had suddenly ballooned his career record to 29-30. A win today brought him even for his career and a Super Bowl win would give him a winning record.

After the Super Bowl, he planned on retiring. This was his chance to go out on top. At the pinnacle of his game. Accomplishing what few coaches only dreamed about. Winning a world championship.

Another irony. The Super Bowl was considered the world championship even though the only NFL teams competing for the coveted prize were from the United States.

Few people gave Buddy the credit for the incredible run, but that hardly mattered to him. Winning was the only thing that mattered. He thanked God every night in his prayers that he had Cole Dillinger leading his team. The man was the best player Buddy had ever coached. The best he'd ever seen play for that matter.

How did he get so lucky? Buddy couldn't help but wonder if things were too good to be true.

He tried to push aside every worry and focus on today's game. Although one of the NFL's strongest believers in Murphy's Law, Martin was confident. His defense was suspect, but his offense made up the difference.

The game plan was set. His team was prepared. Cole Dillinger could win the game against the New York Giants with one arm tied behind his back. As long as it wasn't his throwing arm.

Buddy was in the conference room of the team hotel at the *Regency Hotel* in downtown Chicago. He was putting the final touches on the game plan with his offensive coordinator. They were poring over the plays to call in short yardage situations.

"The secondary of the Giants is full of holes," coordinator Jim Glass said. "We should pass the ball as often as we can. Even in short yardage."

"I don't disagree. But we have to keep the defense honest," Buddy said. "Throw in a running play every now and then."

Buddy had always been a proponent of 'three yards and a cloud of dust.' In other words, run the ball on almost every down. His offenses had always been boring. Based on pounding the ball down the opposing team's throats and wearing them down.

Coaching Cole Dillinger had taken some getting used to for the old ball coach. Dillinger's strength was passing the ball. And the Bears defense wasn't good enough to get into a defensive struggle. They had to outscore their opponents. Which Cole Dillinger was able to do.

So Buddy made the adjustment and the team thrived.

"I will run the ball some," Coach Glass said, "but stopping the run is the Giants' strength. They're vulnerable to the pass. I think we can hit some deep balls early and open things up. They'll have to take those big linebackers out and put in an extra defensive back. I wouldn't be surprised if they start out that way."

"Let 'em stack the secondary. We'll hit them with underneath routes. Out routes. Bubble screens. The tight end will be open all day long."

"Cole doesn't like to throw to the tight ends or running backs. He likes to go for the home run. You know how he is."

"I think the home run will be there. The Giants can't stop him."

"I agree," Coach Glass said with a confident smirk. "Cole is going to have a field day. I predict he'll throw for five hundred yards and five touchdowns."

"That'd be nice. I think the record is five touchdown passes in an NFC championship game. Six in the playoffs including the Super Bowl."

"I'd like to break those records."

Glass also had a lot riding on the game. He wanted to use the success to springboard into a head coaching position. The two men needed to keep the eye on the main goal. Win the game. There was no legacy for Buddy and no head coaching job for Glass if they didn't.

Vince Lombardi, one of the greatest coaches of all time, famously said, 'Winning isn't everything. It's the only thing.'

The only goal should be to get to the Super Bowl.

"If we get up by three or four touchdowns in the second half, you should put Dixon in," Glass said.

Buddy let out a groan. Deuce Dixon was the backup quarterback.

"I don't know," Buddy retorted. "We'll have to be up by at least four touchdowns for me to even consider it. We could put Dixon in, but if he throws a pick six, the Giants are right back in the game. Too big a risk."

"The bigger risk is Cole getting hurt. We'll need him for the Super Bowl. You don't want to risk an injury when the game's already decided."

"I hope we have that problem. We can make that decision when the time comes. Truthfully, I don't want to play Dixon even in a mop-up role. The guy stinks."

"I'll have him hand off the ball and run out the clock. He doesn't even have to throw a pass."

That sounded like a good idea.

Before Buddy could respond further, the door to the conference room opened and the quarterback's coach, Ken Thomas, entered the room.

"Have you guys seen Dillinger?" he asked.

"He should be downstairs," Buddy said. "At the team meal, with everyone else."

"I just came from there. He wasn't with the team. That's why I'm asking."

Buddy's heart skipped a beat. He wasn't sure why. There could be a hundred reasons why Cole wasn't there.

"Did you ask Moose?" Buddy asked.

Moose Crowley was the starting left tackle and Cole's roommate when the team traveled or stayed at the *Regency Hotel* for a home game.

Ken nodded.

"I did. Moose hasn't seen him. He said when he woke up this morning, Cole was already gone."

"Check down at the fitness area," Buddy said in an annoyed voice.

He wasn't sure why Ken was bothering him over something so trivial.

"I did. He wasn't there."

A lava of anger boiled up inside of Buddy.

"Look again!" he barked. "How would I know where he is? He's here somewhere. Check the pool. Check his room. Check the lobby. He might be talking to a pretty girl down there. Leave us alone! We're in the middle of something here."

Ken's shoulders sagged. "I'll look again," he said, and skulked out of the room.

Buddy rubbed his eyes. He hated interruptions. It made him lose his train of thought.

"I wonder where Cole is," Coach Glass said.

"He's probably down in the fitness room pumping iron. Maybe he's in the hot tub getting his body loose. Or on the training table getting a massage."

"He's supposed to be with the team. The team meal is mandatory."

Technically, a player was fined if he missed the team meal. Ten thousand dollars for the first offense. Buddy wasn't even considering it. Not on Championship Sunday. Normally, he wouldn't want to show favoritism to his star quarterback, but no one would fault him for ignoring a minor discretion in this instance.

After the Super Bowl, he was out of there. Between now and then, he didn't want any distractions for his team. He wanted Cole

Dillinger in the right frame of mind. Not fuming over a ten thousand dollar fine.

Besides, Cole was as dependable as it got. He was always on time for meetings and never missed an offseason workout. He was a vocal leader on the team. He'd been named team captain for a reason. The players loved him. They'd probably be more upset than Cole if the coach fined his starting quarterback.

"He's probably in the film room," Coach Glass speculated.

"That's a thought. I think you're right. That's got to be where he is. Thomas ought to be there with him. Not chasing his tail around the hotel."

Cole Dillinger was a film junkie. In some ways, he over prepared for a game. He spent too much time watching film. That's just how he was. Meticulous in his preparations. He studied game film until his eyes hurt. That's one of the things that made him so great.

"I wonder if Dixon is with him in the film room," Buddy joked, already knowing the answer.

Deuce Dixon was the antithesis of Cole. He only did what the coaches made him do. He'd never step in the film room unless required to do so.

A career backup, Dixon earned two million dollars a year to hold a clipboard on the sideline and was happy doing it. One of the least motivated football players Buddy had ever met. They only signed him because he knew the playbook. He'd been the third stringer on Glass's old team where they ran the same offense.

That's why they signed Dixon. To be the third string quarterback. The last resort. To have an extra body at practice.

When their backup quarterback got hurt in training camp, Dixon moved into that position. They tried to find someone else, but all the best players were already on other teams. Dixon was the best choice they had.

Buddy made peace with it and held his breath every time Cole Dillinger took a big hit. Thankfully, they made it through the season, with Cole only suffering minor bumps and bruises. Two more games and they were the Super Bowl Champs and Buddy could ride off into the sunset as a winner and quit worrying about Cole Dillinger's health.

Ken Thomas appeared at the doorway again.

"Cole's not downstairs," he said. "I can't find him anywhere."

Buddy let fly a flurry of expletives. Neither Glass nor Thomas flinched. They were used to it.

Buddy stood from his chair and said, "If you want something done right, you have to do it yourself. I'll find Dillinger. You go back down to the cafeteria. I'll send him there when I find him."

After Thomas left, Buddy sat back down.

"Are we done here?" Buddy asked roughly.

"I think so," Glass said after taking a minute to look through his notes.

"Good. I'm going to go find Cole."

As they exited the conference room, Ken Thomas was on the other side of the door talking to another one of their assistants.

The conversation sounded intense.

"What are you doing?" Buddy asked Ken. "I told you to go be with the team."

"You need to go back to the conference room," Thomas said. His voice sounded as serious as a terminal illness diagnosis.

"Why?"

"Turn on the television. You'll see why."

Buddy and Coach Glass went back into the conference room. The remote to the television was on the conference table. Buddy picked it up and pushed the on button.

What was so important that he needed to see?

His knees wobbled when he saw the large red headline news alert on the screen.

COLE DILLINGER DEAD AT AGE 24.

4

The crime scene looked staged. Even Julia noticed it.

"Something doesn't seem right," she said. "The body seems off. Like it doesn't fit there."

Cole Dillinger was lying on his bed in the master bedroom. Face down. His right arm to his side. His left arm above his head, which was turned to the right. His right leg was bent slightly. In an awkward sleeping position.

He was also wearing sweatpants, a T-shirt, with no socks or shoes. A bullet hole was clearly visible on his back. The white T-shirt had a slight red dot below his shoulder blades. Near where his heart would be.

At first glance, it looked like he was in bed asleep and was shot in the back. But that didn't seem right.

Cliff also noticed that Julia didn't seem herself.

"Are you okay?" he asked her.

She was as white as a sheet.

"I need some air," she said, and took off with no hesitation toward the sliding glass doors leading to the outside.

Those doors opened out into the pool area. Julia walked through them like she couldn't wait to get out of there. Which seemed strange. Was she queasy from seeing the dead body?

Julia had seen several dead bodies while with him on a case. This crime scene was not nearly as bad as most.

Something was bothering her. He put it out of his mind and went to work but reminded himself to ask her later.

"What can you tell me?" he asked Jan, the forensic team member who was examining the body.

"Hello, Detective Ford. It's good to see you again."

He nodded.

"I'd say the subject has been dead for about an hour and a half."

Cliff looked at his watch. It was getting close to ten. That meant the time of death was about eight thirty that morning.

"He died of a gunshot wound to the back," Jan added.

"I see that. Did he die here?" Cliff asked. "The body looks staged."

He couldn't pinpoint a reason why he thought that. He just knew something was off. In his subconscious. It could be anything. His mind had a certain expectation when he saw a crime scene. For whatever reason, alarm bells were going off inside causing him to be skeptical of it.

"He was killed on the bed," Jan said.

Oh well.

Sometimes his eyes played tricks on him.

"I also think the body was staged," she said.

Cliff felt his heart rate increase by a few beats per minute. He was right. Now he was anxious to find out why she thought so too.

Jan motioned for him to come closer and stand next to the bed. She touched Cole's head and pushed back some strands of hair. Cliff could see matted blood. Not visible before because of Cole's thick head of hair.

Jan continued her explanation in a scientific sounding voice. Something you'd expect from someone with her experience. The Lieutenant had called in the best of the best to work the scene. Cliff was glad to have her. There wouldn't be any mistakes.

"The subject suffered a blow to the head," she said. "With some kind of blunt object. The coroner will have to render a guess on what that object might be. I think the blow knocked him out and the subject was carried to the bed. Still alive. Then, he was shot in the back. The body was arranged into this position."

That scenario matched what Cliff was seeing.

Cole's shoes and socks were also strewn on the floor at the foot of the bed. That didn't match what he expected to see. The rest of the house was immaculate. Perfectly kept. Cliff could see Cole's closet which was off the bedroom. The door was open, and a dozen shoes were perfectly organized.

The quarterback didn't seem like the type to just toss his shoes on the ground and lay down in bed to take a nap with all his clothes on. And why would he be napping at eight thirty in the morning, on the day of the biggest game in his young career?

He wouldn't.

"Anything else I should know about?" Cliff asked.

"I think that's all."

That was a lot. More than he usually had to work with. Often forensics didn't provide any useful information for weeks. After drug toxicology tests were performed and DNA and fingerprints were processed in a lab. Although, with this high-profile case, Cliff could push some buttons and the powers-that-be would see that the labs turned around their results in twenty-four to forty-eight hours.

Cliff hoped to have the case solved before then. He often did. He never waited for forensics. He put more weight on the investigation. Questioning witnesses. Looking people in the eye. Developing suspects. That's where the breaks usually came from.

As soon as possible, he needed to dive into every aspect of Cole Dillinger's life. To find out who would have a motive. The twenty million New Yorkers comment by Julia aside, he could narrow it down fairly quickly by questioning the right people.

He just needed to know who they were. A list had already formed in his mind. Coaches. Players. Family members. Love interests. He'd definitely pursue the gambling thread.

The most obvious place to start was the person who found the body. A pool worker. The Lieutenant had filled him in. The man was sitting outside by the pool with instructions not to leave until he gave a statement to the investigator.

Cliff's first question to the pool guy would be, why does Cole Dillinger need a pool worker in January? The weather in Chicago was brutal that time of year. Although, the city was having a heat wave at the moment. The high today was a balmy forty-eight degrees.

Cliff thanked Jan, and exited the master bedroom, out the same door Julia went through. When he saw steam rising from the water, he got his answer as to why Cole Dillinger needed a pool guy in the wintertime. The pool was heated. A hot tub was also off to the side and would need maintenance as well.

Julia was standing to his right and not looking so good. Her eyes looked pained, and her normally chipper smile was absent.

He'd check on her after he questioned the pool worker. The man sat on a pool chair to Cliff's left with a goofy smile on his face.

As Cliff approached, the man stood and stuck out his hand offering a handshake. Cliff didn't take it. After he questioned the man, he'd have forensics check the man's hands for gunpowder residue. He didn't want to do anything to contaminate them by touching him.

Cliff flashed his badge.

"My name is Cliff Ford. I'm a homicide detective. I want to ask you a few questions."

"My name's Justin Jackson. Ask away."

The pool guy seemed awfully cheery for someone who'd just discovered a body.

Justin Jackson was six foot two or so and weighed about one eighty. Sandy blonde hair. California surfer dude type, although Cliff didn't like to profile someone too soon in the process. First impressions were often wrong.

"I discovered the body," he blurted out.

That seemed strange. Most people waited for Cliff to ask questions before offering information.

"What time was that?" Cliff asked.

"About eight forty-five this morning."

Jan said the time of death was around eight thirty.

"Tell me what you saw."

"I arrived at the house and came directly to the backyard to work on the pool. I saw that the door to Mr. Dillinger's bedroom was open. Those sliding glass doors."

He pointed at them, and Cliff instinctively looked. He also saw Julia still off to the side pacing around the pool, with her hand on her stomach.

"I went to check it out," Justin said. "That's when I found Mr. Dillinger lying on the bed. I checked for a pulse and then called 911."

"Why is your head wet?" Cliff asked.

"I took a dip in the pool."

"Why?"

That struck Cliff as an odd thing for a professional pool worker to do.

"It's a nice pool, man. It's also part of my job. To check it out. Make sure everything's in working order."

"Do you usually go for a swim in the pools you service?"

He shrugged his shoulders. "The boss man don't mind if I use the pool."

Cliff wasn't sure if he was referring to his own boss or to Cole Dillinger.

Either way, the explanation made sense. This was a luxury house. Jackson wouldn't be the first hired hand to help himself to the amenities. It still seemed too cold to take a swim and then get out with wet hair and work on the pool afterwards. Why not take the swim after he was finished working on the pool?

"Did you get in the pool right away?" Cliff asked.

"As soon as I got here."

"I thought you got here and saw the sliding doors open and went inside and found the body."

Jackson became slightly agitated.

"No man. When I got here, I jumped in the pool and took a swim. I saw the sliding doors were opened while I was still in the pool. I got out and looked inside."

Cliff made a mental note to have forensics test the carpet in Cole's bedroom for pool chemicals. He didn't want to get bogged down in the minutia right off the bat and there were more pressing questions to ask, so he moved on.

"How long have you worked for Mr. Dillinger?"

"Six months."

"Do you know if the house has a security system?"

Cliff knew it did. He'd seen it when he came inside. He'd never seen a house that size that didn't. The house had cameras everywhere. As soon as he was done with the pool guy, he wanted to see the main system and look at what was recorded. The tapes would verify the pool guy's story. One way or the other.

More importantly, Cliff wondered when the alarm was turned off. Did Cole do it?

"It does have a security system," Jackson answered.

"Do you know if it was on?"

"It was on when I got here."

Not the answer Cliff expected.

If the system was on, then why didn't the alarm sound? Wouldn't it go off when he entered the house? It should've gone off when the sliding glass doors were opened by the murder.

Nothing was making sense.

"Was the alarm going off when you arrived at the house? Is that how you knew it was on?"

"No, man."

Cliff put his hand to his forehead. He was confused. He also didn't like being called, man, in every response. At least it was better than dude, which Cliff imagined was also one of the other words in Justin Jackson's limited vocabulary.

"If the alarm was on, why didn't it go off when you entered the sliding glass doors?"

"The alarm was off."

"You just said it was on!"

"I said it was on when I got here. That was around seven in the morning. I shut it off when I arrived."

A thousand alarm bells were going off in Cliff's head. The pool guy was clearly being evasive.

"You told me you got here at eight forty-five!"

Cliff didn't like it when stories changed. Sometimes people were confused. Sometimes they were having a hard time keeping their stories straight. Inconsistencies were the main thing he was looking for when he questioned someone. That and body language.

Justin was rocking back and forth on his feet. His body language was nervous and he was trying to act like he wasn't.

"No, man. I got here at seven. That's when I turned the alarm off."

"Was Mr. Dillinger here at seven?"

"No, man. Mr. Dillinger wasn't here."

"Let me get this straight. You got here at seven and turned off the security system?"

"That's right."

"Why did you say you arrived at eight-forty-five?"

"Because I did. I came at seven and then left."

"Where did you go?"

"I got hungry, man. I went and got a coffee and an egg bagel sandwich."

"What coffee shop?"

"Java Brews."

Cliff was familiar with it.

"Did you eat your sandwich there or bring it back to the house?"

There were no empty coffee cups lying around the pool.

"I ate it in my car. While I was driving back."

Cliff wondered why he hadn't offered this information from the beginning.

"So you got here at seven. Turned off the alarm. Got hungry. Went and got a coffee and an egg sandwich. Came back to the house. Took a swim. Saw the sliding glass doors were open. That's when you found Mr. Dillinger dead on the bed. Is that your story?"

"Yeah. That's right."

"You went swimming right after eating?"

Jackson waved his head dismissively. "That's an old wives' tale, man. I'm from California, dude, I went surfing after I ate all the time. It don't hurt you."

Cliff was right about the California connection. And dude being a prominent part of his vocabulary.

"Did you see anyone suspicious hanging around the house? A strange car in the neighborhood?"

"Nope. Nothing."

"How well did you know Mr. Dillinger?"

"Pretty well. I mean, I've seen him around. He pays me a good wage to keep his pool clean."

"Was he happy with your work?"

"He never complained. I'm still here, aren't I?"

Answering a question with a question showed defensiveness.

"Was Mr. Dillinger seeing someone? Did he have a girlfriend?"

Jackson paused and became even more nervous.

"Yeah. He was seeing someone. Katherine. Katie. Kate. Ms. Reynolds. She and Mr. Dillinger were seeing each other."

Cliff heard a twinge of anger in the comment. Maybe jealousy. Maybe nothing.

Either way, he had his first suspect. There was more to Justin Jackson than met the eye. His story seemed suspicious. Cliff just didn't know what or why.

Where's Julia?

Cliff looked around. She wasn't outside. He hadn't seen her leave.

"Excuse me for a minute," Cliff said, then went inside to look for her.

He couldn't find her. Anywhere. She wasn't in the house. Or the car. A downstairs door was closed. A bathroom.

Cliff lightly knocked on it.

Julia answered. "Busy."

"Are you okay?" Cliff asked.

"You can come in. It's open."

Cliff opened the door slowly. What he saw caused him to swallow hard. Julia was on her knees in front of the toilet. Leaning over it. Clearly sick to her stomach. He closed the door behind him and locked it.

"I'm sorry I'm contaminating your crime scene," she said, forcing a smile.

She flushed the toilet and stood to her feet. Then walked over to the sink and splashed water on her face.

"I don't think forensics is going to find anything in the powder room toilet," Cliff said.

He put his hand on her back and moved it around in a comforting manner.

"Did you eat something that didn't agree with you?" he asked.

They never did eat at the bar. Cliff's stomach had been growling ever since they got to Cole Dillinger's house. As far as he knew, she hadn't eaten anything all day. Neither had he.

"No."

She had a faraway look on her face.

"What is it?"

She turned and faced him.

"I was going to tell you at the party this afternoon. It was supposed to be a surprise."

She let out a sigh.

He wanted to, but he was holding his breath until she told him what was wrong.

"This is not how I wanted you to find out," she said, avoiding eye contact.

"What is it?"

"I'm pregnant."

That was the last thing he expected her to say.

5

"You're pregnant!" Cliff said, hardly able to believe the words coming out of his wife's mouth.

"I am," Julia said. She forced a smile.

They were still in the powder room of Cole Dillinger's house. It explained her strange behavior and her upset stomach.

"How did that happen?" Cliff asked.

Julia twisted her lips to the side in a sort of clown face.

"I thought you knew how babies were made," she quipped, as a genuine smile pushed past her pained look.

"I mean. When? When did you get pregnant?"

"Probably when we went to Wisconsin for the weekend."

"I don't mean when did you get pregnant. I mean when did you find out?"

Cliff's sentences weren't even making sense to him. He'd just gotten the biggest news in his entire life, on the same day the biggest Chicago murder case in the last fifty years was thrown in his lap.

Who could blame him if he suddenly felt a little overwhelmed?

"I'm about two weeks late," Julia explained.

"Why didn't you tell me?"

"I wanted to wait until I knew for sure. This morning I took a pregnancy test and confirmed it. The morning sickness started today. I'm not feeling good. I think I need to eat something."

"I'll get us out of here as soon as possible."

She touched his arm.

"Don't worry about it. I'll be fine. Finish what you need to do here. We can talk about this later."

"I want to talk about it now. This is huuuuuuge. We're going to have a baby!"

His shock was turning to excitement. Slowly, but delight was overcoming the trepidation.

"I know. Can you believe it? Are you happy?"

She didn't sound excited. Cliff wasn't sure if it was because she wasn't feeling well or was upset about being pregnant. Or both.

He took her into his arms and her head immediately collapsed on his chest. He could feel her crying.

"I'm happy," he said. "I really am. Are you?"

He could feel his polo shirt getting damp from the tears.

"Are those tears of joy?" he asked when she didn't respond to his question.

"I'm scared."

"You're going to be a great mother," Cliff said, reassuringly.

Julia lifted her head. Her eye makeup was slightly smeared. Some was probably on his shirt but now wasn't the time to look.

"Do you think so?" she asked.

"I know so. Our child is going to be blessed to have you as his mom."

"I'm glad you're happy."

"Who wouldn't be? I mean. We talked about it. We both want kids. I think it'll be a good thing."

They stopped using birth control six months before. The doctor said it'd likely take six to eighteen months to get pregnant. Maybe longer. That's why it came as such a shock. Cliff expected to get this news someday. Just not today.

How was he supposed to concentrate on the Cole Dillinger murder?

"I need to show you something," Julia said, bringing his mind back to the case. "Out by the pool. Two things, actually."

"Okay."

Cliff opened the door to the powder room, and they walked out into the hallway.

"Let's go through the kitchen," Cliff said. Left took them back to the master bedroom. Right took them through the kitchen to another set of sliding doors that led to the pool area.

Cliff took Julia's arm and led her to the right. The coroner was preparing to move the body. He didn't want her to see it in case that would make the morning sickness worse.

As they neared the kitchen, Julia stopped walking. Her face was white again. She was clutching her stomach. Lurching her head forward like she was about to gag. She turned around and walked back toward the powder room.

"I'm sorry. I'll meet you outside," she said.

Then closed the door to the powder room behind her.

Cliff had an idea.

He continued on to the kitchen. As expected, he found an oversized pantry. Bigger than his walk-in closet. He'd never seen one this big. Most of the shelves were bare which made sense. As far as Cliff knew, Cole and his girlfriend were the only ones who lived in the monstrosity of a house. He only knew about the girlfriend because of the pool guy.

On one of the shelves was a box of crackers. The box was open, but one of the long skinny packages on the inside was still sealed shut. He took one of the unopened packages, left the pantry, and sat the crackers down on the massive island that took up most of the kitchen.

He opened the refrigerator and found a six pack of Ginger Ale and another six pack of Coke. He thought Julia would like the Ginger Ale better. The carbonation might help with the nausea.

He sat it down on the island as well but left it unopened so it wouldn't go flat. He waited for Julia to finish in the bathroom.

An uneasiness came over him. Partly because he needed to get back to the investigation. Also, because he was stealing food from a dead man.

An action that could get him suspended. At least written up.

It seemed worth the risk. No one was around and he had a good reason for it. Cole certainly wouldn't need it.

He could leave a few bucks on the island, but who would he be repaying?

As long as the Lieutenant didn't see him, he'd be okay. As if on cue, he heard the familiar voice in the other room.

His heart jumped.

It did a flip flop when the Lieutenant rounded the corner and saw him in the kitchen.

"You're just the person I'm looking for," the Lieutenant said, as he walked toward the kitchen with a purpose.

The Lieutenant grimaced when he saw the crackers and soda on the counter. "Are you hungry?" the Lieutenant asked sarcastically.

"These aren't for me. I just found out Julia's pregnant."

Cliff lifted the crackers and soda in the air.

"She's feeling some morning sickness," he said apologetically.

"I'm sorry to hear that," the Lieutenant said.

"Are you sorry to hear that she's pregnant or that she has morning sickness?"

"Both."

The Lieutenant's disdain for kids was well known among the detectives. According to the rumor mill, the Lieutenant had been married and divorced four times and was estranged from his own kids. Which wasn't a surprise. The Lieutenant was married to his job. Which he was good at. Better than parenting, by his own admission.

"I'm just joking with you," the Lieutenant said, although Cliff wasn't sure he was. "Congratulations."

It seemed like he meant it.

Surprisingly, the Lieutenant walked around the island and slapped Cliff on the back and gave him a quick man hug. He was a big man. Not tall but burly. Big boned. He could easily simulate a bear hug if he wanted, but that much warmth and friendliness wasn't in his nature.

"Thank you," Cliff said sincerely.

"Where's Julia?" he asked, looking around. "I thought I saw her earlier."

"She's in the restroom. She's feeling sick. That's why I borrowed the crackers and soda from the pantry and fridge."

"Let's hope the baby looks like his mother," he added, surprising Cliff again. The Lieutenant wasn't big on making jokes.

"We're definitely praying for that."

"How's your investigation coming?" the Lieutenant asked.

The real reason he'd been looking for Cliff. Something that was annoying. He'd been on the case for less than an hour and could already feel the pressure. He'd better get used to it. This same question was going to be asked a hundred times a day until the case was solved. Unnecessarily. If Cliff had something important to report, the Lieutenant would be the first he'd tell.

"I do have my first suspect," Cliff said.

Suspect was a strong term to use to describe Justin Jackson, the pool guy, but it's all he had at the moment to show the Lieutenant he was making progress.

"The pool boy?" the Lieutenant asked.

"Yeah. His story doesn't square. I'll follow up on it."

"I thought the same thing when I met him."

"I have more questions for him."

"What do you need from me?" the Lieutenant asked. "I think it goes without saying that I'm here to help in any way I can. Don't think you're on an island. I'll give you whatever you need to solve this case."

"I have some questions for Mr. Dillinger's teammates and coaches."

The Lieutenant shook his head from side to side in an exaggerated manner.

41

"That's not going to happen," he said. "Not until after the game."

Cliff felt anger rising inside of him. What happened to 'I'll give you whatever you need to solve this case.'

He couldn't help but voice his concern.

"Are you telling me that we're putting a murder investigation on hold because of a football game?"

"This is not just a game. This is *the* championship game. For the right to go to the Super Bowl. The team needs to be focused."

"You know as well as I do, that the first few hours of an investigation are the most important."

"The interviews will have to wait."

Cliff was pacing now. In the limited space behind the island.

"That's not acceptable. I'm the lead investigator. I need to talk to the team."

"What do you think you'll find out from them?" the Lieutenant asked sharply. "They all have alibis. They were at the team hotel."

"That's the main question I want answered. Why wasn't Cole with them? Was he at the hotel last night? If so, when did he come to his house and why? The players and coaches should know the answers."

"Those are good questions to ask. Tomorrow."

"I need to look the players in the eyes and see what I see. Make sure none of them are involved in the murder."

"They aren't."

"How do you know that for sure?"

"Cole Dillinger was their meal ticket. The players needed him to get to the Super Bowl."

"Stranger things have happened."

The Lieutenant clenched his jaw. While he didn't mind pushback to a point, Cliff felt like he was nearing that line.

"The team is off limits," the Lieutenant said roughly. "That's not my call, by the way. It's coming from the mayor's office. And from my boss. They don't want you talking to the team until after the game. For obvious reasons. If the Bears win, which seems unlikely now. But if they win, going to the Super Bowl means hundreds of millions of dollars for the city."

"Since when did money become a consideration in a murder investigation?"

The Lieutenant held up his hand to stop Cliff.

"I don't disagree with you. You can talk to them tonight. After the game. Or tomorrow morning."

Julia walked up around that time. The color had returned to her face.

"I hear congratulations are in order," the Lieutenant said.

He held out his arm and gave her a warm hug and a kiss on the forehead.

Julia glared at Cliff while in the embrace. He realized why. They hadn't talked about when to start telling people. Cliff knew women were touchy about that subject.

"Thank you," Julia said, flashing the Lieutenant a smile. "I'm about six weeks along. They say I'm due in August. Right in the middle of summer. I'm not looking forward to being pregnant in the hottest part of the year."

She was more talkative which told Cliff she was feeling better. She came and stood next to him behind the island.

"I found some crackers and Ginger Ale for you," Cliff said, hoping that would bring him back into her good graces. Also confirm to the Lieutenant that they weren't for him.

Her face lit up. If she was mad, she was past it. She ripped open the package of crackers, took one out, and shoved it in her mouth letting out a satisfying moan.

Cliff popped the top to the soda and handed it to her. She took a long swig while the cracker was still in her mouth. Something she never did.

"This will help," she said, talking with her mouth full.

Another thing she never did. She took out another cracker. Then a third. She was devouring them like a bear just out of hibernation.

With Julia temporarily taken care of, Cliff was anxious to get back to the conversation with the Lieutenant. His boss must've sensed it because he got in the first word, "The Bears coach is addressing the team." He looked at his watch. "Should be right about now."

Cliff looked at the clock on the wall.

11:05.

It suddenly dawned on him. He was too late anyway. Even if he went to the stadium, he'd have to deal with the traffic. He could use his blue lights to get there faster, but it'd still take forty-five minutes to an hour if he left right away. When the team arrived, they'd be getting into their gear. Then they'd take the field for warmups.

The Lieutenant was right. He wouldn't be able to interview them. What was he going to do, go on the sidelines and talk to them between plays?

"The coach is going to ask the team if anyone knows anything that would be helpful to the investigation," the Lieutenant added. "If so, they're to report it immediately. They'll call me if they have anything. If I hear from them, I'll be on the horn to you, Cliff, right away. I can assure you of that."

Cliff was resigned to the decision and ready to drop it.

He remembered that Julia wanted to show him something out by the pool. A good excuse to get away from the Lieutenant.

He rubbed her shoulder.

"Are you feeling better?" Cliff asked.

"Much better," she said. "The crackers are settling my stomach."

She'd eaten at least a half dozen of them. His stomach was growling as well, but he wasn't about to eat one in front of the Lieutenant. His throat was also parched, and a Coke would taste good about now.

"You said you had something to show me," Cliff said. "Out by the pool."

"I do."

"Do you need anything else from me, Lieutenant?" Cliff asked. "I want to get back to the investigation. I have some more questions for the pool guy."

"I'm good," he said. He then walked behind the island and gave Julia a second friendly hug.

"Good luck on your pregnancy," he said. "You already have that beautiful glow. Are you hoping for a boy or a girl?"

"I just want him or her to be—"

"Healthy." The Lieutenant finished her sentence.

"I'll be in touch." He pointed at Cliff.

Cliff remembered something.

"Lieutenant, there is something you can help me with. How would I go about finding out if there were any large bets made on the Giants this morning?"

The Lieutenant furrowed his brow in thought.

"That's good thinking, detective. Let me look into it. I may be able to help you with that."

"Thanks."

"Anything else?" the Lieutenant asked.

"I don't think so. Let me know if you hear anything from the team."

The Lieutenant left and Cliff and Julia were alone in the kitchen.

"Are you good?" Cliff asked.

"Much better, thanks."

"Sorry for telling the Lieutenant about the baby. I should've talked to you first."

"I don't want to tell people until after my first sonogram. A lot of women lose their babies in the first trimester."

"That's not going to happen to us. But I completely understand. It won't happen again."

She ate another cracker and took the last sip of the soda. Cliff took the can from her and put it in the trash. Julia clutched the bag of crackers like they were diamonds.

"What do you want to show me?" Cliff asked.

"It's out by the pool."

They walked through the kitchen and out the sliding glass doors to the pool area. Cliff noticed that Justin Jackson wasn't there. It appeared he left. Without his permission.

Cliff was fuming on the inside.

He'd have to track him down tomorrow. When he did, he intended to ratchet up the questions and see how he held up to more intense scrutiny.

Julia walked over to the right side of the pool area and Cliff followed. She pointed to the concrete.

"Is that blood?" she asked.

Cliff bent down and looked more closely. His heartbeat noticeably increased.

"I think it is," he said. "You have a good eye. I'll be right back."

Cliff went inside and told Jan about the blood. She came out and marked it for her team to examine.

"This is probably where the victim was struck in the head," Cliff said.

"Probably," Jan replied. "We haven't found the blunt object in the house."

Cliff looked around the pool area for something that might qualify. He didn't see anything.

"You said there were two things you wanted to show me," Cliff said to Julia after Jan went back inside. "What was the other thing?"

She pointed. To the north.

A fence separated Cole's property from the neighbor's estate.

Cliff could feel his eyes widen.

Attached to the fence was a large New York Giants logo flag. Flapping in the breeze. Clearly in a place to send a message.

"It looks like I need to pay the next-door neighbor a visit," Cliff said.

6

This was the hardest thing Coach Buddy Martin has had to do since the day he buried his wife of thirty-six years, a few years before. He walked slowly to the microphone at the front of the meeting room where his team had just finished their team meal. The chatter in the room was slightly below a dull roar.

Obviously, the news of Cole Dillinger's death hadn't made it to the players.

The team was excited. They always were before a game, but Buddy had never seen them this amped up. To be expected. Most of them had never participated in a game this important. Neither had he. He'd coached in one playoff game, but never in the championship round.

This was the closest the people in that room had ever been to a Super Bowl and the odds were good that most of them would never get this close again. Buddy couldn't help but wonder if that opportunity died the moment Cole Dillinger took his last breath on this earth.

They'd know in a few hours.

In the meantime, in less than a minute, his words were going to crush his team's spirit. The enthusiasm would be sucked out of the room like a high-powered commercial vacuum cleaner. With one sentence from him, their worlds were going to come crashing down and their hopes and dreams disintegrate like an exploding rocket.

In the same way his had.

About twenty minutes ago. When he got the news that Cole Dillinger was dead. Murdered. He still couldn't believe it.

But he had a job to do. Tell the team. It fell on him. He was the coach. That's why they paid him the big bucks. To be a leader. He'd feel better if he knew what to say. He should say that some things are more important than a game. That's where he would start. This was one of those times.

Life is fleeting. Nothing on this earth is guaranteed. We're not promised tomorrow.

A dozen clichés were clanging around in his head.

He took a deep breath and began.

"Listen up everybody," Buddy said into the microphone. His assistant coaches were standing off to the side of the room. He told them about Cole's death a few minutes before they came into the room. They were still in shock. Their faces were already somber, like they were at a funeral, and not an NFL pregame meal.

Some of them were fighting back tears and he hadn't even started talking.

The team chatter in the room continued. Not lessening at all. Most of the players hadn't noticed him standing at the microphone. Getting their attention by speaking into the mic wasn't going to work.

Buddy put his fingers to his lips and whistled right into the microphone. A skill he'd learned from forty years of coaching. The feedback from the amplifier was shrill and intense, and a number of players put their hands to their ears.

It worked. He got their attention.

When the team saw the coach standing at the front, they let out a cheer. The opposite of what he wanted them to do. Buddy raised his hands and moved them up and down to try and quell the enthusiasm. The players ignored him for a good ten to fifteen seconds. When the din began to quiet down, a few of the players let out some whoops and hollers and the cheering started up again.

"Sit down and shut up!" Buddy said, losing his patience.

Everyone quieted down immediately and sat back down. He could imagine that they were confused by his tone of voice. He saw it on their faces.

"I have some bad news," Buddy said, getting right to the point.

The room got so quiet you could hear a penny drop on the carpeting.

Buddy had no idea how to form the right words. The grief was overwhelming him. He felt like he'd lost a son. His knees were weak. It felt like a semi-truck was barreling down on him so fast that there was nothing he could do to keep from getting crushed by it.

"I'm afraid that... I have really... terrible news." His voice cracked as he said it.

The players were now fully focused. He had their attention. Their eyes were on him. Their faces shared his gloomy expression even though they didn't know why.

"A few minutes ago, I learned that um,... Cole Dillinger was found dead at his home this morning."

A murmur went through the crowd.

"What? Cole? What happened? No way?"

He could hear them voicing their disbelief. Some were looking around the room for Cole. As if somehow the coach had gotten it wrong.

The murmuring intensified.

Buddy didn't try to quiet it.

The players deserved a moment to let it sink in. They probably had the same burning question that was searing in his mind. Why was Cole at his house when he was supposed to be with the team?

Buddy's grief was mixed with anger. The pause allowed it to begin raging inside of him again like a roaring furnace.

Why did Cole leave the hotel? He was with them last night at the team meeting. Buddy saw him with his own eyes. As far as he knew, Cole was in his room at curfew which was at eleven.

This was why the team stayed at a hotel the night before a game. Even for home games. So nothing bad could happen to the players. So nothing could go wrong. Some thought coaches were being overprotective. That these were grown men who didn't need a curfew. Buddy wasn't one of them. If players were allowed to spend the night at their houses, any number of things could happen. None of them good.

They might be late to the team meal the next morning. God forbid, they might get in a car accident driving to the game. They could have a fight with their spouse or girlfriend and not be in the right frame of mind to play a football game. They might stay up late or even go out on the town the night before. Get drunk. Drive drunk. Hookup with a woman.

Any of those things could affect their performance on the football field. A chance Buddy wasn't willing to take. Having the players in a cocoon gave Buddy peace of mind and protected the players from themselves.

Buddy was so angry he could spit. So much in despair, he could cry.

Something fell through the cracks. Somebody screwed up. Cole Dillinger never should've been at his home. If he'd been with the team, he'd still be alive. Buddy wanted to blame somebody, but he didn't know who was at fault. His assistant coaches didn't know Cole was gone. Nobody noticed he wasn't there until around ten o'clock that morning. How was that possible? Their job was to keep track of the players. Not his.

Buddy waited until the murmuring died down. He also needed the time to regain his composure. It finally did and the din slowly subsided.

"The details are sketchy," Buddy said. "I don't know a lot at this time. It appears like Cole was murdered."

More intense murmuring.

Buddy could hardly believe he was using the word murder. He barely believed it when it was told to him.

This has to be a nightmare.

Buddy halfway expected to wake up and find the whole thing was a dream. Or a film crew was going to burst through the door and say 'Candid Camera,' or some such stupid thing.

He looked at the doors in the back of the room. What he wouldn't give for Cole to walk through them at that very moment.

It wasn't going to happen. Cole Dillinger was dead. Denial wasn't going to bring him back. Neither was wishful thinking.

He let the anger show in his next words to the team. "If *anybody* has any information that might help the authorities find out who murdered Cole Dillinger, tell me or one of your coaches. Right away."

Buddy took another deep breath. He felt a sudden strength come on him. He remembered a plaque on the wall of his office.

TOUGH TIMES NEVER LAST BUT TOUGH PEOPLE DO.

This was a tough time. His team needed him to be a leader.

"Look men," Buddy said, "we have a football game to play. It's not going to be canceled or postponed. In a few hours, we're going to take the field wearing the Bears logo on our helmets and chests."

He took a deep breath so he could increase the intensity of his words.

"We owe it to our fans to play the game of our lives. For all those people who bought tickets and are watching us on television. You are playing this game not only for them but for your friends and families. For yourselves. For Cole. Knowing him—"

Buddy rubbed his eyes when a tear escaped and the emotion filled his throat making him unable to talk. He could see others around the room having the same reaction. He decided to let the emotion overwhelm him.

"Knowing Cole, he'd want us to play the game," he said, no longer fighting back the tears which were now streaming. "And he'd want us to win. That's what we're going to do."

A cheer went up among the players.

Buddy rubbed the tears off his cheeks and out of his eyes. He waited for the cheer to subside. When it didn't happen right away, he raised his hands to make it.

He desperately wanted to continue. This was the speech of his life. The words were suddenly flowing. He felt the energy behind them.

"We're Bears!" he shouted into the microphone. "The bear is the toughest animal on the planet. Our fight song is *Bear Down, Chicago Bears*. As you know, it's played every time we score. We've got to bear down, men. Fight for our lives. It'll take everything we have to win this game!"

The team was nearing a frenzy.

"Some of you might not know the origin of the song," he said after the roller coaster of noise calmed.

Buddy remembered reading about it.

"The song was written in the early 1940's."

The room was totally silent again. The players were fixated on his every word.

"When the *Monsters of the Midway* were in their heyday, the Chicago Bears played the Washington Redskins in the championship game. The same game you're about to play in."

"Yeah!" a cheer erupted and just as quickly subsided.

"The Bears were huge underdogs. I consider us underdogs now. No one expects us to win this game. No one expected the *Monsters of the Midway* to win either, some eighty years ago. Do you know what happened?"

"What?" was the cry that went up all over the room.

"The Bears won 73-0!" Buddy raised his fist in the air when he said it. "That's the largest margin of victory of any game in the history of the National Football League! It was a Bear who did it!"

The loudest cheer of the day erupted. Then applause. The *Monsters of the Midway* were household names in Chicago. Every player had at least heard of them.

"We're going to go out there and we're going to shock the world today. I don't know if we're going to win 73-0, but we're going to win. For Cole!"

Another cheer rose up filling the room with more excitement than Buddy had ever seen in one room before. He'd felt it in the stadium on occasion. Never like this. The whole demeanor of his assistant coaches had changed. That's what he wanted. He needed everyone in the room to believe that they could win the game.

He quieted the team. They were getting better at following his lead. He had one further thing to say. Most of what he had said wasn't planned. This was.

"Will you all join me for a moment of silence, as we remember Cole and his family during this difficult time."

The players wearing caps took them off.

For a good minute, they all stood there in silence. Their heads bowed. Some had their eyes closed. Some didn't.

He heard sobbing throughout the room.

Buddy had no tears left to shed.

Back to business. They had a game to get ready for.

"The bus leaves in forty-five minutes for the stadium," Buddy said, after the moment of silence was over. "Get your stuff packed and be downstairs ready to go. Quarterbacks, come to conference room B. We're going to talk about a revised game plan."

The game plan was simple and already solidified in Buddy's mind. Don't let Deuce Dixon beat them. They were going to go to a ground and pound game. Let the game be won in the trenches. Their backup quarterback was going to hand the ball off to the running backs. Only throw a pass when absolutely necessary.

It was their best chance to win the game. Hopefully, the defense would play above their heads. The Giants weren't the most potent offense in the NFL.

It might actually work.

"As soon as I dismiss you," Buddy said, "I want the defense to stay here. You're going to meet with your coaches for ten minutes or so. When you're finished, you can go and pack."

He searched his mind to see if he had forgotten anything.

He couldn't think of anything.

"That's all. And go Bears."

After Buddy left the microphone, the murmuring ramped up again. The disbelief was back.

He felt good about the speech. The words were inspiring. Were they enough? They wouldn't know for several more hours. It could go either way. The team could come out and play the game of their lives, or be so emotionally drained that they had nothing left in the tank. No energy to draw on.

Buddy felt the unease. He still felt like he'd been punched in the gut. The team almost certainly felt the same emotions.

Somehow, they had to snap out of it. They had a game to play.

One of the wide receivers, Rocket Mustang, approached Buddy. His face was as serious as a man on a beach who'd just seen a tsunami approaching.

"What is it, Rocket?"

"I know why Cole went home."

"Why?" he asked.

"I saw him in the lobby."

"When?"

"This morning."

"About what time?"

"Around eight. He was in a hurry. Said he had to go somewhere."

"Did he say where?"

"He said he got a text and had to go home. He'd be back in time for the team meal. He wanted me to cover for him. I told him I would. I'm sorry."

Buddy wanted to explode. He could feel his blood pressure rising to the point of boiling.

But he resisted the urge. Railing on his star wide receiver and one of Cole's best friends, seemed pointless now.

"Thanks, Rocket. Go get ready for the game."

Buddy immediately walked over to the General Manager. He related the information to him. Word for word. Exactly as Rocket had given it to him.

"I'll call the police commissioner," the GM said.

"Thanks."

Buddy couldn't help but wonder what was on that text.

7

Cliff knocked on the neighbor's door. The one flying the New York Giants flag on the fence between Cole Dillinger's property and his own.

Julia wanted to wait in the car. She asked for another Ginger Ale and Cliff got it for her. After consuming most of the package of crackers, Julia felt much better which was the main thing.

Cliff was mindful of the fact that he needed to get her some real food. He wanted some as well. He hadn't eaten anything all day. A box of power bars was in the pantry, but he resisted the urge to take one.

As soon as he finished questioning the neighbor, he'd take Julia home. They could eat there. Most of the restaurants and bars would be packed by now. The game was only a few hours away.

A man answered the door.

Cliff sized him up. Five ten. Wearing tan slacks and a collared country club logo shirt. Preppy looking. Early fifties. Fit. A little gray around the ears. He looked like the type of person who thought a lot of himself.

Cliff flashed his badge and gave him the standard introduction.

"I'm Senior Detective Cliff Ford, with the Chicago PD. I'd like to ask you a few questions."

The man's response wasn't what Cliff was expecting.

"I'm not answering any questions unless my lawyer is present," he said matter-of-factly.

"I don't think you need a lawyer, sir. I just wanted to ask you about your flag in the backyard. It'll only take a minute."

"Like I said, I'm not answering any questions unless my lawyer is present."

He sounded like a broken record.

"Why did you put the flag on Mr. Dillinger's fence?" Cliff asked, trying to maintain a casual tone, but more curious now than he had been when he first knocked on the door.

"That fence is part of my property."

"I get that. I'm not saying you don't have the right to fly the flag there. I'm just wondering why you would. I can understand that you're a Giants fan and want to support your team, but why not fly the flag in front of your house where everyone can see it?"

"I'm not a Giants fan. I'm a Bears fan."

"That makes it even more curious. Were you trying to send Mr. Dillinger a message? Was your real motive to stir up trouble? To get a rise out of him?"

"Like I said. I'm not answering any questions without my lawyer present."

"Was it meant to be a joke? Were you trying to be funny? Are you and Cole Dillinger friends and you were only joking around with him?"

Maybe asking multiple questions at once, would get him off his standard response.

"What part of I'm not answering questions without my lawyer present do you not understand?"

That response didn't sit well with Cliff. He could feel the anger rising inside of him like a fever on a thermometer.

"Why the animosity toward me?" Cliff asked.

The man stood there tight lipped.

THE CLIFF HANGERS: THE QUARTERBACK

"Was there some kind of feud between you and Mr. Dillinger? Is that why you put the flag there? To make him mad. It sure seems like it."

His stare was steely and resolved.

"What's your name, sir?"

"Austin Mayfield."

Cliff wrote it down in his black book.

"How long have you lived in this house?"

If Cliff could get him to answer some simple questions, he might be able to slip in the important ones. Especially if he asked them at a rapid-fire pace.

"A little over a year."

"Any kids?"

"I don't see the relevance."

"I don't see why you won't answer a simple question."

"I want an attorney."

"Is there some reason why you think you need an attorney?"

"I'm not answering that."

"Why not?"

"It doesn't matter why. It's my constitutional right."

"That's not exactly true. You don't have a constitutional right to obstruct justice. You have to answer my questions. Unless you're pleading the fifth. You do have the right not to incriminate yourself. But I haven't asked you any questions that would be related to a crime."

"You're on my property. I don't have to talk to you."

"We can go down to the station and you can answer my questions there."

"I know my rights."

"Why are you concerned about incriminating yourself? I asked if you have any kids. The last time I checked, it's not a crime to have kids in America."

Maybe sarcasm would work.

"I think you should leave."

"My wife just told me she's pregnant," Cliff said in a joking tone. "About thirty minutes ago. How about that. I'm going to be a father. Our first. I'm positive that I'm not breaking the law by having a kid. You aren't either. So answer my question. Do you have any kids?"

Mayfield simply stared at Cliff. Even humor wasn't working.

"Let's try some questions that would be more related to obstruction of justice. Where were you at eight thirty this morning?"

"I'm not answering."

"Did you see anything suspicious at Mr. Dillinger's house this morning?"

Silence.

"Did you hear a gunshot?"

He crossed his arms in front of himself.

"Have you seen any strange people hanging around the neighborhood?"

He stared past Cliff refusing to make eye contact.

"Have you seen any suspicious cars that you didn't recognize?"

He looked at Cliff and frowned.

"Do you have any kids?"

Mayfield moved his neck from side to side like he was relieving tension in it.

"Did you murder Cole Dillinger?" Cliff asked roughly.

Maybe shock would work.

"No."

At least he answered one question.

Cliff closed his black book. He pulled out one of his cards and handed it to Mayfield who looked at it then turned it over and looked on the back which was blank.

"Have your attorney call me at this number," Cliff said. "I'm much more interested in talking to you now than I was before. It's your fault, you know. You could've made this easy on yourself and answered a couple of simple questions. Then I would've been on my way. Seems like you prefer to do things the hard way."

Cliff had to be careful not to let his frustration turn into badgering.

"Your evasiveness has me curious, though. It makes me wonder if you're hiding something. I think it's a good idea for you to have your attorney there when I question you. Because it's going to get extremely uncomfortable. I promise you that."

Cliff probably crossed the line, but his head was throbbing now. A headache had crept up on him. Probably from not eating. His blood sugar might be falling as well.

His patience was certainly falling and nearing a breaking point.

Mayfield closed the door in Cliff's face which only made him madder.

He had a second suspect.

The man's behavior was strange at the very least. Perhaps criminal.

Cliff walked back toward his car to ask Julia if she wanted him to take her home. He still had more work to do. Checking the security camera videos was the next thing on his list.

To get to his car, he had to walk past a group of reporters who were congregated behind a yellow police tape. When they saw him, they began shouting questions in his direction.

He ignored them.

One particular reporter, Starr Olson, was trying desperately to get his attention. He knew her fairly well, so he walked over to her. The rest of the reporters became almost manic, shouting out questions, trying to outdo the others.

He easily tuned them out.

Cliff lifted the tape so Starr could walk under it. A policeman was assigned to monitor the area and he held out his hand and gave orders to the rest of the group to remain behind the tape.

"How are you, Starr?" Cliff said, after they were out of earshot of her peers.

If they were at a social function, he'd give her a hug. That's how well they knew each other. She knew Julia as well. In front of the other reporters, they needed to maintain their professionalism and distance.

"I'm fine, detective. How are you?"

Starr was your typical television reporter. Pretty. Tough minded. Had a chip on her shoulder. Determined to hold her own in a male dominated world. She'd been in Chicago for a while, but Cliff could see her career springing forward and her leaving at some point to bigger and better things. They'd talked about it. Starr would only leave a market as big as Chicago if the big networks came calling. So far they hadn't.

"I'm up to my eyeballs in a huge mess," Cliff admitted. "Mr. Dillinger's death is a real tragedy for all of Chicago."

"That's why I wanted to talk to you. I might have some information that could be helpful to your investigation."

His curiosity piqued.

Cliff knew the game. Starr would want something in return. He didn't have anything to give her other than a pool guy who only knew two words, man and dude, and an arrogant neighbor who was a major jerk.

"What do you want in return for this information, Starr? I just started looking into this. I don't have much to give you at this point."

He really wanted her information, though. If Starr said she knew something important, she meant it. Some reporters lied and said they had something actionable when they didn't. They were just trying to weasel information out of him.

He almost never talked to reporters for that reason. Starr was a straight shooter. That's why he was talking to her now.

"I want to be there when you make an arrest," she said.

He thought she would want access to the house. To take pictures of the crime scene. Something he couldn't do. He was relieved she wanted something in the future, even though he couldn't give her that either.

"You know the policy is no reporters at an arrest. That's for your safety."

"I'm willing to take the risk."

"Why don't you tell me what you've got? For old times sake. We've been friends a long time. If the information is good, I'll throw you a bone at some point."

"I love you, Cliff. But I'm not giving up a source, without something guaranteed in return."

That's what he thought she'd say.

The chess match continued.

"Give me a hint as to what you have."

"Trust me. You're going to want to hear this."

"If it's related to the murder, it could be considered obstruction if you don't tell me."

She laughed.

"Cliff Ford, I'm surprised at you. Don't play that card with me. You know I'll go to jail before I reveal a source."

"I know," he smiled so she knew he wasn't threatening her.

"Here's what I'll do," Cliff said. "When we make the arrest, I'll make sure that you're the first to know about it. I'll give you enough head start that you can be there when we bring him in. Before everyone else even knows about it."

"That's not much."

"That's all I got. If I can do more later, I'll call you."

"Fair enough."

"What you got?"

She moved in closer to him, so she was speaking directly in his ear.

"One of the neighbors is pitching a story. He says it's bombshell information on Cole Dillinger."

Cliff thought of the neighbor flying the flag. Things were starting to make sense. That's why he only wanted to meet with Cliff with an attorney present. He and his attorney were shopping a story. They wanted to tell that story to the press. Not to police investigators. That'd make the information less valuable.

Austin Mayfield's interview moved to the top of the list of priorities.

"I know about Mr. Mayfield," Cliff said with a sigh of resignation that the information hadn't turned out to be more helpful.

"That's not the man's name."

Cliff pointed at the house. "Mr. Mayfield lives over there."

"That's not the neighbor who is shopping the story. The man lives there."

She pointed to the neighbor on the other side of Dillinger's house.

"His name is Harold Potter," Starr added.

Cliff turned his head to the side to let her know it sounded like a made up name.

"I'm not kidding. His name really is Harold Potter. He kind of looks like him too."

"Did Mr. Potter give you a hint as to the nature of the information?"

"He did not. But he said it's juicy dirt. Those were his words."

Starr moved in close again and lowered her voice. "He's asking one million dollars for the information."

"A million dollars!"

Cliff almost said it too loud. Several of the reporters looked their way.

"What could he possibly have that would be worth that kind of money?" Cliff asked, whispering this time.

"I don't know. It's too rich for my editor. If it wasn't, I wouldn't be telling you about it. I'd get the scoop myself. I'm telling you because I don't want any of my competition to get it. So far, nobody is willing to pay the money."

"That's a lot for an exclusive story. Even if it is dirt on Cole Dillinger."

"I think he'll get it. Once the national media gets involved, and they will, they might start a bidding war and he'll get more than a million dollars. If it's as juicy as he says it is."

"Thanks for the heads up, Starr. I think I'll pay Mr. Potter a visit. I owe you one."

"You already owe me four or five. But who's counting."

"Thank you."

"You're welcome. Remember me when you come across something big. I'd love to scoop the big guys."

"I will."

As Cliff walked toward his car, his phone rang.

The Lieutenant.

"I just heard from the general manager of the Bears," he said. "One of the players told the coach that Cole Dillinger got a text this morning, around eight a.m. Cole said he had to go home. It seemed urgent. That he'd be back in time for the team meal."

"That's interesting."

"It may be important. Check out his phone."

"I'm on it."

Cliff hung up.

Instead of continuing to the car, he got Julia's attention and pointed to the house. She seemed to understand, and he changed direction and went back inside to find Jan, the lady leading the forensics team.

"I need Mr. Dillinger's cell phone," Cliff said.

"I don't believe we have it."

She happened to have the evidence log in her hand. She flipped through the pages.

"No, sir. We didn't find a cell phone."

"Did you look in his car?"

"We processed the car. There wasn't a cell phone in it. We didn't find any evidence in the car that could be linked to the murder. Everything we found was either by the pool or in the master bedroom."

"But no cell phone?"

"No."

Cliff knew better than to question Jan. She was as thorough as a queen bee building a hive. If there was a cell phone in the house, she would've found it. Cell phones and computers were some of the first things they looked for.

That could only mean one thing. The killer took it.

Was the killer also the one who sent the text to get Cole back to his house?

8

Cliff's things-to-do list was getting longer by the minute.

Find Cole Dillinger's cell phone.

Interview Harold Potter for the first time.

Interview the next-door neighbor with the Giants flag and the pool guy for a second time.

Look at the security cameras at the house and at the guard gate entrance into the subdivision.

Talk to the Bears' players and coaches.

Take care of his pregnant wife.

The last one being his priority at the moment. He couldn't expect her to wait in the car while he worked his way through the list.

"I'm going to take you home," Cliff said to Julia when he finally made it back to the car after all the distractions.

"I don't want to go home," she replied. "I want to stay with you."

"I may be a while. I have more interviews to conduct. I need to look at the security cameras. I don't know how long that'll take."

"I don't care. I don't want to be alone. I want to be with you."

She clutched his arm. Normally, Julia was as independent as a cow grazing in a pasture. Cliff could only attribute her clinginess to the pregnancy. For whatever reason, she was feeling the need to be with him.

He wanted to be with her as well. They had so much to talk about. He didn't know exactly what to expect from the pregnancy. He had a million questions. He really didn't want to be alone either.

Cliff wasn't sure what to do. The pressure to solve Cole Dillinger's murder was staring him in the face. As much as he wanted to be with her, he didn't want any distractions. Not at this critical juncture in the investigation.

Julia must've sensed his waffling, because she said, "I'll go to the interviews with you. Maybe I can help you with something. If not, I'll stay out of your way."

"Aren't you hungry?"

"I had some crackers. I'm fine."

"I'm starving."

She took the package of remaining crackers out of the side console of the car and handed them to Cliff. He instinctively looked around to see if his Lieutenant was around, even though he knew he wasn't. Satisfied, Cliff pulled three crackers out of the package and scarfed them down. Saving the last three for Julia.

An unopened bottled water was in the center console. He gulped it down in no time.

"That was good," Cliff said.

"You're so easy to cook for," Julia quipped, with a wide grin.

Cliff was glad to see her sense of humor was back. She must be feeling better. He was feeling better as well. Maybe having her around was a good idea.

"You're such an amazing cook," he said, matching her wide smile and squeezing her hand.

He was still hungry, but the crackers would tide him over until they could get something with more sustenance. If they hurried, they might even be able to watch the game together.

"Tell me where you are in the investigation," Julia said.

He filled her in on what he had learned to that point. She listened with intense interest. Especially the part about the neighbor with the flag, since she was the one who had pointed it out to Cliff.

"I agree. The pool guy and the neighbor are suspects," she said.

"That doesn't mean they committed the murder," Cliff replied, stating the obvious.

"No. But they have information they aren't telling you. It might lead to the murderer."

Technically, Cliff wasn't supposed to disclose the details of an investigation with anyone outside the department, but Julia was an exception. He valued her input, and could count on her to keep things confidential.

The Lieutenant even knew she helped him on occasion. He remarked once at a Christmas party in front of a group of people that he should've hired her instead of Cliff. His exact comment was, "She's the best undercover detective we have on the force. Of course, Cliff is the only one who has seen her under the covers."

The Lieutenant roared at his jokes. They all had a hearty laugh and Julia took it in stride. If she was offended, she didn't let anyone know it. Cliff had heard a lot worse off-colored jokes in his ten years on the force.

After he finished briefing her, Julia said, "Where do you want to start?"

She was rubbing her hands together like she was getting her second wind. He was still dragging. The headache made his head throb, and his stomach still cried out for real food.

"Let's start with the neighbor," he answered.

"Which one?"

"Harold Potter. The one hawking his story. Let's see what he thinks is considered juicy dirt worth a million dollars."

"I still can't believe that's his name."

Cliff looked in the direction of his house. He noticed for the first time a large P on the front door, so he assumed Potter really was his last name. Starr's information was usually spot on.

They got out of the car and walked that way, which was to the left of Cole Dillinger's house, if they were standing on the street facing the houses.

When Cliff knocked on the door, he got a burst of energy. That happened when he felt like he was getting close to a break in the case. The anticipation of finding out what Harold Potter knew was exhilarating.

More than likely, he'd be underwhelmed by it, or the man would refuse to disclose it, but that didn't dampen the enthusiasm of the hunt. Either way, it felt good to be investigating the case again without having to worry about Julia.

The front door opened and Cliff's first thought was, *He does look like Harry Potter*. Julia looked at Cliff and smiled like she was thinking the same thing.

"Mr. Potter, my name is Cliff Ford. Senior detective with Chicago P.D. This is Julia. Do you mind if we ask you a few questions?"

He wasn't going to mention that Julia was his wife. Potter would probably assume she was another detective.

"I don't mind at all," he said in a friendly manner. A sharp contrast to the flag neighbor. "Please come in."

Julia went in first and Cliff followed. They waited in the entryway for him to close the door and direct them where to go. Cliff had forgotten to show him his badge, but it didn't matter since it was on his belt and clearly visible.

The house wasn't as impressive as Cole Dillinger's but qualified as a mansion. Julia was noticeably checking out her surroundings. The huge chandelier in the foyer was stunning. The massive paintings on the wall and the marble floor and staircase, made the entryway look like an art gallery.

Potter led them into what Cliff would consider a den. The furniture was made up of antiques and the curtains and carpeting were ornate. Harold Potter seemed to have a thing for crystal vases which were all over the room. Or perhaps his wife was the one with the obsession.

The house appeared to be less than ten years old. Newer but had a lived-in feel.

The house was on a hill, higher than the others in the neighborhood and looked down on Cole Dillinger's house. Cliff tried to imagine the view from the backyard. He surmised that it overlooked Dillinger's pool area. He would work that into his questions. Hopefully, even be able to see it.

"Did you know Mr. Dillinger?" Cliff asked, getting things started without chit chat.

"Yes."

"Were you friends?"

"I'd like to think we were. His dog is in my backyard."

That surprised Cliff.

Potter didn't wait for a follow up question to explain. "I watch Cole's dog when he's gone. You know. When he has a game and all. Our dogs are best friends."

"When did you get Mr. Dillinger's dog?"

"Yesterday afternoon. Right before he left for the team hotel."

"Did you see anything suspicious this morning?"

Potter suddenly became nervous. He changed positions in his seat. Crossed his legs. Then uncrossed them. Wrung his hands together.

"I didn't see Cole get shot, if that's what you mean."

"How did you know that Mr. Dillinger was shot?"

"It's all over the news."

Cliff wondered how that leaked out so fast. Probably from someone at the coroner's office. Maybe one of the cops on the scene. Those kinds of leaks infuriated him. It made it harder for him to do his job. He liked to have information that only he and the killer knew.

"What did you see?" Cliff asked, putting the leak out of his mind. He had his black book out and was ready to take notes if Potter said anything significant.

"Do I have to answer your questions?" he asked.

"Why wouldn't you want to?"

"I don't know who shot Cole. I couldn't even venture a guess. Well, maybe I have a guess."

"I don't want you to guess. I only want to know what you saw."

Actually, Cliff was interested in his guess. He made a quick note to ask him about it at the right time.

"I'd rather not say."

Sirens were going off in Cliff's head with such intensity, they were overriding his headache.

"That's concerning to me," Cliff said sternly. "I'd like to know why."

Potter hesitated again.

Cliff leaned in closer. To invade his space. He didn't want a repeat of the fiasco with the other neighbor. He'd put pressure on Potter if necessary. Harold Potter seemed weaker. Like he'd cave easier.

Potter was sitting on a side chair in the den next to the couch where Cliff and Julia were sitting.

"I'd rather not say what I saw. Do I have to?"

"Why don't you want to?"

"I have my reasons."

"Make me understand them."

Potter's demeanor changed so it was like that of the flag guy. He folded his arms in front of his chest. Clenched his jaw. Like he was digging in.

Cliff decided to drop the bombshell and let Potter know he wasn't fooling around.

"I know you're trying to sell your story to the press."

His eyes widened.

"For a million dollars."

They widened further. "How did you—"

Cliff cut him off.

"There are a lot of things I know," Cliff said strongly. "I will also know if you're lying to me or keeping something from me. That's not a good idea. You could be charged with a crime."

"What I know is not related to Cole's murder."

"I'll be the judge of that. It may be related to my investigation. It might help lead to the murderer"

"Maybe."

In Cliff's mind, Potter had just admitted that he had important information that might solve the crime. Breaks like this didn't come this early that often. He had to convince Potter to talk.

"If I tell you what I know, it'll leak to the press. Then it won't be worth anything."

Cliff shook his head no.

"I don't leak to the press. They'll never know what we talk about."

He rolled his eyes in a feminine sort of way. "Yeah. Right. I know who you guys are. The police are the worst ones. They leak like a sieve."

"Not me."

"I saw you talking to that reporter."

"It wasn't related to the case."

"I don't know that I can trust you."

Cliff was about to come unglued. He wanted to grab Potter by the shirt, shove him against the wall, and make him talk. He only did that in his dreams.

He also didn't know how to defend the police. Potter was right. They did leak like an umbrella with holes in it. It was ironic that Cliff was trying to convince the man they didn't leak information, when the fact that Cole Dillinger had been shot had already been leaked.

Still.

What happened to the days when people wanted to get involved? When they wanted to help the police. When they weren't more concerned about making a profit on a tragedy.

Cliff tried to maintain his composure. He never leaked unless it was conducive to the investigation to do so, but how did he convince Potter of that fact? He couldn't give him a guarantee. Other people in the department would know about the information. One of the elected officials might leak it. Probably would.

Potter was also perceptive. He saw Cliff talking to Starr Olson about the case. A reporter. Cliff wasn't about to disclose that she was the one who told him about the million dollars. Potter would never trust him.

"Nah. I think I'll wait and tell my story to the press," Potter finally said, predictably.

Cliff was beside himself but didn't let Potter see it.

What was it with these two neighbors? Obstructing his investigation. Made worse by the fact that he couldn't do anything about it. What was he going to tell the judge? Mr. Mayfield wouldn't tell him how many kids he had, and Mr. Potter wouldn't disclose information that he had already told Cliff wasn't related to the murder of Cole Dillinger.

The two neighbors were royal pains in his already throbbing neck. In different ways. Mayfield was as arrogant as a peacock strutting around a zoo. Potter was as weak and nerdy as the worst basketball player on the worst high school team in America.

Cliff put his black notebook away. He should take Julia to get something to eat. He'd grab some aspirin on the way for his headache.

He was just getting started on his investigation and already needed to regroup.

"You should consider this," Julia said out of the blue.

Cliff bit his lip to keep from asking what Potter should consider. His wife didn't often interject herself into an interrogation. When she did, it was generally insightful and impactful.

They both waited for her to finish her sentence. Cliff found himself holding his breath.

"You should consider the reward," Julia said.

What reward?

Cliff made a conscious effort to keep his mouth from flying open.

"I didn't know there was a reward," Potter said what Cliff was thinking.

"You know the Chicago Bears are going to offer a reward for information leading to the arrest of Cole Dillinger's killer."

"I hadn't thought about that."

His wife was brilliant.

She continued with that thought. "The reward could be a lot more than a million dollars. You can have your cake and eat it too. Tell Cliff your information and collect the reward money and sell your story to the press."

He was obviously thinking about it.

Julia turned on the charm. "You'll be a celebrity, Mr. Potter. You're Cole Dillinger's best friend. The one who helped find his killer. You could write a best-selling book. A picture of you and Cole's dog could be on the cover. You'll be a hero in Chicago. You'll never have to buy a drink in a bar again. The Bears will give you seats in the owner's suite."

Potter's eyes lit up. The man was already clearly rich. Julia throwing out the celebrity idea was nothing short of genius.

"You might be right," he said, pensively.

"I am right," Julia said.

"Will you vouch for me?" Potter asked, looking straight at Cliff. "With the reward money and all?"

"If you give me information that helps me solve this murder, then I'll vouch for you."

"Do you promise you won't leak it to the press?"

"You have my word."

"If Cliff Ford gives you his word, you can take it to the bank," Julia said.

"Okay. I'll tell you what I know."

Cliff got his black book out again.

9

Thanks to Julia, Harold Potter was willing to tell them what bombshell information he had on Cole Dillinger that was worth a cool million dollars.

Thanks to Julia, the interview was now on hold. Something Cliff was not happy about.

"Tell us what you know," Cliff had said to Mr. Potter.

"Cole Dillinger's killer lives in this neighborhood," he replied, emphatically.

"Do you know who this person is?" Cliff asked.

"I think so, yes."

Then things went off the proverbial rails.

Before Harold Potter could state who killed Cole Dillinger, he abruptly said, "Would either of you like something to drink?"

"I'll take something," Julia said so quickly Cliff had no chance to decline the offer.

"I have some pound cake as well, if you'd like a snack."

"That'd be great," she answered.

"I'll be right back."

Just like that, Harold Potter left the room. His words, 'Cole Dillinger's killer lives in the neighborhood and I think I know who it is,' was left hanging in the air like a loud burp.

Cliff glared at Julia.

"What?" she asked. "I'm hungry."

"So am I, but did you hear what he said?" Cliff whispered roughly. "That he knows who the murderer is."

"He'll tell us when he gets back. What difference does it make if it's now or five minutes from now?"

Cliff bit his lip and turned his head away to avoid saying something that Harold Potter might overhear in the other room. He also wanted to be careful not to say something to Julia he might regret.

Stopping the interview in midstream was never a good idea. A good investigator would never let a witness off the hook when he was about to disclose valuable information that could break a case wide open. What if Harold Potter had second thoughts while he was away from them in the kitchen? They'd be back to square one and Potter might clam up again.

Julia wasn't a detective and wouldn't know that, but still. She should keep quiet. Although, he reminded himself that Potter wouldn't even be talking if not for her.

The situation was also complicated because Julia was carrying his child.

Why did that make a difference? Was he not allowed to get upset at a pregnant woman? Could he no longer raise his voice if she annoyed him?

They hadn't talked about it, but he felt like they were living under new rules.

Cliff decided the silent treatment was the best approach. To keep his mouth shut. He sat on the couch holding his black book, waiting impatiently for Potter to return. He couldn't help but feel like a deflated balloon. Like all the air had been let out of the room. They'd lost valuable momentum that he'd have to work to recover.

He wouldn't feel better until he learned the information.

Cliff did feel better when Potter returned, and he took a bite of the warm pound cake with some kind of icing on top. Then a large gulp of the best sweet tea he'd had in a while.

Julia devoured hers like a woman who'd just been rescued from a deserted island.

Did pregnant women eat more? Julia didn't eat dessert often. Rarely in the middle of the day. Was this a new normal?

"Would you like some more?" Harold Potter said.

"No thank you," Cliff quickly said.

Julia had better say no or she'd hear about it later. Pregnancy or not.

She did say no.

Thankfully.

That didn't mean Harold Potter was in a hurry to tell his story. He wasn't finished with his cake. He sat in his chair eating it slowly. Daintily. With sophistication. He'd take a bite and then dab at the side of his mouth with a napkin. Take a sip of tea. Then start the whole process over again in the same order.

Like he was having dinner and high tea with the Queen of England and her husband.

Potter was relaxed. Calm. Like he didn't have a care in the world.

His demeanor seemed odd. Why was there no sense of urgency? His friend and next-door neighbor was found murdered. Wouldn't he be as anxious to tell what he knew as Cliff was to hear it?

Cliff had enough anxiety for the both of them. His heart was pounding. He could feel it in his ears like someone was standing directly behind him beating a large bass drum.

There was nothing he could do to move the process along without seeming too anxious. It didn't seem appropriate to ask Potter questions while he had his mouth full of food. So Cliff tried to relax. To keep things casual. He did know that witnesses, and suspects for that matter, were more talkative when they were comfortable. Potter seemed as comfortable as a Shih Tzu laying on his owner's lap.

It took ten minutes, but Potter finally finished.

Cliff flipped through his black book, giving notice to everyone that he was ready to get back to business. Hopefully, Potter was still willing to talk. If not, Cliff would blow a gasket in his high-strung detective engine.

"Here's where we left off," Cliff said, pretending to read from notes in the black book. In reality, the page was blank. Hopefully, not for long.

"You were saying that you know who killed Cole Dillinger."

"I believe I said that I *think* I know."

"Yes. That's right. Who is it?"

Potter let out a contrived sigh. Like he was already in front of the cameras doing an interview for the media. At least practicing for it. He clearly intended to play this for all it was worth. To heighten the drama.

He leaned back in his chair and crossed his legs, holding the glass of tea in his hand. He stared off in the distance.

"It's one of three people," he said reflectively.

Cliff wanted to wring his neck.

Potter didn't know who killed Cole Dillinger. He was guessing. Unless his reasoning was sound, his conjecture was basically useless.

"Cole was having an affair with a married woman."

Now they were getting somewhere.

"Her husband would be the first likely suspect in my mind," Potter said.

Cliff didn't disagree. A large percentage of murders were committed by spouses. More often than not, infidelity was involved.

"Who is the woman?" Cliff asked.

"Marsha Blackburn. She lives across the street."

Potter pointed at the window. The den was on the street side, and they could see a large mansion through the window on the other side of the street.

"That's where Mrs. Blackburn and her husband live."

"How do you know she was having an affair with Mr. Dillinger?"

"I've seen them together. Cole would sneak over to her house. Sometimes she'd go to his house. Always when her husband was at work or out of town. They were very secretive."

"What does Mrs. Blackburn's husband do?"

"He's a plastic surgeon."

That statement dislodged a memory in Cliff's mind. He'd heard of Leon Blackburn. The most prominent plastic surgeon in Chicago. Women from all over the region came to him.

"Is his name, Leon?"

"Yes."

Cliff scribbled their names in his black book. He had an impeccable memory when it came to crime scenes and interviews, and he'd make more detailed notes later. But he liked the visual of the witness seeing him write things down.

Only for a few seconds though. He didn't want to interrupt the flow by taking a long time between questions.

Things were making more sense now. Potter did have dirt on Cole that would be worth a million dollars. Probably more. Maybe not from the major networks, but the tabloids would pay several million for a story this salacious.

"The husband knows about the affair," Potter said.

Cliff felt his right eyebrow raise, which was a habit that he'd tried to break, but couldn't. He preferred his witnesses and suspects see a stone-cold face. He couldn't help it when something was said to pique his interest.

Right now, his interest was through the roof.

"How do you know this?" Cliff asked.

"I saw Mr. Blackburn this morning. In front of Cole's house. He and Cole were arguing."

"What time this morning?"

"Eight-fifteen. I know this because my alarm went off. I have it set to feed the dogs at the same time every morning."

Cliff's interest was not only through the roof, it was soaring in the sky. Barreling towards outer space.

He now had a third suspect. A jealous husband. One with motive. A timeline that fits.

"Could you hear what Mr. Dillinger and Mr. Blackburn were arguing about?"

"No. But I have a pretty good idea."

So did Cliff. He searched his mind for the next logical question.

"What did you see next?"

He went with a generic one.

"Mr. Blackburn got in his car and sped off. Cole got in his car and pulled into his garage."

A question suddenly popped into Cliff's mind.

"Did you see Mr. Jackson any time this morning? Mr. Dillinger's pool man?"

"Yes."

"When did you see him?"

"Around seven o'clock this morning. I was having coffee on my back patio. I can see the pool from my deck."

That corroborated Jackson's story. He said he arrived at the house at seven.

"What was Mr. Jackson doing?"

"He was swimming in the pool with Cole's girlfriend, Kate. They were naked."

Cliff almost fell off the couch.

"Do you know Kate's last name?"

"Reynolds. She's a supermodel."

Cliff remembered the pool guy mentioning Kate. He called her several names. Katherine, Kate, and Katie. Then Ms. Reynolds. Jackson seemed to have a familiarity with her. Now he knew why.

"What happened next? After you saw them in the pool?"

"I went back inside my house. I'm not a voyeur."

"What did you do then?"

"I sent Cole a text. From one of my burner phones."

The bombshells continue to rain down. Like pieces of hail. The puzzle was starting to come together.

"What did your text to Mr. Dillinger say?"

"That his girlfriend was cheating on him with the pool guy. Right then. He should think about coming home."

"Why would you send him a text?"

"I thought he should know. I regret it now. In some ways, I feel responsible for Cole's death. If I hadn't texted him, maybe he wouldn't have come home, and he'd still be alive."

Potter was emotionless. Monotone. His expression didn't match the words. Like he was telling them what he had for lunch yesterday. Not relating scandalous details of affairs and murder.

"So you think Justin Jackson might've killed Cole?"

"He's one of the people I suspect did it."

Julia wasn't saying anything. She was slowly sipping her tea. Also looking at the plate on the coffee table. Like she wished she had another piece of pound cake.

Cliff wondered what she thought of all these revelations and the unbelievable tale Potter was spewing out of his mouth. He now had two viable suspects. Justin Jackson was firmly in his crosshairs along with Mr. Blackburn. They both had motive and opportunity. Cliff needed to get both of them to the station as soon as possible.

As soon as they were done with Potter, he intended to go directly across the street to the Blackburn's house. To interview the husband and wife. He needed to figure out a way to interview them separately.

He also wanted to talk to Kate Reynolds. Cole's girlfriend. Where was she? He hadn't seen hide nor hair of her. Why not? Surely, she'd heard the news of Cole's death by now. Wouldn't she have rushed back home?

Not if her boyfriend killed her boyfriend.

What a sordid tale of deceit.

Cliff searched his mind for the next question. He found a more specific one.

"Did you hear a gunshot?" he asked.

"No."

"Did you see Mr. Dillinger confront Mr. Jackson? Around eight thirty?"

"No."

"Did you hear them arguing?"

"No. I don't think Mr. Jackson was there."

"Why do you say that?"

"I saw him leave the house about eight o'clock. I guess after the deed with the girlfriend was done."

"Before Cole came home?"

"That's correct."

"Did you see him return?"

"No. But I did see his car in the driveway a little later. Like around eight-forty-five."

It fits Jackson's version of events. Jackson said he went to get something to eat. Came back and took a swim. Saw the open sliding glass doors to the master bedroom and discovered the body.

He didn't mention he'd gone swimming with Cole's girlfriend an hour earlier.

Cliff could envision another scenario. Cole came home. Confronted Kate. The pool guy showed up. An argument ensued. The pool guy hit Cole on the head with a blunt object. Moved him to his bed and then shot him.

Kate helped him. Then she left.

Another scenario was also demanding attention in his mind.

Mr. Blackburn found out his wife was having an affair. He was leaving his house when he saw Cole Dillinger drive up. He got out of his car. They argued. Almost came to blows.

They didn't. Blackburn drove away. Parked his car somewhere in the neighborhood. Snuck around to Cole's house. Struck him in the head on the patio by the pool. Then moved him to the bed and shot him. Then left.

The pool guy came back to the house a few minutes later and discovered the body.

The most important unanswered question was overwhelming all the others. Where was Kate Reynolds while all this was happening?

"Did you see Ms. Reynolds at all?" Cliff asked. "After you saw her in the pool?"

"No."

"Did you see her leave the house?"

"No. But like I said, I tried to avoid looking over there. I didn't really want to invade their privacy. I mean. She's not my girlfriend or my wife. Who am I to judge what she does with another consenting adult?"

"But you wanted Cole to know."

"He's my friend. I thought he had a right to know what was happening in his own house. You know. While the cat's away, the mice will play."

Cole did care enough to leave the team hotel and go home. That much was certain.

"Can you give me Cole's phone number before I leave?"

"Of course."

That'd make it easier for Cliff to find Cole's phone. At the very least, he could subpoena the phone company for Cole's text and call records.

"Why do you have a burner phone?" Cliff asked.

"For my work. Sometimes I travel and don't want to take my personal phone."

"What do you do for a living?"

"I'm the President of a software development company."

"Are you married?"

"Going through a divorce."

"I'm sorry to hear that."

"Don't be. It's been a long time coming. Although, I don't recommend it. It can put a huge dent in your finances."

"Is there anything else you'd like to add?"

"That's all I know."

"You said there were three suspects," Julia interjected. "That's only two."

"That's right," Potter said.

"Who's the third?" Cliff asked.

"Austin Mayfield."

"The man who lives next door to Mr. Dillinger?"

"That's correct.."

"Why is he a suspect in your mind?"

"I heard him say it."

"Say what?"

"That he was going to kill Cole Dillinger."

10

Thirty minutes ago, Cliff had two possible suspects in the murder of Cole Dillinger and nothing more than flimsy evidence against either. Now he had three strong suspects. All with plausible motives.

Justin Jackson. Leon Blackburn. Austin Mayfield.

Although the jury was still out, so to speak, on Mr. Mayfield. According to Potter, the neighbor threatened to kill Cole Dillinger. Cliff needed details. The four W's. When did he make the threat, where was he when he made it, who heard it, and why was the threat made?

He wouldn't have to pry it out of Harold Potter. Once the man started telling his compelling gossip of which novels were made, the words flowed out of him like water from a broken fire hydrant.

The first thing out of his mouth was that Austin Mayfield was at the top of his list of suspects. More likely the murderer than even Mr. Blackburn or the pool guy. Cliff was desperate to know why he thought that.

Potter began his narrative.

"Cole and Austin have been feuding for almost a year," he explained. "Pretty much since Austin moved in."

"What about?" Cliff asked.

Harold Potter took a deep breath like he was going to be talking for a while.

"The first issue was related to the fence."

Cliff already knew something was up with that.

"Neither of them are the original owners of their houses. Austin's was built first. Then Cole's. The man who built Cole's house wanted to put up a fence. The neighbor liked the idea and the two of them went in on it together."

"How long ago was this?" Cliff asked, breaking a cardinal rule of interviewing witnesses. Once you get them talking, don't interrupt with a trivial question. He made a mental note to stop doing it.

"Eight years ago," Potter answered, then paused, waiting for another question.

"Go ahead."

Harold Potter struggled to regain his train of thought, which was why Cliff shouldn't have interrupted him.

"The two homeowners decided to go in together to build a fence," Julia said, helping Potter remember where he was in the story after his pregnant pause.

Cliff fought back a smile at the pun that had popped into his head out of thin air.

Potter continued. "When the fence was built, it wasn't right on the property line. The contractor messed up. The fence was built too far to the north. It encroached onto Austin's property by two feet. Nobody knew it until Austin bought his house and had it surveyed."

Potter paused again and looked at Cliff to see if he was going to ask a question. Cliff kept his mouth shut this time.

"Austin wanted the fence moved. He approached Cole about paying for it."

"What difference does it make?" Julia asked. "The houses are on five or six acres."

"That's what Cole said. He refused to pay for it."

Cliff forced back another grin.

He could imagine two multi-millionaires arguing over a ten-thousand-dollar fence. He hoped it hadn't led to murder. So far, he hadn't heard anything to make him believe it had.

"Austin kept making a big deal about it. Cole's lawyer told him not to pay to move it or agree to let it be moved, even if Austin paid for it. Apparently, if a fence has been in place longer than seven years, then that becomes the new property line. The theory of acquiescence, I think, is the legal term."

"That hardly seems like a motive to kill someone," Julia said.

Cliff knew that wasn't true. A few years back, a man in south Chicago killed his neighbor over a property line dispute. He didn't work the case, but every detective in Chicago had seen a murder committed over a lot less.

"I'm getting to the good part," Harold Potter said.

Cliff couldn't wait to hear it. Potter would already be there if Cliff and Julia didn't keep interrupting him. Julia shouldn't be expected to know not to interrupt the witness. He could hardly be upset with her since he'd done the same thing.

And she was carrying his baby.

Why did his mind keep going back to that?

He smiled lovingly at his wife, and she returned it.

Knowing she was pregnant had brought out an instinct in him that he didn't know he had. It made him want to protect her. That wasn't the right word. He'd always been protective of Julia. This new compulsion was to be gentle with her. Like he would be with a newborn baby. Cradle the baby's head. Hold his or her neck in place. Check on the baby several times a night. Take the baby to the doctor at the first sign of a sniffle.

A fatherly instinct was raging inside of him, which he was now transferring on to Julia.

She'd kick his rear-end if she knew.

Julia wasn't the kind of woman who wanted to be pampered. She was as tough as a railroad nail spike. He'd keep these newfound kid gloves a secret. She'd hit the ceiling if she knew he was purposely babying her.

The second mental pun in the last thirty seconds caused Cliff to smile and Harold Potter to frown when he saw it. Considering the seriousness of the discussion, a smile was inappropriate.

"Please continue," Cliff said, to try and get things back on track. "I want to hear the good part."

Cliff buried his head in his black book to reestablish his detective demeanor.

"Cole likes to mow his own yard," Potter said. "He says it keeps him in shape during the offseason."

Cliff didn't see how riding a lawn mower around a five-acre tract kept an elite athlete in shape.

"He uses a push mower," Potter said. "Cole plants his own trees and trims his own bushes."

All the more reason not to say anything. Potter was good at filling in the blanks and answering the questions in Cliff's head. Cliff pretended to be writing notes in his black book, even though Potter hadn't said anything meaningful.

"When he mows his grass, sometimes the clippings get on Austin's yard. That makes Austin mad. They get in mine as well, but I don't say anything. My yard-guy simply cleans them up. No big deal. But it was a big deal to Austin Mayfield."

Cliff did write that down.

Property line dispute. Grass clippings in yard. Austin mad.

"Austin confronted Cole about it back in July. He was already peeved about the fence. Cole said he'd stop. A week later, Cole was mowing his yard and the same thing happened. Grass clippings sprayed out of his mower, and flew into Austin's yard."

Cliff wondered how Potter knew all this but refrained from asking. If Potter didn't say how he knew, then Cliff would bring it up later.

"Austin came charging out of his house and got in Cole's face."

Potter's pause was longer than it should've been.

"What happened next?" Cliff asked, to get the story moving again.

"Cole struck him. In the face. He gave Austin a black eye. Austin called the police."

Cliff made a note to look for a police report.

"The police didn't do anything because Austin didn't want to press charges."

There'd be no police report. *Darn.*

Cliff drew a line through the note in his black book.

A 911 call would be in the log. Cliff would look it up. It's not that he didn't believe Potter, it's just the more minor details he verified, the more credence he could give to the more important aspects of the story. Like the affair with Mrs. Blackburn. Seeing Cliff's girlfriend in the pool with another man.

"After the police left, that's when Austin threatened Cole. He said he was going to sue him for everything he had and make Cole pay. If Cole touched him again or ever came on his property, he'd kill him."

"Did you hear Mr. Mayfield make the threat?" Cliff asked.

"No. I wasn't there."

"How do you know about it?"

"Cole told me."

Cliff's heart sank a couple of inches in his chest.

The whole thing was hearsay and inadmissible in court. With no police report, Cliff would have a hard time proving the altercation actually took place unless Mayfield was willing to talk about it. Cliff doubted the neighbor's lawyer would let him. Threaten to kill a man who ends up murdered a few months later, and Cliff had no doubt Mayfield's lips were going to be as tight as the lid on the barrel of a drum filled with nuclear waste.

"With all due respect, Mr. Potter, you didn't actually see Mr. Dillinger hit Mr. Mayfield and you didn't actually hear him make the threat."

"I thought you might say that. Austin filed a lawsuit against Cole. There'd be a record of that."

Cliff scribbled a few notes in his black book. A civil lawsuit was public record, but he doubted one had actually been filed. If it had, that information would already be all over the news. The NFL had a personal conduct policy. If Cole struck a neighbor, even if provoked, he would've been suspended or fined by the league.

"How come we never heard anything about it?" Julia asked the obvious question, showing her perceptiveness once again.

"I don't know," Potter said. "Maybe the judge sealed the records."

Cliff shook his head.

"A judge seals a record after a settlement has been reached."

"They did reach a settlement. Cole paid him money. I don't know how much, but I was told it was a lot. Cole wanted to make it go away."

Cliff shook his head no again.

"Money might've exchanged hands, but that doesn't mean the lawsuit was *actually* filed. The judge only seals the records after a lawsuit is on his docket. That means, there'd be a public record of the complaint. The press monitors every lawsuit filed in the city of Chicago, which would have jurisdiction. If Mr. Dillinger's name showed up on a lawsuit, they'd be all over it. The press would be camped outside your house. Like they are now."

Harold Potter grimaced.

That didn't mean the events didn't take place exactly as Potter described them. Even the lawsuit. Cliff knew how the cutthroat lawyers worked. They prepared a lawsuit and then made a phone call to Cole or his attorney. Threatened to sue him unless he paid money. Probably even sent him a copy of the lawsuit to scare him.

Legal blackmail.

Cliff could see Cole paying whatever to make it go away. The parties would sign a confidentiality agreement and the whole thing would be swept under the rug. Never to see the light of day. No one would know about it. Not the press, nor the NFL.

Except, apparently, a nosy neighbor. Cliff wondered why Cole would divulge these details to Potter. Maybe he regretted doing so.

He would now, if he knew Potter was trying to parlay that information into a big payday.

At least he would if he weren't dead.

Regardless, the thread was definitely worth pursuing. If Potter was lying, he had a vivid imagination. The story was probably embellished, but Cliff expected that from witnesses. Especially ones like Potter who had a financial motive for making it as titillating as possible.

After a few more questions, Cliff felt like he had enough to end the interview.

His focus was already on Mrs. Blackburn. A number of questions were already formulating in his mind. If she admitted to having an affair with Cole Dillinger, that'd go a long way toward solidifying Potter's credibility and making Mr. Blackburn a prime suspect.

Cliff and Julia managed to leave after another offer of cake, which they both declined. Potter seemed like he didn't want the interview to end. As if he was enjoying it.

As they were walking away from the house, Cliff asked Julia, "Do you think he's telling the truth?"

She didn't answer right away. Julia was not a shoot-from-the-hip kind of girl. To answer a question that provocative, she'd want to think about it first.

"To be honest, I don't know what to think," she said. "I was a little overwhelmed."

"I know what you mean."

"It was so much to process at once. My first reaction was that it couldn't all be true."

"That's exactly what I was thinking. Great minds think alike."

Julia cracked a weak smile. It seemed like she wasn't feeling well again.

"You're the one with the great detective mind," she said. "I'm just along for the ride."

"I trust your instincts."

"I don't trust them right now. My brain's in some kind of pregnancy fog."

"That's to be expected. You haven't eaten anything of substance. It's been a stressful day."

"That's true. After I ate the pound cake, I got this sugar rush. Now I'm crashing."

"Do you want me to take you home?"

"No. I want to stay with you. Besides, we're about to get to the good part. Mrs. Blackburn might blow this case wide open. A few minutes from now, you might be arresting her husband for murder."

Cliff chuckled.

"That'd make the Lieutenant happy. Unfortunately, it doesn't happen that way very often. This isn't a one-hour TV show where the killer is found before the last commercial."

"I suppose."

"That's what I mean about your instincts being good. You're right about Mrs. Blackburn. We might not solve the murder in the next ten minutes, but if Mrs. Blackburn was having an affair with Cole, that'd prove one aspect of Harold Potter's story was true."

"A big part."

"For sure. That'd give the rest of his story even more credibility."

Before they could cross the street, Cliff's phone vibrated on his hip. He pulled it out and looked to see who was calling.

The Lieutenant.

"How are you coming on the case?" his boss asked after the obligatory greeting.

"I've made significant progress since the last time we talked," Cliff said.

He wasn't about to go into the details while standing on the sidewalk. Not with Julia next to him feeling fatigued.

"So have I," the Lieutenant said.

Cliff's ears perked up. He was suddenly feeling the same sugar crash as Julia. The Lieutenant calling with progress, sent a jolt of energy through him, like he'd consumed a large soda loaded with caffeine and sugar.

"Your idea about the wager was a good one," he said. "I talked to a source over at *I Bet Sports Gaming*. He said that a five-million-dollar bet was placed on the New York Giants this morning. Guess what time?"

He didn't wait for Cliff to answer.

"Eight twenty-eight. While the line was still sixteen points."

"The coroner said the murder likely occurred around eight thirty."

"Close enough."

Cliff felt adrenaline pulse through him like a geyser in Yellowstone rushes through the ground on the way to the surface.

"Write down this name and number," the Lieutenant said.

Cliff pulled out his black book and tried to write it down as fast as the Lieutenant was reciting it. He read it back to him to make sure he got it right.

"He goes by Rizzo," the Lieutenant added. "I want you to meet with him right after the game starts."

"Can I meet with him now? I can be there in twenty minutes."

"Nope. He's knee deep in cow manure at the moment. As you can imagine, the betting line has flipped. The Giants are the favorites. Rizzo is busy trying to find a way to keep them from losing their shirts."

"What is Rizzo going to tell me?"

"The name of the person who made that bet."

11

When Mrs. Marsha Blackburn opened the front door, Cliff had his answer. She was having an affair with Cole Dillinger.

Her eyes were swollen and puffy. She clutched a wad of wet tissues tightly in her hand.

"Are you Mrs. Blackburn?" Cliff asked.

"Yes. Who ar… are you?" Her voice cracked as she said it, but she managed to contain the tears that still watered her eyes.

"I'm Detective Cliff Ford, Chicago P.D. This is Julia. We'd like to ask you a few questions. May we come in?"

She closed the door slightly and leaned against it. "I'm home alone and I don't know anything about Mr. Dillinger's death."

"Would you prefer I come back when your husband is home?"

Her eyes widened in fear, and she said, "No. Now is fine."

He thought she might say that.

Her house was a monstrosity. Even Cole Dillinger's house paled in comparison. Business must be good. From the looks of it, Mr. Blackburn got a lot of business from his wife. She appeared to have had every plastic surgery known to man.

She could also be a poster child for her husband's abilities. Most people who'd had that much work, looked clown-like. Unnatural. The forty something woman had perfectly carved features and was stunningly gorgeous.

Well endowed. Not by the creator, but by her husband.

"I take it you've heard about Cole Dillinger's murder?" Cliff asked, after she led them into a den, and they sat down.

When he mentioned Cole's name, a sob almost escaped her lips, but she held it back.

"Yes, sir. I did hear about it."

"How would you describe your relationship with Mr. Dillinger?"

No use beating around the bush.

"We were acquaintances."

"Do you always cry this hard over acquaintances?"

She seemed surprised by Cliff's directness. Her eyes shifted up and to the left. A tell that she was searching for an excuse.

"I have allergies," she said.

Mrs. Blackburn was a bad liar.

"You have allergies in January?" Cliff asked.

She shrugged her shoulders and faked a cough but didn't respond.

He wasn't going to let her drag him into the weeds questioning her about something as ridiculous as allergies.

"Where's your husband?" he asked instead.

"He's at the office."

"On a Sunday?"

"He goes into the office every Sunday morning. It's quieter. He gets more work done. Paperwork mostly. Things like that. He's a surgeon. He'll be home in time for the game."

"What time did he leave this morning?"

"Around eight fifteen."

Another part of Harold Potter's story was now verified.

"What were you doing at that time of the morning?"

"I was sleeping."

"Then how do you know when he left?"

"He came in and kissed me on the cheek. I looked over at the clock. That's how I know."

Cliff didn't have his black book out on purpose. He wanted to keep his eyes fixated on the woman. Study her like a hawk eyes prey on the ground. Ready to swoop in at the first opening.

"How long have you been married?"

"Two years."

"Have you been married before?"

"Yes. Twice."

"Kids?"

"One son. He's seventeen. He lives with his father."

"Were you married to someone else when you met Mr. Blackburn?"

Her shoulders sagged slightly. "Yes."

Cliff had taken a wild guess that turned out to be right. He could see her defenses weakening. It wouldn't take long. He expected her to admit what he already knew. That she was romantically involved with Cole Dillinger.

The problem was getting it out of her right away. From his experience, the longer an interrogation went on, the more witnesses dug in and stuck to their story. When that happened and they gained confidence, it could take a long time to shake them out of their foxhole.

Before he could continue his barrage of questions, Julia suddenly blurted, "When did you and Cole Dillinger start having an affair?"

Mrs. Blackburn's eyes widened. To the extent they could, considering how swollen they were and how tight they were from her surgeries.

Cliff couldn't help but admire how Julia had phrased the question. Rule 101 of police interrogation. When did you stop beating your wife? Makes it much harder to prove a negative.

Mrs. Blackburn tried.

"We weren't having an affair! I'm a married woman."

The denial was not the least bit believable. Mrs. Blackburn flashed the huge rock on her finger to try to give it more credibility.

"Why would you even ask me such a thing?"

"Because we know you were," Julia said. Not accusingly, but with an air of certainty. "I've seen a lot of grief. I've lost a loved one myself. You don't seem like a woman who just lost an acquaintance."

"I'm an emotional person."

"You wouldn't be this upset," Julia continued, "if Cole didn't mean something special to you. You were in love with him, weren't you?"

Mrs. Blackburn burst into tears.

Julia stood and walked around the coffee table to sit beside her. She put her hand on Mrs. Blackburn's hand to console her.

"It's okay. You can tell us."

"Are you going to tell my husband?" she asked, after Julia gave her a few seconds to compose herself. "He'll kill me if he finds out."

Cliff sat straight up. Was she saying that figuratively or was she genuinely concerned for her life?

Mrs. Blackburn must've seen Cliff's expression because she clarified her statement. "I don't mean that he would actually *kill* me."

"What do you mean?" Cliff asked. "Is your husband a violent man?"

"No. I promise he's not."

The words 'I promise' were a telltale sign that a witness was lying.

"Has he ever hit you?" Julia asked, in a better tone than Cliff was capable of mustering to a witness who was lying to him.

"No. I mean, he has. But not in a while. And only a couple of times. He gets jealous when other guys look at me."

More alarm bells were sounding in Cliff's head.

The tears suddenly dried up and Mrs. Blackburn's mouth opened as wide as her collagen enhanced lips would allow.

She began to ramble.

"Do you think my husband killed Cole, do you? I don't think he would. I mean. He doesn't know about Cole and me. He would've said something."

She rolled her eyes. Obvious even through the caked-on makeup.

"Actually, he's oblivious to what I do. I could have sex with another man in the other room and he wouldn't have a clue."

She said the last words with a clear hint of bitterness.

"I don't think my husband is capable of murder," she added. "Do you think he is?"

"I don't know what to think," Cliff said honestly. He had no definitive proof that Leon Blackburn killed her lover and would never speculate or offer a witness his opinion, even if he had one.

"My husband has a temper but I don't think he'd hurt someone."

"He hurt you," Julia said in a gentle tone.

"That's different. I deserved it. I can be too flirtatious. I don't blame him. Why should he trust me? Our relationship started out as an affair. I came on to him. I'm sure he's worried that I might cheat on him too."

Cliff wanted to state the obvious but resisted. Whatever fears her husband had about her fidelity, or lack thereof, were well founded. But having an affair wasn't against the law. His job was not to investigate moral behavior or judge what happened between two consenting adults. He wasn't even tasked with judging a murderer. The court system did that. His sole responsibility was to find the killer and enough evidence to get a conviction.

"When did your relationship with Mr. Dillinger start?" Cliff asked the question Julia had asked, but Mrs. Blackburn hadn't answered.

"About six months ago."

"How often would you see him?"

"A couple times a week when he was in town."

She buried her head in her hands. "I know. I'm a horrible person."

Cliff knew the road from guilt to shame was a short one. Shame to self-condemnation was even shorter.

"How did it start?" Julia asked.

"Cole knocked on my door. A piece of our mail was in his mailbox. He was returning it. I invited him in. We had an instant attraction. That was the first time."

"Do you know he has a girlfriend?" Julia asked.

Mrs. Blackburn's entire demeanor changed.

"He doesn't love Kate! She doesn't make him happy like I do."

Cliff could hear the bitterness in her voice. If he was investigating the murder of Kate Reynolds, Mrs. Blackburn would be a prime suspect.

He looked at his wife admiringly. A woman so stunningly beautiful, she didn't need plastic surgery. Now that she was with child, she was even more attractive to him. If that was even possible.

"She's prettier than me," Mrs. Blackburn said, "She's a supermodel. Did you know that?"

Cliff nodded although he'd never actually met the woman. Something he was anxious to do.

"Cole and I are soulmates!"

The tears started flowing again and she didn't even try to hide them.

Not until we heard the voice of her husband in the other room.

"Honey. I'm home."

Cliff hadn't even heard the garage door. Probably because it was on the other side of the house. Seemingly a city block away.

Mrs. Blackburn roughly pushed the tears out of her eyes and off her face.

Cliff stood to his feet when Mr. Blackburn entered the room. His botoxed forehead attempted to furrow to the extent it could.

"Mr. Blackburn, my name is Cliff Ford. I'm a detective with Chicago P.D. I'm investigating the murder of Cole Dillinger."

Mr. Blackburn walked over to Cliff and extended his hand. Cliff shook it and looked him straight in the eye. He was taller than Cliff. Had perfectly manicured hair. Handsome features surgically and chemically enhanced as well.

"I just heard about Cole's death," he said. "It's a real tragedy."

Mr. Blackburn looked over at his wife and became immediately concerned because he bolted right toward her.

"Are you alright?" he asked, taking her hand in his. "You've been crying."

Without notice, he suddenly directed anger toward Cliff. "What did you say to upset her so badly?"

"We just wanted to ask your wife some questions. I have a few for you as well."

"In the future, I'd prefer that I be here when you talk to my wife."

Cliff nodded. For all practical purposes, his interview with Mrs. Blackburn was over and he had no more relevant questions for her.

Julia stood and moved from the couch and circled the coffee table to sit next to Cliff on a loveseat that sat across from the couch. Mr. Blackburn sat down next to his wife and put his arm around her. Her head collapsed on his chest, but her eyes were in constant motion.

They flitted back and forth. Between Cliff and Julia. Then out of the corner of her eye at her husband. Back to Cliff. Her expression was almost pleading with him not to tell her husband about the affair.

He had no intention of telling him. Not yet anyway. He liked knowing things a suspect didn't know he knew.

"Mr. Blackburn," Cliff said.

"It's Dr. Blackburn."

"Of course. Dr. Blackburn can you tell me where you've been this morning?"

"At my office. I'm a cosmetic surgeon."

"Did anyone see you at work?"

"No. I was the only one there."

Cliff had his black notebook out now and pretended to take notes.

"What time did you leave the house?"

"About eight fifteen. I don't know if this is relevant, but I actually saw Cole as I was leaving this morning for work."

"Did you talk to him?"

"I did. I was a little surprised actually. With the game today, I figured he'd be with the team."

"What did the two of you talk about?"

"I wished him luck. Told him we'd be watching and pulling for him. Then I drove away."

The first contradiction he found in Harold Potter's account of things. That meant one of them was lying. Someone lying meant someone had something to hide. Not necessarily a murder, but something.

"Cole seemed to be in a hurry," Mr. Blackburn said in a believable voice. "Looking back at it, he kind of had a worried look on his face. Like he was preoccupied. Troubled."

"Did either of you get out of your car?"

"No. I rolled down my window. He pulled up next to me, and we talked through the windows of our cars. I mean, the conversation lasted all of ten seconds. He thanked me and I drove away."

"Did you stop anywhere on the way to work?"

"No."

"Did you see anything suspicious?"

"Not that I can think of."

"Have either of you seen any strange vehicles in the neighborhood? Anyone loitering around?"

"There are workers here all the time," Dr. Blackburn said. "That's always concerned me. Why have a gated subdivision if anybody can come in under the guise of working construction? But other than that, I haven't noticed anyone. What about you honey?"

Mrs. Blackburn shook her head nervously from side to side. She refused to even look Cliff's way. Her stare was affixed to her hands which were still clutching the tissues and resting on her knees, which were also tensed.

"Are you aware of a feud between Mr. Dillinger and Mr. Mayfield?"

He shook his head. "I'm not aware of any problems in the neighborhood, though I don't know my neighbors that well. I work way too much."

From the expression on her face, it seemed like Mrs. Blackburn might've known.

"Do you own a gun?" Cliff asked.

"I own several."

"What kind are they?"

He rattled off the makes and models of three rifles and two handguns along with a couple of antiques.

"Where do you keep them?"

"In the gun cabinet in my den."

Cliff stood to his feet. Abruptly. Startling everyone including Julia.

"I don't have any further questions."

Cliff pulled out his card and handed it to Mr. Blackburn.

"If either of you think of something that might be useful to my investigation, please call me at that number on the card."

"We will."

In less than two minutes, Cliff and Julia were back in their car.

"Why did you stop questioning Mr. Blackburn?" she asked.

"I wasn't going to get any more information out of him. Anyway, his story is easy enough to corroborate by the security camera at the guard gate. If he drove out of the subdivision before the murder occurred, then I can pretty much rule him out as the murderer. There's simply not enough time for him to get back to Cole's house and kill him. Then dispose of the weapon."

"I imagine some of the houses have cameras as well."

"Probably all of them."

"Do you want to look at the cameras in Cole's house first?"

Cliff shook his head no while he started the car.

"They aren't there anymore. I'm sure they've already been taken down to the evidence locker. I'll look at them later."

He drove straight to the entrance of the subdivision and pulled into a parking space. One lone guard manned it. He wore a long sleeved white shirt with a patch on it. His belly hung over his two-sizes too small pants. The gun on his belt meant someone powerful pulled some strings down at the city to get permission for him to man the gate with a weapon.

Cliff introduced himself.

"What time did you come to work today?"

"Nine. We come in later on Sundays."

"I'd like to take a look at the videos on the security cameras, if I may."

"I already have."

Cliff acted surprised, even though he wasn't. If he worked at the guard gate and a murder occurred in his neighborhood, that's the first thing he'd do.

"What did you see?"

"Nothing."

"Did you see anyone suspicious coming in or out of the subdivision between eight and eight thirty this morning?"

"I didn't see anything at all."

"Did any of your residents enter or leave during that time?"

"When I say I saw nothing, I mean I literally saw nothing. The tape has been tampered with. Everything from seven in the morning until eight-forty-five is a black screen. I called 911 to report it."

That message hadn't gotten back to Cliff.

The new information changed things. Dr. Blackburn's story could no longer be verified. Neither could the pool guy's. It felt like a major setback. That's exactly what the killer wanted.

12

I Bet Sports Gaming
Downtown Chicago

The Chicago Bears led the New York Giants 9-0 at halftime. Much to the shock of even the most die hard Bears fan. The game had turned into a defensive struggle. The only scoring were three field goals by the Bears All-Pro kicker.

Cliff and Julia were interested in the game, but more consumed with gorging themselves on the huge buffet in the VIP lounge of the *I Bet Sports Gaming* establishment. The place was wall-to-wall with sports fans and professional gamblers who were as excited as a thousand kids in a pizza arcade.

They found Rizzo, the contact given to Cliff by the Lieutenant, but he didn't have the name yet. Apparently, the five-million-dollar bet on the New York Giants wasn't made by an individual, but by a Finnish corporation through a bookie. They were having a hard time tracking down the source of the wager. Rizzo was confident they'd be able to do so and he'd have it for them soon.

Since they had to wait, Rizzo offered them access to the VIP lounge, normally reserved for high rollers. The seventy-five hundred square foot suite was modern and posh. Large big screen televisions provided multiple vantage points to watch the game from plush chairs and various sized tables throughout the suite.

The all-you-can-eat smorgasbord buffet had Cliff and Julia's full attention. The only thing they'd eaten that day were crackers and a slice of pound cake. They attacked the buffet like they'd just been rescued off a deserted island.

They chose from bacon wrapped beef tenderloin, prime rib, Osso Bucco stuffed pork chops, wrapped pork loin in raspberry chipotle sauce, seared scallops and shrimp served on a bed of zebra pasta with a lobster cream sauce, and at least a dozen starches, soups, and vegetables.

More traditional football fair was also available. Buffalo Coca Cola Chicken wings, hamburger sliders, mozzarella cheese sticks, fried macaroni and cheese balls, and cheese fries.

They hadn't even made it to the dessert table which ran along an entire wall.

"You're going to have to carry me out of here," Julia said.

"Then who's going to carry me out?" Cliff grunted.

"It's back to the gym for me tomorrow," Julia said.

"Do you think that's a good idea?"

"Is what a good idea?"

"Going to the gym. Shouldn't you take it easy while you're pregnant?"

"I'm having a baby, not open-heart surgery."

"I know that, but you're a workout maniac. It might not be good for the baby."

They both were intense fitness fanatics. Cliff's BMI was 10 and Julia's was slightly better. Although, that was measured before they had consumed three days' worth of food in the last thirty minutes.

"God made it so that the baby is well protected in my womb," Julia said. "I'm not going to hurt the baby by working out. In fact, it's good for me. All the experts say exercise during pregnancy is important. It'll keep me from gaining too much weight."

"How much do you think you'll gain?"

"What I've read is that twenty-five to thirty-five pounds is ideal."

She pushed her cheeks out, so her face looked bloated. "I gained half of that tonight," she said. "That's why I've got to hit the gym tomorrow."

"Don't overdo it."

Julia gave him a playful glare. "You're cute when you worry about me," she said. "You should be more worried about the Bears. We need to pull them through."

With the score 9-0, Cliff was less worried than he was earlier in the day when he thought the Bears had no chance of winning. His mood regarding the game had gone from despondent to cautiously optimistic.

"The Bears might actually win this game," Cliff said, looking around at the large television screens throughout the lounge. The Giants were about to kick off to start the second half.

"I wouldn't get your hopes up yet," Julia said. "There's a whole half to play. But they are looking good."

"The defense is playing out of their minds," Cliff said.

"How is Deuce Dixon doing?" Julia asked, speaking of the backup quarterback who was the biggest concern going in.

"Surprisingly well. He hasn't made a costly mistake. Not that they're giving him a chance to screw up. He only attempted six passes in the first half. Completed five of them. For nineteen yards."

"Oh. That's not so good."

"It's good enough. As long as they win, it doesn't matter how many yards he throws for. The Bears need to stick with the plan. Keep handing the ball off, play good defense, and they can win this game. How incredible would that be?"

A huge cheer went up in the room.

"What happened?" Julia asked.

Cliff was cheering with them. He was standing. His hands were high in the air. It felt good to stretch his midsection and all the food that had settled in it.

"The Bears returned the kickoff for a touchdown," Cliff said excitedly, caught up in the emotion of the room. He had to practically shout so Julia could hear him.

The electricity generated by the crowd could light up a city block. Julia raised one fist in the air to join them in the celebration.

"The extra point is good," Cliff said. "The Bears lead sixteen to nothing."

The din subsided to a level slightly below a frenzy.

"If we stepped outside, I bet we could hear the crowd cheering at the stadium," Julia said.

Cliff nodded. They were less than a mile from Soldier Field.

"Wouldn't it be ironic if the Bears covered the spread without Cole Dillinger?" he said.

"That would be. It's still tragic, though."

"Of course. Think about this. What if the gamblers were the ones who killed Cole? Then as soon as they got confirmation he was dead, they placed the bet. Five million bucks on the Giants. Almost a sure thing without Cole. They got the Giants plus sixteen points, because no one else knew Cole was dead. Once the news broke the line changed and the line went down. But their bet was locked in."

"That's like insider trading," Julia said.

"Exactly."

"What if the Bears win by more than sixteen points?" Cliff said. "The gamblers lose their bet. How great would that be?"

"Sounds like they'd get what they deserve."

"That and a lifetime in jail if I have anything to say about it."

It made Cliff angry just thinking about it. He didn't need added motivation to solve a murder. He was wired with an intense resolve to find killers.

"Do you think the gamblers killed Cole and not someone close to him?" Julia asked.

"I go back and forth."

"I have some theories," Julia said.

Cliff's mind was a jumbled mess. He wanted to watch the game, but the case was a major distraction. His brain was processing all the possible scenarios faster than a high-speed computer. Talking about them with Julia might bring him clarity.

The Bears seemed to have the game firmly in control anyway. The reaction of the room would tell him what was happening on the screens. Every play had some sort of emotional reaction. They cheered when the Bears did something good and groaned when they didn't. If it was really bad, they responded angrily. Cussed and screamed at the television sets.

"Let's start with the pool guy," Julia said. "He's having an affair with Cole's girlfriend."

"Allegedly."

"Whether he was or not, Cole thought his girlfriend was cheating on him, based on the text he received from Harold Potter."

"Cole gave the text enough credence that he left the hotel and rushed home. On the day of a big game."

A groan went through the crowd and Cliff immediately turned his head toward the televisions.

The Giants kicked a field goal. The score was 16-3.

Nothing to worry about, yet. Still a big lead.

Julia was oblivious to the game. She was more focused on her theory.

"Cole arrives home and confronts his girlfriend," she said. "The pool guy shows up and gets in an argument with Cole. It turns physical. The pool guy hits Cole over the head with a blunt object and knocks him out."

"Maybe the girlfriend hit Cole. While Cole was distracted."

"That's possible. Point well taken. That's why you're the detective. Anyway, Cole's not dead, and they don't know what to do. So, they carry him into the bedroom where they shoot him. Then stage the body to make it look like he was killed in his sleep."

Julia's scenario brought something into focus for Cliff. Whoever shot Cole wasn't a professional.

"The murder wasn't well thought out," Cliff said. "Whoever did this wasn't a professional."

"Exactly. That's why I wondered if one of the neighbors did it rather than a professional gambler. Whoever you're looking for probably hasn't killed before. That fits the suspects in the neighborhood."

"Don't forget the bet. Whoever placed it, either had inside information or got incredibly lucky. If he had inside information, then he either committed the murder, or was involved in a conspiracy to commit it."

"Wouldn't a professional gambler who bet five million on the game, spend a little bit of money and hire a professional hitman?"

"Maybe."

"So let's go back to the people who had motive and opportunity," Julia said. "Like the pool guy."

"He said he didn't get back to the house until later. After eight thirty. That'd be after Cole was killed."

"Maybe that's a lie."

Cliff groaned.

"Unfortunately, I don't have the security tape to know when he arrived."

"I think it's a safe assumption that whoever doctored the tape is the same person who committed the murder."

"That's probably true. So back to your theory. How does a pool guy doctor a security tape? He wouldn't have access to it. He doesn't live in the neighborhood."

"He could pay the guard."

"I wouldn't think the pool guy has a lot of money. It'd take some serious cash to get a security guard to help cover up a murder of a prominent member of the neighborhood. The star quarterback of the Bears."

Julia stared off at the television screens. Not watching the Bears. Clearly, deep in thought.

"Which brings up another point," Cliff said. "What does Cole's girlfriend see in the pool guy? She's got a rich good-looking boyfriend"

"Mrs. Blackburn has a rich, good-looking and successful husband," Julia retorted.

"My point exactly. She wanted the young stud. The professional athlete. Isn't that what all women want."

"The heart wants what the heart wants."

"Why would Cole be interested in Mrs. Blackburn? A woman twenty years older? When he's dating a supermodel? It doesn't make sense."

"Love doesn't have to make sense. You know that. Look at me and you."

Cliff frowned.

"I'm just kidding. You're perfect for me. You're my soulmate."

The frown was still on Cliff's face.

"Besides, you don't have to worry about that anymore," Julia said. "Now that I'm pregnant, no good-looking guy is going to give me a second look."

"I'll give you a second look. And a third. A fourth. A thousand looks."

"Thank you, Cliff. But you know my body isn't going to look like this for much longer. Can you handle it?"

"Baby. I plan on handling it more than you want me to."

She rolled her eyes.

"I know. You can't keep your hands off of me. I wonder if that'll be the case when I'm sticking out to here and I don't lose my baby fat right away."

Her hands made a motion to simulate her late-term stomach.

"I think you'll be even more attractive to me."

"That's sweet. Back to the suspects. Mr. Blackburn is obviously a major suspect."

"Dr. Blackburn."

She rolled her eyes again. "It takes an arrogant man to correct you to your face for calling him mister instead of doctor."

"He is the epitome of arrogant."

"Arrogant enough to think he can get away with committing murder?"

"He beats his wife, so you know he has a proclivity to violence."

"He's also the jealous type."

"And he owns guns."

"Why didn't you ask to see his guns, Cliff? I thought you would."

"Mr. Blackburn is an intelligent man. I doubt he'd kill Cole and then put the gun back in his gun safe. He'd get rid of it. He would want me to see his safe to prove his innocence. What I really wanted to do was see the security tape. If it backed up his story, then I could rule him out and wouldn't need to see the safe. If the tape showed that he didn't leave the subdivision when he said he did, then I could get a subpoena to search the whole house. Right now, I don't have enough evidence to get a judge to sign off on one."

Julia stood up.

"Where are you going?" Cliff asked.

"To the restroom."

"Is the baby pressing against your bladder?"

"The baby is the size of a peanut. It's two helpings of garlic mashed potatoes that are taking up all the room in my midsection."

Cliff stood up as well.

"Where are you going?" she asked.

"To the dessert bar. It's free. Might as well take advantage of it."

She let out a moan like she couldn't believe he was going to eat dessert. Then said, "Get me a few bites of something."

Cliff filled a plate with one of everything that had chocolate on it. Chocolate mousse, chocolate cheesecake, and two chocolate brownies. He also added a couple of things he thought Julia would like. Bomboloni which were Italian miniature donuts filled with jelly and cream with powdered sugar and a hazelnut spread on the top. Also a thin slice of lemon chiffon cake.

Julia grimaced when she got back to the table and saw the plate sitting in the center.

"I can't eat another thing," she said, as she picked up a fork and took her first bite.

"Did you know that Chicago is the home of the chocolate brownie?" Cliff asked as he took a bite of one. They were his favorite food growing up.

"I think you told me that before."

"The fourth quarter is starting," Cliff said, pointing at the television. "The Bears are still ahead 16-3."

"Don't celebrate yet."

He took a deep breath, then dug into the desserts. Between the two of them, they made a big dent in the plate within a few minutes. They finally started to slow down before anything more was said.

"Do you want to talk about the case some more?" Julia asked.

"No. I want to watch the last quarter of the game. Maybe that'll take my mind off the case for a few minutes."

Wishful thinking.

Watching the Bears reminded him of something. An image that haunted his mind. Cole Dillinger lying in a cold morgue. Instead of where he should be. Playing in the game.

It made Cliff angry to even think about it. But he needed to put it out of his mind and enjoy the game. He was in that wonderful suite with his beautiful wife who was carrying his child.

Being at the game wasn't as good as this. The VIP lounge was a balmy seventy-two. The fans in the stadium were cold. The food here was free. A hot dog and soda at the game cost fifteen bucks. With parking, he could pay out a day's salary for the entire experience, even if the tickets were free.

In his mind, he had the best place to watch the game. He reached over and took Julia's hand. Rizzo suddenly appeared. With a yellow file folder.

"Did you get enough to eat?" he asked.

A cheer went up in the crowd before they could answer. Cliff looked over at the television. The Giants were punting the football. There was less than five minutes left in the game. Still 16-3.

We're going to win.

"No," Cliff said jokingly. "I didn't get enough." He smiled widely, so Rizzo knew he was kidding.

"I'm actually eating for two," Julia said.

"She's pregnant," Cliff clarified, when Rizzo looked confused.

"Congratulations."

"You'd think I was eating for four," she said. Then took another bite.

"Maybe, you'll have triplets," Rizzo quipped.

Julia looked down and Cliff knew why. Triplets ran in her family. She was actually an identical triplet. Something extremely rare. She had two sisters who looked just like her. One was an FBI agent killed in a drive-by shooting. The other sister, Anna, was married and living in New York.

A deafening groan went up in the room.

The Bears fumbled the punt. The Giants recovered.

Shoot. Don't blow this.

16-3 is a big enough lead. Not much time left on the clock. We should be fine.

"Here's the name of the company that made the five-million-dollar wager," Rizzo said.

Cliff opened the file and looked for the name.

Dursley Enterprises.

"Do you know who owns the company?"

Rizzo shook his head. "I have no way of finding out."

"Thank you for this," Cliff said.

He didn't know how to find out the name of the owners of a foreign corporation either.

"I hope you find Cole's killer," Rizzo said sincerely.

"I will," Cliff said.

An angry roar went through the building. Cliff almost felt the room shaking. Rizzo excused himself.

"What happened?" Julia asked.

He looked over to see.

"The Giants scored a touchdown. The score is 16-9. 16-10 if they make the extra point."

They did.

Cliff was suddenly feeling very nervous. About the case and the game.

13

The tension in the VIP lounge of the *I Bet Sports Gaming* room was as thick as the uneaten dish of tofu at the buffet bar. The Bears led 16-10 with 2:16 left in the game. The Giants were lining up to attempt an onside kick. They were out of timeouts.

Cliff and Julia were standing. As was nearly every patron in the lounge. The sound on the television was turned up so they could hear the announcers. Longtime NFL broadcaster, Buzz Adams, was providing the play-by-play, and former quarterback and NFL Hall of Famer, Mike Salts, provided the color commentary and analysis.

Julia had her fingers crossed in front of her and against her chest just under her chin. She bounced up and down on the toes of her feet in nervousness.

Cliff liked to pace when he was nervous. He couldn't because they were shoulder-to-shoulder with all the other tense gamblers and fans. Most of the outcome of the bets had been decided. The Bears weren't going to cover the sixteen-point spread. It seemed like most people were watching more as fans than as gamblers.

They were caught up in the excitement. Rooting for the Bears to win. After all the team and city had suffered that day, a trip to the Super Bowl would take a little of the sting out of it. It wouldn't bring Cole back, but maybe the city of Chicago would have something to celebrate over the next two weeks rather than just mourn Cole's death and the loss of the game.

The Bears were two minutes away from going to the Super Bowl. If they recovered the onside kick, all they had to do was run out the clock and they'd win. If the Giants recovered, they still had time to drive down the field for the winning score.

Cliff could feel the tension rise another couple of notches. If that were even possible.

"Here we go," Buzz said through the surround sound speakers strategically placed around the room. "The Giants need this without any timeouts."

"The Bears have all their good-hands players up on the line," Salts said.

Cliff could hear the excitement in their voices.

"I see a couple of receivers and running backs lined up to recover the kick."

Salts explained what he meant. "You want the best people up close. The ones who know how to catch the ball."

Buzz described the action.

"The Giants kicker, Curtis Fields, puts the ball on the kicking tee. He leans it back on the tee. He's obviously going to squib it. Here we go. He approaches the ball. It's bouncing on the ground."

Cliff could feel himself holding his breath.

"It's still loose! There's a huge scramble! Nobody has it!"

What was happening? Who has it?

"A Bears player kicks it! It bounces back towards the Giants goal line! There's a huge pile up! At least a dozen guys dove on the pile. I honestly don't know who recovered that football."

"It was a perfectly executed onside kick," Salts said, excitedly. "A Bears player had it, but then he got blasted by a Giant player and the ball came loose. Then it was like a hot potato. At least six different people had their hands on the ball and a chance to recover it. I don't know how the refs are going to get the mass of men out of the pile."

The refs tugged at the players who were on top of each other. Many of them were wrestling on the ground in a big scrum trying to gain an advantage and keep the opposing players away from the ball.

"Everything hinges on this call," Buzz said.

Nervous tension filled the room like a San Francisco fog fills the bay. Cliff's hands were up on the back of his head. He wanted to turn away, like you would from a car crash. If the Giants recovered, it'd feel like he'd just witnessed a car wreck.

"Still no signal," Buzz said.

"Come on. Come on. Come on," Cliff muttered to himself.

Julia's eyes were peeled to the screen. Her crossed fingers were now over her mouth.

What's taking so long?

"I think the Bears have it," Salts said.

Cliff felt his heart skip a beat.

"They do! Bears ball! Bears ball!" Buzz shouted. "The ref is pointing in the direction of the Chicago Bears. Listen to this crowd. They're going crazy. The Giants players are arguing, but it won't do them any good. The Bears have it. They can take a knee three times and punch their ticket to the Super Bowl."

The crowd in the bar was going crazy with the fans in the stadium. The whole city of Chicago was no doubt sky high with euphoria.

"This is unbelievable!" Cliff shouted. "I just knew the Giants had recovered the ball."

"Give the Bears players credit," Salts said. "That ball was on the ground. They fought for it. I've been at the bottom of those piles. It's not fun. Somehow, they came out of there with the ball."

"The whole stadium just let out a collective sigh of relief."

Cliff and Julia clasped hands and were jumping up and down. He threw his arms around her and picked her up in the air. Then wondered if he should since she was pregnant. He sat her back down. Gently.

They started high fiving the people around them. Cliff didn't remember ever feeling this much excitement in one room.

"The city will be celebrating tonight," Salts said. "Two minutes and four seconds is showing on the clock. That's how long the Bears need to hold on to the ball. Then they can punch their ticket to the Super Bowl."

"The Bears are going to win!" Cliff shouted to Julia.

The room was still buzzing.

"There's still time," Julia said. "Don't count your chickens yet."

"The Giants don't have any timeouts. The Bears can run out the clock."

Buzz Adams contradicted Cliff on the television. "The Bears can't run out the clock. Even though the Giants don't have any timeouts, the clock will stop at the two-minute warning. If they don't get a first down, the Bears will still have to punt. How much time will be left on the clock, Mike?"

"I expect the Bears to hand the ball off on the first play," Salts said. "Then they'll likely take a knee two straight times. According to my rough calculations, there'll be roughly seventeen seconds left when they get to fourth down."

"It's not over yet," Julia said.

"It's over," Cliff said. "Even if the Giants get the ball back, they'll only have ten seconds or so left on the clock."

"We need to get a first down, so we can put it away."

The tension had returned to the room like a bad cough that won't go away.

The final two minutes played out as Salts predicted. The Bears ran a handoff up the middle of the line for an eight-yard gain on first down.

"That was so close!" Cliff said. "He almost got the first down. Dang!"

The clock stopped for the two-minute warning. Nine seconds ran off the clock. 1:55 was left.

"Don't do anything stupid," Cliff said aloud to the Bears players as if they could hear him.

"They should try to get the first down," Julia said. "It's only two yards. If they get it, the game is over."

Cliff shook his head contradicting her. "Too risky. If they fumble the handoff and the Giants recover, they still have time to drive down and score. The safest thing to do is simply take a knee. Run out the clock."

The Bears took a knee on second down as Cliff predicted.

They were facing third down.

1:03 left.

They took another knee.

Fourth down.

The refs reset the ball at 57 seconds and restarted the clock. The play clock ran for forty seconds. They now had fourth down with five yards to go to get the first down.

"There's a seventeen second differential between the play clock and the game clock," Buzz said. "The Bears will have to run one more play."

The television screen showed Deuce Dixon standing next to the official. When the clock hit 18 seconds, he called a timeout. Right before the play clock expired.

"Are they going to kick a field goal?" Julia asked. "They're in range."

Cliff did the math, and the field goal would be a forty-five yarder. Well within their kicker's range. He thought about it and then shook his head no. "I don't think they'll kick a field goal. They won't take the risk."

"I think they should. If they make the field goal, they'll have a nine-point lead, and the Giants can't win," Julia argued.

"If the kick is blocked, the Giants could run it back for a touchdown. Stranger things have happened. You could have a bad snap. Too risky."

The announcers were having the same discussion.

"What do you think Mike?" Buzz asked. "You were a quarterback. You've been in this situation. What do the Bears do?"

"You could punt or try a field goal, but it could get blocked. That's too risky."

"You just said that!" Julia said, pointing at Cliff, who could feel his face beaming.

Salts continued with his analysis.

"The clock stops on a change of possession. The Bears could take a knee, but then the Giants would have roughly thirteen seconds left on the clock. Enough time to run two plays. I think the Bears should have Dixon take the snap, then run around for several seconds. Take as much time off the clock as possible. When he's about to be tackled, he should get on the ground to avoid taking a hit and eliminate the risk of a fumble."

"Dixon has a history of fumbling," Buzz said. "Do you think they should take the path of least resistance? Take a knee and rely on their defense to stop them. What are the odds that the Giants can go sixty-five yards in thirteen seconds with no timeouts?"

"I agree with Buzz," Julia said. "They should take a knee."

Cliff disagreed. "I agree with Salts. They should run Deuce on a bootleg and try to get the first down. If it's not there, then he should run time off the clock. After five to ten seconds, he should fall to the ground. It's the safest play."

"I actually think they should kick a field goal. Win it outright."

Cliff didn't respond. It didn't really matter what either of them thought the Bears should do. He wanted to pace but still couldn't because of the limited space. His heart was pacing around his chest instead.

The timeout was over. The Bears offense was back on the field. That meant they weren't going to punt or try a field goal.

Deuce Dixon was under center.

"I can't watch," Julia said, covering her eyes.

Cliff could see her peeking through her fingers.

Buzz Adams described the action. "Dixon takes the snap and rolls to his left."

Cliff saw it before the announcer said it.

"The ball is on the ground! Dixon lost the football! Oh my goodness! He stumbled and fumbled. The Giants recovered!"

Cliff couldn't believe what he just saw with his own eyes.

The replay came on. Salts explained what had happened.

"Dixon came away from center. It looks like Burlingame, his big right guard, number 74, tripped him up. He was on backside protection. He pulled out of his stance quicker than Dixon could get on the edge, and their heels clicked. Dixon started to fall. He tried to catch himself by putting the ball on the ground. It's a bang-bang play. He lost the football when it hit the ground."

"It was Haney, the Giants safety who recovered the fumble," Buzz said. "The Bears were fortunate he didn't return it for a touchdown. He had a clear path to the endzone, but somebody got a big paw out and tripped him up. Otherwise, the Giants would've scored."

"The Bears still have this," Cliff said. "There's only seven seconds left. The Giants have to go sixty yards with no timeouts."

"This is not a complete disaster," Salts said. "The Giants have to go sixty yards with no timeouts."

Julia looked at Cliff, then pointed to the screen. "You just said that!"

He smiled, nervously.

The Giants offense was back on the field.

"It all comes down to this one play," Buzz said.

You could suddenly hear a pin drop in the room.

"Here we go," Buzz said. "Giants quarterback, Coy Majors is in the shotgun. Three receivers are to the left. Two to the right. He's going to heave it to the end zone."

"He's got the arm to get it there," Salts said.

"Majors takes the snap!"

Cliff's eyes were glued to the screen. It's like it all happened in slow motion.

"He scrambles to his right."

"Get him," Cliff shouted at the big screen.

"He's under pressure."

He heard Julia let out a scream. Barely perceptible over the shouts of the rest of the patrons.

"Majors avoids the rush."

He's going to get it off.

"He lets it go. A high rainbow to the end zone."

It felt like the ball was suspended in the air for two minutes even though it was only a few seconds.

"There's a battle for the ball! It's tipped up in the air!"

"Knock it down!" Cliff shouted.

Cliff watched as a Giants wide receiver came up with the ball.

"It's caught! Oh my goodness!" Buzz shouted.

"Miraculous!" Salts said.

Cliff's heart sunk to the bottom of his chest.

"Dante McGee went up high in the air! The Giants receiver is six foot three. He jumped over the defenders. The ball was tipped. He went up there and got it. What an incredible play to end the game!"

"The Giants are an extra point away from winning this thing."

"Unbelievable!" Cliff said angrily.

Julia had her hands over her mouth in disbelief.

"The air has been let out of this stadium," Buzz said. "The Bears fans are stunned. They can't believe what just happened."

"Miss the extra point!" Cliff shouted. If they missed the extra point, the game would go to overtime.

"The kick is up! It's good! Giants win! Giants win! Giants win! The New York Giants are going to the Super Bowl. In one of the most unbelievable comebacks in NFL championship history."

The Giants players stormed the field. Several of them lifted their coach in the air and carried him onto the field. The announcers were silent for several minutes, while the cameraman panned the stadium to capture the moment. The thrill of victory for some, the agony of defeat for most.

"The Bears had this game won," Buzz said, when he finally began commentating again.

"What an incredible finish," Salts said. "I'm emotionally exhausted. I can only imagine how the Bears players are feeling. They fought their hearts out. All Deuce Dixon had to do was hold onto the ball and run out the clock. He fumbled the ball on a simple running play. I'm sure that's why the coach kept the ball in Dixon's hands. So he wouldn't risk a fumble on a handoff. He fumbled anyway."

"The Bears snatched defeat out of the hands of victory," Buzz said.

"What an amazing comeback!" Salts said. "The Bears will look back on this as a heartbreaker. They'll remember it for the rest of their lives"

"The whole city will remember this tragic day. What a roller coaster of emotions. They lost their quarterback this morning under tragic circumstances. If they had Cole Dillinger, this game wouldn't have been close. Then to get this close to winning. It'll take the city a long time to recover from this loss."

Cliff slumped back into his seat and turned his back on the television. He couldn't take watching anymore.

"Do you want to leave?" Julia asked.

"Let's wait thirty minutes or so until the traffic thins out."

They had to drive back toward the stadium to get home.

Julia sat down in her seat.

Thirty minutes later, rioters and looters had taken to the streets. The city of Chicago was on fire.

14

Watching the end of the Chicago Bears game was painful. Seeing the horrifying images of the rioters and looters on the streets of Chicago destroying the city on the same television screens was downright excruciating.

Rizzo had changed the channels in the VIP lounge to the local feeds. The reporters on the ground and in the air were capturing the utter lawlessness that had taken over. Several hundred rioters spilled onto the Dan Ryan Expressway including portions of Interstates 90 and 94, bringing traffic to a standstill. The violent mobs were forcing people from their cars, robbing, and beating them.

That was the way Cliff and Julia would've gone home.

Chicago's downtown shopping district, the Magnificent Mile, was under siege. Looters broke windows and were ransacking a number of high-end shops. Video feeds captured untold numbers of people coming out of the stores carrying televisions, computers, expensive designer clothing and handbags, and whatever else would fit in their arms or in garbage bags.

There were unconfirmed reports of shots fired.

Helicopter crews showed fires throughout the city and suburbs. Several explosions had been heard. Rioters were throwing makeshift fire-bombs and rocks at police. An unmarked squad car was set on fire at State Street and Haddock Place. Several police cruisers were overturned and set on fire at Madison and Dearborn streets.

More unconfirmed reports said an officer was down.

Hospitals had instituted state-of-emergency protocols and were calling on all workers to come in. Ambulances and emergency vehicles could not move around the city safely and had been ordered by the mayor to stay in their stations until further notice. Cliff wondered how the injured were going to get to the hospitals.

They weren't.

The fires were left to burn.

The injured would die on the streets.

God forbid someone had a heart attack or went into labor. He could only imagine what he'd do if it was happening to Julia at that moment.

It had to be happening somewhere. To someone.

Cliff said a quick prayer for the madness to end. Julia's lips were moving, and she was staring off at the other side of the room. She might've been doing the same thing.

Hundreds of rioters flooded the streets near Millennium Park. Destroying businesses, defacing public buildings with graffiti, looting convenience stores, and wreaking havoc with unsuspecting patrons trying to leave the local restaurants and bars.

More reports of injuries in that area.

Citywide, the number of injured could grow to hundreds if not thousands and the damage to property in the billions. If the rioting wasn't stopped soon, the death toll could become unimaginable.

Chicago looked like a war zone.

The worst part was that the police had been ordered to stand down and told not to try to stop the hoodlums.

Cliff's lieutenant called him and warned him to stay put.

"There's no direct route back to the station or to your house," he said. "Any way you turn, you're going to run into rioters."

"Can I help?" Cliff asked. "I'm willing to man a riot line."

"No!" he said emphatically. "Ivory Martin has ordered the police not to respond to rioters. Police aren't allowed to use their weapons.

Not even pepper spray. I'm not sending my detectives out on the streets with their hands tied."

Ivory Martin was the mayor. Someone the Lieutenant didn't hold in high regard. He'd been highly critical of her 'defund the police' movement. The Lieutenant was old school. In his view, lawlessness should be met with overwhelming force. Not brutality, but with whatever force was necessary to restore law and order.

Knowing the Lieutenant, he was anxious to man a riot line as well.

Cliff was included in the stand down directive. He could only fire his weapon if fired upon.

Stupid.

A policy put together by a politician who'd never been on the front lines.

The mayor had her armed guards and was no doubt barricaded in a secure place.

Such a hypocrite.

Didn't she know that a rock could kill you as easily as a gun? Almost anything these days could be used as a weapon. A skateboard. A baseball bat. Cloth lit on fire. A bottle filled with gasoline, then set on fire. Even firecrackers thrown into a police line could do serious damage.

Common sense in law enforcement had been thrown out the window.

The motto of the Chicago Police Department was 'At danger's call, we'll promptly fly; and bravely do or bravely die.' Had been since 1856. That was no longer the case.

He didn't want to get into a long discussion with the Lieutenant about it. It'd just make them both angrier.

The Lieutenant also didn't ask him about the Cole Dillinger case. It seemed minor compared to what was happening that night. Cliff picked up the file with the name of the corporation that placed the five-million-dollar bet so he could keep it safe. Important information that needed to be guarded.

"We'll stay here as long as we can," Cliff assured the Lieutenant. "But I don't know how safe we are."

Violent mobs were within one block of their location.

"If you run into trouble, let me know," the Lieutenant said. "I'll do what I can to send someone to help."

Cliff didn't intend to stay there. He got Julia's attention so she could help him develop a plan.

"Can we get to Roosevelt?" she asked. "From there we can go east to the 41. Then head north. We can get out of Chicago all together. We'll find a hotel somewhere and let things die down."

"The hotels are probably all booked because of the game."

"We'll drive all the way to Wisconsin if we have to."

He nodded.

Cliff studied the map on his phone.

"According to my GPS, 41 is a parking lot," he said. "That's where a lot of the fans leaving Soldier Field are trying to get to."

"I guess 55 is out."

That's the road leading west.

"I don't think we can get there either," Cliff said. "Besides, the last place we want to be is on a freeway. You never know when a mob is going to flood an interstate and shut things down."

A news reporter came on the television with an announcement.

"The Mayor of Chicago, Ivory Martin, has issued a curfew effective immediately. She's also suspended all public transportation in and out of downtown Chicago until further notice."

"That's just great!" Cliff said with exasperation. "What good is a curfew going to do? Does she think people who break the law by stealing and looting are going to obey a curfew? And the police can't arrest them anyway. What a load of crock!"

"Shutting down the subways and trains is going to strand people in downtown Chicago," Julia said, almost matching his intensity. "That's only going to make things worse. How are people who live in the suburbs going to get out of downtown?"

"It's insane. She needs to call the governor and have him bring in the National Guard and restore order."

"Too late for that now."

They heard a crashing sound.

Julia let out a scream.

So did dozens of others in the main lounge on the other side of the closed doors.

The next sounds they heard were windows breaking.

Rizzo said they barricaded the front entrance and locked the doors, but he wasn't sure if it would hold. Apparently, it hadn't.

Cliff could envision it in his mind. The entire front entrance of the *I Bet Gaming* was glass so people could see inside and want to come in.

That's why Cliff didn't feel safe. The looters would eventually make a beeline for their building. The dozens of big screen televisions and posh furnishings easily seen from the street were worth a small fortune.

Rizzo suddenly appeared through the doorway.

Frantic. Shouting.

He was waving his hands in the air.

"Get out of here! Out the back entrance."

Cliff had his gun and thought about taking up a position at the door to hold the rioters off until everyone could get out. But then he remembered what the Lieutenant had said and it'd do no good to point his weapon if he couldn't use it. The mob would realize he was impotent to stop them and they'd overwhelm him within seconds.

Cliff was relegated to fleeing out the back door with everyone else. A problem in and of itself. The back door was now a logjam.

The first of the violent mob entered the VIP lounge. Cliff instinctively reached for his weapon. Fortunately, they seemed more interested in fighting each other for the televisions than they were at chasing them.

Cliff and Julia managed to get out the back door into an alley. He didn't see any immediate threats on the outside. Their car was around the corner in a parking lot, and they needed to get to it. With no public transportation available, it was the only way out of the city.

He couldn't think of anywhere in the city that was safe. Except maybe the police station, which was only a few blocks away and had a perimeter of cops around it. He might be able to get them there and through the barricade by flashing his badge.

Then what would they do? Hunker down and wait? That didn't seem like a good option. The best thing was to get out of town altogether. He'd somehow find a way.

They practically ran to their car. On the way, he racked his brain trying to come up with a plan. When one formulated, he sprang into action.

"I know which way to go," Cliff said. "I know a back way."

"Where are we going?" Julia asked.

"Through the neighborhoods. My guess is that the rioters will focus on the businesses first. That's the low bearing fruit, so to speak. Hopefully, order can be restored before they get to the neighborhoods."

"That sounds like a good plan. Which neighborhood?"

He didn't answer. She'd know soon enough. And he wasn't positive he knew the best way to go to avoid the rioters and traffic. In his mind, he could picture a thin corridor of homes between the businesses that might provide an escape.

Cliff exited the parking lot and went the opposite direction of the main street where the rioters had come from. A couple of turns and they were on a residential street, headed toward a wealthier neighborhood. He intended to wind his way through the maze of homes to the other side, then through another high-end subdivision, exit that one on the other side, drive under the interstate, and eventually make it to the 41.

They'd be north of the city. At that point, they could continue driving until they found a hotel. Like Julia said, all the way to Wisconsin if necessary.

As long as he didn't have to make a turn in either direction, he'd be okay. East took him back toward the businesses. West took him towards the freeways and more businesses. Either direction was risky. For all practical purposes, they were surrounded by rioters on either side. As long as he stayed on the side streets and headed north, they were safe.

Very few cars were on the road in that area. They were able to make it through the first neighborhood without any trouble. Cliff wasn't surprised to see the neighborhood practically deserted. It appeared that everyone was locked down in their homes with the lights off.

When they exited the neighborhood, Cliff sped up and crossed a major thoroughfare when he didn't see any trouble either way. When he reached the entrance to the next subdivision, he rounded a curve and started to turn in.

Julia let out a scream.

He slammed on his brakes.

The subdivision entrance was blocked. Several homeowners had taken it upon themselves to park their vehicles at the entrance. Side by side, so no one could drive through it. About half a dozen men stood behind the cars with guns. They motioned for him to keep driving.

Cliff pointed like he wanted to drive through.

Their guns were pointed at the ground, but Cliff didn't know what they'd do if he got out of the car to talk to them. One of them, the leader, kept motioning with his gun for Cliff to move on.

He decided not to argue with them. It'd take several minutes to clear the barricade, even if he was able to convince them to do so. Which he doubted.

And what if they did? The other end of the subdivision was probably blocked as well.

Even though he was angry, Cliff could hardly blame them. That's what he would do. Protect his property.

"Which way?" Julia asked.

"East."

He turned that way. They'd have to take their chances on the 41.

Two blocks over they ran into a police barricade. This time, Cliff did get out of his car. He showed the cop his badge.

"You can't go this way," the man in blue said.

"I need to. I've got to get to the 41."

"You'll have to go a different way. I've got orders to stop all traffic from going on these streets."

Cliff wasn't sure why.

The cop pointed in the direction he wanted Cliff to go.

"I can't go that way. It'll lead me back to where they are rioting."

"You aren't going this way."

Cliff paced around in a circle trying to decide what to do. He got back in his car. Still not sure. He couldn't go back. That'd only lead to where they'd come from. He imagined the scene at *I Bet Gaming* was more chaotic now than it had been when they left.

He drove slowly in the direction the policeman had told him to go. At the next intersection, he wanted to turn left, but it was a one-way street. He could only go right. That was not the best way to go.

His only hope was that the rioters and looters were already past that area.

At first it looked like they were.

Then he came to a major intersection where all hell had broken loose. Cars were overturned and on fire. Windows on business were broken. The street was littered with debris.

Cliff hesitated.

He was at a dead end. He couldn't turn left or right without running into a mob of people.

The only thing he could do was back up and go the way he came. An idea came to him. He'd go back to the subdivision with the barricade. He'd help them man it. They could stay in their car tonight, or maybe one of the people in the neighborhood would let them stay in their home. Especially if he helped protect them.

Before he could put the car in reverse, he heard a loud bang behind him.

Julia let out a muted yelp.

A group of thugs were pounding on the trunk of the car.

"Get out of the way, or I'll run you over!" Cliff shouted.

Fortunately, they didn't hear him. The last thing he needed to do was incite them further.

A rock came smashing through the back window.

This time Julia's scream wasn't muted.

Screw them.

Cliff tried to back up slowly. He couldn't without running over the group of rioters. He could potentially kill or maim a half dozen of them. At that point, he hardly cared. Except that they'd drag both of them out of the car and beat them to death.

He couldn't take the risk of drawing more rioters to their position.

It didn't matter. They were already there.

A teenager with his shirt off jumped on the hood of his car and was dancing, slinging his shirt in the air like a lasso. Within seconds another rioter was on the roof. Jumping up and down. The sound of metal banging echoed through the car with a deafening sound.

This is not good.

They needed to get out of the car.

But was it safer inside or out?

He wasn't sure.

The vehicle was rocking back and forth now. Several people were on Julia's side trying to tip it over. It was too heavy for them, so they stopped and started banging on her window instead.

Definitely safer outside the car.

Evil and hate filled their eyes even though they had no reason to hate Cliff or Julia. They'd never done anything to them. So what if the Bears lost. It was only a game.

Julia screamed.

A couple of the crazy people tried to open her car door. It was locked.

Cliff heard one of them shout, "It's a cop car."

Oh no!

It wasn't safe inside or outside.

15

Cliff had been shot at on more than one occasion, but he'd never felt in this much danger. They were surrounded by an angry mob who had no regard for human life or property and a hatred for anyone in authority. Especially members of law enforcement.

The frenzy intensified when the group of thugs realized Cliff was in an unmarked police vehicle. The throng, many of them masked to hide their faces, gravitated toward his car like a magnet to iron. Because of that, Cliff and Julia were outnumbered at least twenty to one.

A gun was a great neutralizer in that situation, but Cliff wasn't allowed to use it. A dozen or more people were videotaping the scene with their phones. Whatever happened that night was going to end up on social media or the news if it was compelling enough.

In other words, if he made a mistake.

Used deadly force to protect himself.

How could that be considered a mistake when the riotous swarm of amoral wasps attacked him first?

It didn't matter even if his life was in danger. If he shot someone who was unarmed, he'd be arrested and charged with manslaughter or negligent homicide. At the very least. First-degree murder, if the prosecutors wanted to make an example of him and the outcry was loud enough.

He could spend the rest of his life in jail. Only slightly better than being dead.

It didn't matter. He'd do whatever he had to do to protect his wife and their unborn child.

Whatever that was, he had to do it soon.

The car they were in was rocking back and forth more violently. Staying there was no longer an option. At some point, the mob would break the windows and drag them out. Or turn the car upside down with them in it and set it on fire.

At least on the outside, he had a fighting chance.

He considered the best course of action. Cliff was cool under pressure. He was used to making split second decisions.

"Julia, you wait in the car," he said calmly. "I'm going to get out and come around to get you."

"Don't leave me alone," she said. Her voice registered sheer panic. She clutched his arm so tightly it hurt.

"I'm not going to leave you," Cliff said. "But we can't stay in the car. Don't open the door until you see me."

She nodded. He had to pry her hand off his arm.

The rioters pressed against his door and pounded on the window. Cliff took a deep breath, gave himself a pep talk of courage, and opened the door and forced his way out.

He was attacked immediately.

Several blows came at once.

He blocked most of them. One fist grazed his head.

A man tried to tackle Cliff to the ground. Cliff pushed him off, then kicked him in the kneecap sending him tumbling to the ground, writhing in pain.

That infuriated the crowd even more.

Cliff had training in martial arts. He took up the fighting pose. That caused them to pause and try to surround him rather than attempt a full-on assault. A half a dozen more joined them. He moved them away from the car. Away from Julia.

One of the men threw a punch at him. Cliff saw it coming, dodged it, then kicked the man in the midsection. He collapsed to his knees trying to catch his breath.

Expletives were flying from the gang as were rocks and whatever else they could find to throw at him. Nothing found the mark and he was effectively holding them off.

He was about to turn his attention to getting to Julia when a roar came up from the crowd behind him. Cliff looked back to see what was happening. The fight had pushed him further away from the car then he realized. To his horror, one side of his car was in the air. A number of rioters were trying to turn it over.

They succeeded.

The car fell to the ground. Upside down. The four wheels facing upward. The undercarriage was all that was visible.

The crowd let out a huge cheer.

Cliff shouted, "Julia!"

Where was she?

Did she get out of the car or was she still in it?

He didn't see her.

The crowd swelled around the car as onlookers cheered the over-turning of a police vehicle. Several of them lit pieces of cloth and papers and threw them inside the broken windows.

"No!" he shouted.

Panic ran through Cliff like fear of the plague runs through a village.

At least a dozen people were between him and the car. They were holding him back.

He had to get Julia out of there. To do so, he had to get past his own threats. He'd be no good to her if he was on the ground, dead or disabled.

The crescendo of the mob grew into utter hysteria. It's like they were at a college bonfire pep rally before a big game.

Cliff decided that Julia had to have gotten out.

He scanned the area looking for her while keeping an eye out for the next wave of attacks. He noticeably exhaled air when he saw her out of the car. Thirty yards away. Facing off with several rioters.

She kicked one in the groin. Another came up from behind and grabbed her. He pulled her backwards, so her feet were in the air. She kicked her legs back and forth.

Remember your training.

She had the presence of mind to do so.

Julia brought the heel of one of her feet into the man's shin. He let her go and began to hop around in pain.

Good for you!

When Julia's feet hit the ground, she took off running.

Cliff wanted to follow her with his eyes, but had his own threats to contend with. One of the rioters came up from behind and tried to grab his gun. He slapped the man's hand away.

A blow struck his head from behind. He blacked out for a second or two.

Then saw stars.

He felt a kick to his lower body, and Cliff fell to his knees. Emboldened, the mob began to pummel Cliff with punches. He put his hand over his head to protect it and curled up on the ground. They started kicking him. One after the other. Stomping. Alternating between his head and his stomach and side.

He felt the air leave his lungs when one of the blows connected flush to his side. He fought desperately to catch his breath.

He was in real trouble.

A man was on top of him. Trying to get his gun. Cliff grabbed the man's wrists to stop him. That left him vulnerable to more kicks.

The mob sensed that they had the advantage. The opposite was true. The attackers had awakened the lion inside of him.

Self-preservation kicked in. Seeing Julia under attack stoked a rage inside of him like a poker stokes a fire. This was no time for restraint. Losing was not an option. They'd take his gun and use it to kill another cop or an innocent bystander.

He couldn't let that happen.

He took in a deep breath, half expecting his lungs not to accept it. The dizziness cleared as another shot of adrenaline pulsed through his veins and the oxygen gave him a jolt of energy.

He jumped to his feet. Staggered to keep his legs under him but had the presence of mind to begin throwing punches in every direction.

They were connecting.

He kept them going like a windmill in a thunderstorm.

Hitting whoever he hit.

Kicking whoever was in his way.

Kneeing. Elbowing. Scratching. Clawing.

He connected with an uppercut to the closest threat. The man dropped to the ground in a heap. A roundhouse kick dropped another one.

He felt like a prize fighter who'd come off the mat to win a match. Cliff was fighting by instinct now. With no purpose other than survival.

I have to get to Julia.

That was spurring him on as much as anything. The crowd retreated to give themselves some distance. He'd already done serious damage to several of them. They were thinking twice about coming after him again. Several in the crowd were gone now. Looking for an easier target.

One by one they left. Cliff used the opportunity to look around for Julia.

He saw her.

She was on the ground. On the other side of the street. A distance away. A group of three teens with masks on their faces were kicking her. Cliff screamed at the top of his lungs. He started running toward her. He pulled his gun and waved it in the air.

The three thugs saw him and took off running.

Another threat emerged. Three large black men were headed straight for Julia who lay motionless on the ground.

Cliff was still a distance away, but he yelled at them. Threatening them.

"Stay away from her."

They didn't notice him. If they heard his threats, they were ignoring them.

The black men were near Julia now.

Cliff's lungs burned from running. Why was it taking so long for me to get to her? He didn't realize he was limping badly.

One of the men knelt beside Julia. The other two surrounded her. *What were they doing?*

They were protecting her.

When Cliff got close, the two black men standing saw Cliff's gun. They held up their hands.

"Get away from my wife," Cliff said roughly.

"She's hurt," the largest of the three men said. "We've got to get her to a hospital."

Cliff holstered his gun. He knelt beside Julia. She had a pulse but was unconscious. He picked her up in his arms and looked for a place to take her.

"Over there," the largest man said, pointing to a lit-up building. The sign out front read *Union Rescue Mission*. A dozen or so men were in front, protecting it.

Cliff carried Julia inside ignoring his ankle that was throbbing. He laid her on one of the pews and assessed her injuries. Her eye was swollen, and she had a cut on her head. Her arms and hands were cut and bruised. Her breathing was labored. Like she had broken ribs or a collapsed lung.

"Do you have a vehicle?" Cliff asked. "I need to get her to the hospital."

He shook his head. "University Medical is not far from here," the largest man said. "I'll carry her there." The man suddenly picked Julia up like she was a kid's doll before Cliff could object.

"I can carry her," Cliff said.

"I've got her. You're hurt."

"I'm okay."

"You're bleeding."

Cliff touched his head. He felt blood. He also tasted it. He had a busted lip and bruised sore ribs. He had scrapes on his back and elbows from falling on the concrete. He suddenly realized he sprained or broke his ankle. When he tried to put weight on it, he felt a bolt of pain.

Up to now, the adrenaline and shock had overridden all of his injuries. Once he was out of the fray, he could feel every one of them.

The other two good Samaritans went back out on the streets. Cliff didn't get a chance to thank them.

"This way," the man said. Cliff got a better look at him. He appeared to be about six foot six and close to three hundred pounds of sheer muscle.

Cliff followed him out the back door of the mission and down the street. If he remembered right, University Medical was only a few blocks away.

"What's your name?" Cliff asked.

"I'm Pastor Angus. Some people call me Black Angus. But only once."

He smiled broadly when he said it. His face was darker than most, and in the nighttime, his white teeth pierced through the darkness.

Cliff had a hard time keeping up. Angus' large and broad steps were equal to two of his. Julia was limp in his arms. He carried her effortlessly. Like she was nothing more than a sack of potatoes for him.

Julia moaned slightly.

"It's going to be okay," Cliff said to her. "We're going to get you some help."

They were to the hospital in less than ten minutes. They rushed through the doors of the emergency room and were met by a nurse. The waiting room was packed, but the nurse must've sensed that Julia was a priority. That and she saw Cliff's badge that was now in his hand.

"Bring her this way," the nurse said, leading them into the emergency room corridor.

The whole area was abuzz with activity.

"Put her on this gurney," she said to Angus.

He laid her gently on the bed.

Cliff got a better look at her injuries in the light. They were more extensive than he had first thought. The left side of her head had swollen to the size of a cantaloupe. Her left eye was swollen shut.

The nurse did a quick check of her pulse, then her eyes. She whisked her away, leaving them standing there. The look on her face could only be described as deep concern.

"Thank you," Cliff said to Angus. "I'm going to go be with my wife."

"I understand. I can't stay. I have to go back and protect the Mission and help the others. I'm sorry. God Bless You. I hope she's okay. We'll be praying for her."

"I can't tell you how much I appreciate it. You saved her life."

Cliff held out his hand. Angus's hand dwarfed Cliff's. Somehow Cliff managed to pull him into a hug.

"Go be with your wife," Angus said. "What's her name?"

"Julia Ford."

"We'll be praying for Julia. She seems like a fighter."

"She is."

Then he was gone.

Cliff found the room where they took Julia. She was surrounded by a team of doctors and nurses. One of the nurses took one look at Cliff and said, "We've got to get you fixed up."

"That's my wife," he said. "I want to stay with her."

"We're going to take good care of her. You're bleeding. You're going to need stitches. Come with me."

She grabbed Cliff by the arm to lead him out of the room. He tried to resist, but she had a firm grip. Cliff kept looking back at Julia.

"Is she going to be alright?" he asked.

"She's stable. We won't know until we assess her injuries."

"She's pregnant."

"I'll tell the doctor. Let's get you in a room."

She led Cliff into a room and made him sit on the table. A doctor was in the room within seconds. They made him lie down on the table and began to assess his injuries. Cliff had a laceration to the back of his head. No fractured ribs, but a large purple bruise was already forming on his side. It hurt like he'd been hit by a cement truck. He probably had a mild concussion.

"I don't want any pain reliever that makes me sleepy," he said. "I want to be awake when my wife comes to."

They gave him some aspirin and made him keep still. The worst injury was to his ankle. The x-ray showed it wasn't broken, but the bone was bruised. Probably from where he kicked one of his attackers. Maybe where one of them kicked him.

They treated it and then put it in a boot. He wanted to get up and go see Julia, but they wouldn't let him.

"The doctor will come in and update you as soon as he can."

The wait was agony. He kept asking the nurse questions. "How is she? Will she be alright? What are they doing to her?"

Cliff called the Lieutenant to let him know what had happened. He'd get there as soon as he could.

Finally, the doctor came in. If Cliff had been attached to a heart monitor, it would've shown his heart beating wildly. He was expecting the worst, even though he'd prayed for things to be okay.

"Detective Ford, my name is Dr. Peters. I've been treating your wife."

"How is she?"

He was almost afraid to ask.

"She's in critical condition. But she's stable. For now. She suffered severe trauma to the brain. We have her in a medically induced coma to reduce the swelling. At this point, she doesn't need surgery. If the swelling doesn't subside, we're going to have to go in to relieve the pressure. She is being admitted into the ICU."

"Is she going to live?"

The doctor hesitated. That's not what Cliff wanted to see.

"The next twenty-four hours are touch and go," he said soberly. "We'll just have to see how she responds to treatment. She also has two fractured ribs and a punctured lung. She's on a ventilator so we can help her breathe."

"And the baby."

"I'm sorry."

Cliff felt like he'd been punched in the gut again.

16

University Medical Hospital
Three days later

Julia wasn't better, but she also wasn't worse. An encouraging sign, according to the doctors. It didn't seem encouraging to Cliff. Julia lay in the hospital bed, attached to a ventilator, in a medically induced coma.

If they took her off it, she'd likely die.

She looked even worse than she was. Her head was wrapped with bandages and the left side of her face was as black and purple as a rotting eggplant.

Cliff hadn't left her side. Most of the time, his hand was in hers or he was stroking her arm. Rubbing her neck and shoulders. Talking to her. Whispering in her ear. Trying to encourage her. Occasionally, he thought he felt her squeeze his hand. Probably his imagination, but he drew hope from it.

Since the hours had dragged into days, he talked to her about everything he could think of. Their wedding. Vacations they'd been on. Their honeymoon. The life they had together. Her sister Anna. Her work at the women's shelter and how she needed to wake up because the girls needed her.

I needed her.

Cliff didn't tell Julia about losing the baby. The worst part about her waking up would be giving her that news. She'd only known for one day that she was pregnant, but Cliff could tell she was excited about it. The doctor said she was young and there was no permanent damage. There'd be more opportunities to have kids.

The doctor always attached ifs to his statements.

If they can bring her out of the coma.

If she can breathe on her own.

If she still has brain function.

The tests were all promising. No guarantees though.

That was the hardest part. The unknown. Cliff's life had already been turned upside down. What would it be like if Julia was no longer a part of it? In the deep recesses of the night, his hope would fade.

That's when he felt God the most. Comforting him. Increasing his faith.

Still, Cliff welcomed the sunrises. During the day, he could stay busy and control his thoughts.

The Lieutenant came by the hospital the day after the attack. After asking about Julia's condition and offering his words of encouragement, he wanted to talk about the Cole Dillinger case.

"I'm taking you off of it," he had said.

Cliff expected it and had his rebuttals.

"I want to stay on the case. I'm the one who knows it inside and out. I already have three, maybe four suspects."

"You need to focus on Julia," he argued. "Getting her well and home is your first priority.".

"I will. But I can do both."

"Julia needs you."

"She has me. I'll be right here. There's nothing I can do for her other than pray. I'm going stir crazy, sitting around this hospital room with nothing to do. I can get a lot of work done on the case with my laptop and phone."

The Lieutenant persisted.

"Witnesses need to be interviewed. How are you going to run an investigation from a hospital room?"

"I can leave for a few minutes if I need to."

"How are you going to get around wearing a boot?"

Cliff's foot had to be in the boot for two weeks. The ankle had a severe bone bruise.

"I'll manage. I can walk in it."

"Why would you want to? Most people would jump at the chance to get a month off with paid leave. You were injured in the line of duty. I can get you an indefinite leave. You can take as much time as you want."

"I don't want time off. I want to find Cole's murderer. You know I'm the person to do it. That's why you assigned it to me."

The Lieutenant wasn't buying the arguments, so Cliff pulled out his best one.

"Assign Ron to work with me. I'll direct the investigation and show him what to do."

Ron Pearlman was a junior detective. Fairly new in the office, but capable. Cliff and Ron had become friends. They played golf a few times together. Ron and his wife had been to their house, so he knew Julia.

Normally, detectives had partners. Because of the mayor's budget cuts, the department had a hiring freeze. They were understaffed as it was, and they didn't have the manpower to cover all the cases, much less have two detectives working one case.

The Lieutenant would likely reject the idea for that reason alone.

On the other hand, if Cliff took an extended leave, the department would have even less resources. For that reason, the Lieutenant relented. After Cliff assured him he was in the emotional and physical condition to be able to handle the rigors of lead detective.

"If at any time, it becomes too much, I'm pulling you off," he warned.

"It won't be."

Ron came to the hospital later that day and Cliff filled him in on all the details of the case and sent him off with a things-to-do list. Two days later, Ron had already worked through them and was back at the hospital to go through his findings with Cliff.

They met in the cafeteria so they could spread papers out on the table. They chose a table in the corner so they could speak more openly without anyone overhearing them.

"Where do you want to start?" Ron asked.

"Cole Dillinger's girlfriend," Cliff said. "Kate Reynolds. Did you meet with her?"

Of all the things on the list, interviewing the girlfriend was at the top. Cliff really wanted to know what she said.

"I tracked her down and interviewed her at her attorney's office. She was cooperative, even though she had a lawyer present. She seemed shaken by the whole thing."

"What did she say about the affair with the pool boy?" Cliff asked.

"She denied it. She said she barely knew him. He was only an acquaintance."

"Did you believe her?"

He shrugged his shoulders. "Who's to say?"

"Was she at Cole's house the morning he was murdered?"

"Yes."

Cliff sat forward in his chair. His anticipation hadn't waned by the denial of the affair, but knowing she was in the house the morning of the murders, ticked it up another notch.

Ron looked down at his notes. He had typed them up and set a copy in front of Cliff, but he ignored them. He would read the reports later. He preferred to hear it come out of Ron's mouth, so he could get a feel for his tone and inflections when he described the facts and his impressions of her responses.

The next best thing to actually interviewing the witness directly.

Ron began the narrative. "She woke up around six. Said she couldn't sleep. Got up and fixed coffee. She drank it in the den.

Then cleaned up the dishes, went back to the bedroom, and took a shower."

"Did she see the pool guy? He said he arrived at seven."

"Yes. He knocked on the front door around seven. She was still in her bathrobe. He apologized for bothering her. He didn't know she would be there. She let him in and he went outside to work on the pool."

"Harold Potter said she got in the pool with him."

"Somebody's lying," Ron said. "I asked her about it. I mean... I didn't tell her what Potter said. I asked her if she went swimming that morning."

"What'd she say?"

"She was emphatic. Why would I go in the pool? Justin was working on it."

She called him Justin. Cliff remembered the pool guy called her Kate. So they were on a first name basis. Could be nothing, but they seemed to have a familiarity with each other. Perhaps more than just acquaintances. Maybe not.

Ron added, "Ms. Reynold also said that she never went in the pool in the wintertime. It's too cold. She said that she's not really a pool person. She doesn't use it, even in the summer. The sun wrinkles her skin."

"I understand she's a supermodel."

"Oh yes. She's stunningly gorgeous. Skinny as a popsicle stick, though. Her skin does look perfect."

"What did she do next?"

"She got dressed and left."

"What time?"

"Shortly after eight. The pool guy was still there. She went outside and told him she was leaving."

"Where did she go?"

"The Regency Hotel. The player's wives and girlfriends had breakfast there. At eight thirty."

"Did you confirm it?"

"I did. I talked to one player's wife who attended. She said everything seemed normal with Kate. She didn't eat much. But she never does."

That sparked a question in Cliff that took Ron off the subject, but was important, nonetheless.

"Have you talked to any of the other players or coaches?" Cliff asked.

"I tried. But they're all gone. After the game, they scattered. Most of them are in Cabo, or the Bahamas. Someplace warm."

"I was afraid that might happen. I'm sure they wanted to get out of town as fast as possible."

Ron shrugged.

Cliff let out a noticeable sigh. "So it's a he said/she said. Harold Potter's word against Kate Reynold's. I don't know who to believe. Kate obviously has a motive to lie if she was having an affair with the pool guy."

"Yes, she would."

Cliff wished he could've been there for the interview. The junior detective didn't have enough experience to know if Kate Reynolds was lying. It wasn't an exact science anyway. Cliff had been fooled plenty of times. He could interview Kate and not know for sure either.

In fact, it had happened in this case. Harold Potter said Dr. Blackburn had a heated argument with Cole on the street outside his house. The doctor said it was a casual conversation about the game. One of them was lying. Cliff didn't know which. He could hardly expect Ron to know if Kate was telling the truth. That reminded him to ask about Dr. Blackburn's story and his wife's affair.

"Did you check for any security cameras at the doctor's office building?" Cliff asked. He was desperate to know what time the doctor showed up at his office.

"I did. There's a camera right across the street. In another office building."

"Excellent. What did you find?"

"The doctor wasn't there. He never showed up."

Cliff's heart did a couple of leaps in his chest. Then took off racing, like a horse out of the starting gate.

"Are you sure?"

"I watched the tape from eight in the morning until lunchtime. I never saw his car."

"Is there a rear entrance? Could he have come in a different way?"

"I looked. There's a rear entrance and parking lot. But the only way in or out of the parking lot is through the entrance off the street in front of the medical complex. The security camera has a perfect view of the entrance."

"Could he have parked somewhere else and walked over?"

"Why would he? He can park right at the back entrance. His office is also in the front of the building. I never saw any lights or any activity in the building at all."

"So the doctor is lying."

"It appears that way."

Cliff was impressed. Ron was doing a thorough job.

"If the doctor lied about going to the office, he may have also lied about the argument in the street," Ron added.

"True. But that doesn't mean he killed Cole," Cliff mused. "He might've been having his own affair. Maybe he has his own girl on the side that he meets with every Sunday morning and his wife only thinks he goes to the office."

"Or he circled back around and killed Cole."

"Right. Did you check the security cameras in the subdivision? They'll tell us when he left."

"I did. You're not going to believe what I found."

"What?"

"They've all been erased. From eight o'clock to eight forty-five. Same as the guardhouse."

Cliff didn't believe it.

"All of them?"

"Yes. All the homeowners reported it. Everybody is angry with the security company."

"How is that possible? How could someone go into every house and erase every tape?"

Before Ron could answer, Cliff figured it out. "They're all on the same system."

"Yep," Ron said. "Ace Security. They installed the equipment in all the houses and do all the monitoring."

Cliff remembered that Cole Dillinger's system was monitored by Ace. A sticker was on the window by the front door.

"I assume they're all connected to the internet?" Cliff asked.

Ron nodded.

"That explains how someone could delete all of them at once. The killer is also a hacker."

"Every single homeowner who has a security system in the neighborhood, looked at their tapes. Obviously. Wouldn't you? I know I would if there was a murder in my neighborhood. The tapes were blank during those times. Nothing but a black screen."

"I wish at least one of them had his own system."

"The neighborhood went in together with one security company so they could save money on the monitoring."

"Like those people needed to save a few bucks a month."

Ron had no response.

"Should I also assume the backup at the security company was tampered with as well?"

"You should assume so. Since it was. It's erased."

"I guess going with only one system wasn't such a good idea after all."

"Nope."

The conversation ground to a halt. Cliff had been counting on the security cameras to confirm or disprove everybody's story.

"Speaking of backups," Ron said, breaking the silence, "I talked to Rizzo at *I Bet Gaming*. Their entire system was destroyed in the riot. All their computers and equipment were looted. The lowlifes even took the wiring out of the walls. They have a backup system that's off site, but it'll take time to look up who made the five-million-dollar wager. Right now, they're just trying to sort through all the bets and get them paid out. As you can imagine, those are the priority."

Rizzo had given Cliff the file with the name of the corporation who placed the bet. That file was in his car that was destroyed by the rioters. Cliff couldn't remember the name of the company. All he knew was it started with a D and the company was Finnish.

"I assume Rizzo doesn't remember the name," Cliff asked, kicking himself for not writing it down somewhere safe.

Ron shook his head no.

"Julia will remember," Cliff said. "When she wakes up."

As soon as he said it, a pain pierced his heart like he'd been shot with an arrow. Maybe Julia would remember or maybe she wouldn't. Not if she had brain damage. Or amnesia.

If she didn't survive.

He fought back that thought. The emotion building inside of him was about to erupt. He came down to the cafeteria so he could put Julia's precarious situation out of his mind for a few minutes. It wasn't ever going to happen, until she woke up, and came back to him.

He suddenly felt extreme frustration. Either because of Julia, or because the case kept running into roadblocks. Or both. He voiced it. "Do you have any good news for me at all?" Cliff asked, roughly.

Ron smiled. "I do."

"Why didn't you start with it?"

"I saved the best for last."

Cliff wasn't amused, but his mind was fully engaged in the case again.

"I interviewed Mr. Mayfield," Ron said.

"The neighbor who flew the Giants flag on the fence. The one who had a physical confrontation with Cole and sued him."

Cliff thought that might be the most promising lead of all.

"Yep. At the station. With his attorney."

"Good idea to make him come to you. What did he say?"

"Nothing. On the advice of his attorney, he refused to answer any questions."

Why is that good news?

"Did he plead the fifth?" Cliff asked.

"Not exactly. His attorney is smart. He used the confidentiality agreement as his excuse."

"So, he admitted that he sued Cole?"

"Not in those exact words. As I said, he refused to answer any questions. But he insinuated that there was an agreement."

"I think it's clear they had one."

"Agreed. His attorney said they weren't going to answer any questions unless ordered by a judge to do so."

"That son-of-a-biscuit-eater."

Cliff could hardly hide his frustration with Mayfield.

"I wanted to get my hands on that agreement," Ron said, "but the Lieutenant wouldn't sign off on it. He doesn't think a judge will grant permission without some evidence against Mr. Mayfield."

"He probably won't."

"I may have some evidence."

"What?"

"The gun used to kill Cole was a .22 caliber revolver with a subsonic round."

"That explains why no one in the neighborhood heard the gunshot."

"The mob uses that caliber weapon."

"Cole was shot in the back," Cliff retorted. "Near the heart."

From experience, Cliff knew that when the mob used a low caliber bullet, a head shot was more effective. The bullet was so weak, it wouldn't exit the other side of Cole's skull. It'd simply bounce around inside his brain, creating massive damage. Of course, a .22 bullet through the heart, would have the same effect on that area of the body.

"Guess who owns a .22?" Ron asked.

"Mayfield!"

The obvious answer. Otherwise, why would Ron bring it up?

"That's right. I looked it up. He has that gun registered in his name."

"Get a subpoena."

"I did. I've got the gun at the crime lab."

"When will we get the results back?"

"In the next day or two."

That was good news. The lab would fire a bullet from Mayfield's gun and compare it to the bullet taken from Cole's body. If they were a match, then they had the murder weapon.

Cliff smiled for the first time.

"So, your job, Ron, was to eliminate one or more suspects. All you've done is make all three of them look more guilty."

Ron shrugged his shoulders and let out a chuckle.

"Good job," Cliff said. "Good job."

17

Sunday morning
One Week After Championship Game

The doctor's words were penetrating.

"We're going to try to wake Julia up today and see if she's responsive and can breathe on her own."

Cliff suddenly couldn't breathe. He'd been waiting for six days to hear those words. Now that he had, an overwhelming sense of dread came over him.

What if she's not responsive and can't breathe on her own?

At least right now, he could assume she would. Once they try it, if the worst-case scenario became a reality, then he'd have difficult decisions to make.

"Do you think she's ready?" Cliff asked.

"Her lungs are healing," Dr. Moody said.

He was Julia's lead doctor.

"The EEG shows brain activity, and the swelling has gone down. Not as much as we'd like but enough to where we can try it. She'll heal faster if she's awake. I'm optimistic."

Until a minute ago, Cliff had been the most optimistic person in the room. Of course, Julia was going to wake up and recognize him, start the process of making a full recovery, and be home in no time.

Now he wasn't so sure. Self-doubt was stronger than it'd ever been. He had to fight it off and trust God. This was the moment he'd been praying for.

"We'll be back in a little while to get her ready," the doctor said.

How long was a little while?

Cliff looked at the clock on the wall. *7:45 a.m.*

A little while in 'doctor speak' could be thirty minutes or four hours. Thirty minutes would be too soon. He wouldn't be ready. He needed more time to build up his courage. Four hours would be too long. Every minute would be sheer torture.

A knock on the door startled him.

"Come in," Cliff said.

Angus walked in. The pastor of the rescue mission who Cliff credited with saving their lives.

When Cliff saw him, he practically burst into tears.

Angus was next to him immediately. He put his massive hand on Cliff's shoulder. Cliff bolted up from his chair and Angus wrapped his huge arms around him and pulled him into a bear hug.

"They're going to try and wake Julia up today," Cliff said, trying his best to fight back the tears.

"That's an answer to prayer," Angus replied in a surprisingly gentle voice for a giant of a man.

"It is, if she comes out of it," Cliff said. "The doctor says there are no guarantees."

"There are few guarantees in life. At least you'll know."

"What if I don't want to know?"

"You do. You're just scared."

They talked for nearly fifteen minutes. Angus' words were powerful and encouraging. He had a rough side to him. He came from the streets. Spent years in prison for killing a man. When he got out, he was a changed man and started the mission to help others. He talked about how he shouldn't even be alive right now, but God had a different plan.

Then his words turned from encouraging to firm. He basically told Cliff to man up. To be strong for Julia. Don't be a wimp. He didn't use those words, but the message got through loud and clear.

"Never give up. No matter what. Don't give up." The words were as strong as the man behind them.

"I won't," Cliff said, even though he wasn't sure he believed the words coming out of his own mouth.

"I have to go," Angus said. "We have services this morning."

"Thank you for coming by. It means a lot. I want Julia to meet you when she wakes up."

Angus smiled. Like his work was done and he'd helped Cliff regain his optimism. He stood from the chair and walked over to Julia and laid his hands on her. He began to pray. His deep bass voice filled the room.

"Lord, I thank you for healing my sister, Julia. In Jesus's precious name I pray. Amen."

Then he was gone.

Cliff couldn't help but wonder if Angus was real. He'd show up in their lives and then disappear. Almost like an angel.

Regardless, Cliff felt better.

Until the nurses entered the room and began to prep Julia. What they did was painful to watch. Cliff had to turn his head. Thankfully, his phone rang, giving him an excuse to leave the room.

"Hello, Ron," Cliff said. "What are you doing up so early on a Sunday morning?"

Ron should be off today.

"I had an idea," he replied. "I'm going to follow Dr. Blackburn and see where he goes."

Cliff looked at the clock again. *8:15.*

"According to his wife, he leaves his house every Sunday morning and goes to his office," Ron said.

"Every Sunday. Without fail. Those were her words."

"Not last Sunday. He went somewhere else."

"That's a good idea to follow him. Keep me posted."

"I will."

Ron didn't hang up right away.

"A few housekeeping items," he said.

Cliff was glad Ron was still on the line. It kept his mind occupied. Otherwise, he'd be pacing the hospital floor or inside Julia's room driving the ICU nurses crazy with questions.

"None of our suspects have police records," Ron said.

He was talking about Kate Reynolds, the girlfriend, Justin Jackson, the pool guy, Dr. Blackburn, and Mr. Mayfield. Those were the primary suspects at this point, along with whoever made that five-million-dollar bet.

"I didn't think they did," Cliff said with resignation. "But it doesn't hurt to check."

"Neither does Harold Potter. Not even a parking ticket."

Potter hadn't been ruled out as a suspect either.

"I'm not surprised," Cliff said.

The line went silent for a few seconds.

"Anything else?"

Cliff heard papers rattling in the background. It sounded like Ron was in his car.

"Mayfield's gun came back negative. It's not the murder weapon."

"I'm not surprised by that either. Mayfield doesn't seem dumb enough to kill his next-door neighbor and then leave the gun in plain sight in his own house."

"That gun's probably at the bottom of Lake Michigan."

"Yep."

It didn't seem like Ron had anything further, so Cliff said goodbye and hung up the phone.

Good timing. Dr. Moody was coming down the hall toward him. A little while must mean less than thirty minutes to him. He stopped to talk to Cliff before entering Julia's room.

"Do you have any questions?" the doctor asked.

"How long will it take for her to wake up?"

Cliff was proud of the fact that the question assumed she was going to wake up. Angus had helped him renew his faith. Cliff was determined to only speak positive thoughts from here on out. If the worst happened, he'd deal with it when it came. Until then, he'd believe the best and assume she was going to wake up and make a complete recovery.

"Every patient is different," Dr. Moody said. "We'll bring her out slowly. It's not like a light switch that you flip on and off. The drugs are powerful."

Cliff nodded like he understood even though he still didn't know what to expect.

"It's more like a dimmer switch," Dr. Moody continued. "The lights will come on slowly."

What is slowly to a doctor?

"Do you mean, thirty minutes to an hour?" Cliff asked. "A couple of hours?"

"Over the course of the day. We'll see how it goes. Hopefully by this afternoon, or early evening she'll be awake enough to communicate. Either verbally or with signals. At that point, we'll reassess. We'll see how she's doing."

"When will she come off the ventilator?"

"We'll start weaning her off the vent at the same time we're lowering the dosage on the drugs. The nurses will monitor her oxygen levels. If they're good, we'll lower the support until she's off it completely. By tonight, maybe this afternoon, we'll know if she can breathe on her own."

"She will."

He patted Cliff on the shoulder. "Keep thinking those thoughts."

"Do you want me to wait out here?" Cliff asked.

"No. I want you in the room. Keep talking to her. She needs to hear a familiar voice. That'll help her acclimate. When she starts to come to, don't be surprised if she's disoriented at first. She might not even recognize you. That's to be expected. Hang in there. It's a process."

165

"She's going to be fine. Julia's a fighter."

Cliff held the door open for the doctor and they entered the room. One of the nurses said, "She's ready, doctor."

The doctor looked at the monitors. Then her chart. "Her vitals are all good," he said.

Cliff could feel the spark of optimism igniting and becoming a fire inside of him.

The doctor did a physical exam. He looked at the wound on the side of Julia's head. The swelling had gone down considerably. Her one eye was still closed but not swollen shut. He opened the good eye and looked at it.

If he was concerned by anything, he didn't show it. He was as expressionless as a professional poker player.

A person with a white coat entered the room. Cliff didn't recognize her.

"This is Doctor Curtis," Dr. Moody said. "She's an anesthesiologist. She'll be slowly reducing the drugs that are keeping your wife asleep."

Doctor Curtis gave Cliff a nod of the head.

"Thank you," was all Cliff could muster.

"We'll be monitoring the EEG," Dr. Curtis explained. "As long as everything is good, we'll keep lowering the drugs incrementally, based on what we see."

Cliff's phone buzzed. He'd forgotten to put it on silent. He looked down and saw a text from Ron.

DB on the move.

He assumed that meant Dr. Blackburn had left his house. Cliff looked at the clock. *8:20.* That made sense.

"Now it's a waiting game," Dr. Moody said, then abruptly left the room.

Cliff had two waiting games to deal with. When would Julia wake up? Where was Dr. Blackburn going? Fifteen minutes later, he had one of his answers.

Ron called him.

"Dr. Blackburn went to his office. I'm camped outside."

"You don't have to call me unless you know something," Cliff said, in an annoyed voice. "I'm kind of in the middle of something."

"I'm sorry. I thought you'd want to know."

Cliff backtracked. "It's okay. I do want to hear from you. Send me a text unless it's something big. Then call me." Cliff hung up.

The ICU nurses and anesthesiologist were hard at work. They were so intense they didn't even acknowledge he was there. So, Cliff went and stood next to Julia and began to whisper in her ear as the doctor suggested.

He didn't know if she could hear him, but he felt better saying the words. He told her they were going to wake her up from her sleep. He was looking forward to talking to her. He had so much to tell her.

Sometime later, his phone buzzed again. Ron was calling him.

Anger jolted Cliff like a rear-end collision. Why was Ron calling him while he was talking to Julia? It'd better be important.

It was.

"Guess who just walked into Dr. Blackburn's office?"

Cliff wasn't in the mood to guess.

"Kate Reynolds," Ron said.

"Cole's girlfriend?"

Cliff tried to process the information. With everything going on with Julia combined with the lack of sleep, his mind was not in detective mode.

"That's right. Why would she be in his office?" Ron asked.

"It is strange."

"In the interview, I asked Ms. Reynolds if she knew Dr. Blackburn or his wife Marsha. She said she knew *of* them but didn't really know them. She certainly never mentioned that she was having work done."

"We'll ask her."

"Do you want me to ask her now or wait until she leaves?"

Cliff thought about it for a moment. "Don't let her know you're there. We'll ask her later. That's the best way to know if she's lying."

"I'll stay out of sight."

"Better yet. When she leaves, follow her. I'd like to see where she goes next."

"Will do."

Cliff went back into Julia's room. This time the nurses offered him information without him having to ask.

"Everything looks good," Doctor Curtis said. "EEG is good."

"Vitals are all good," an ICU nurse said. "Her oxygen levels are holding steady even though we decreased the vent."

"I'm so glad to hear that."

Cliff was by Julia's side again. Talking to her. "You're doing well. I'm proud of you."

The next couple of hours were tedious. Cliff's mind wandered between the circumstances in the hospital and trying to figure out why Cole's girlfriend was at Dr. Blackburn's office.

Could they be having an affair? How ironic would that be? Stranger things had happened through the years.

With Julia awake, he'd have more time to spend on the case.

Was that true?

He had no idea how much time she'd need. Things could go back to normal, or he could be dealing with a wife in a vegetative state who needed constant care. He had to at least consider that possibility. It wouldn't matter. His vow was in sickness and in health. Until death do us part. He intended to honor that commitment. He'd quit his job and take care of her full-time if he had to. She'd do the same for him if the circumstances were reversed.

Cliff tried to put all the hypothetical scenarios out of his mind. Why waste mental energy until he knew?

Ron sent him another text.

Girlfriend on the move.

By Cliff's estimation, Kate Reynolds had been at the doctor's office for more than an hour. A lot could happen in that amount of time. He tried not to let his imagination speculate on what happened while she was there.

Cliff responded with his own text.

Follow her.

Twenty minutes later, Ron called Cliff. "She went to a restaurant. Guess who she's meeting?"

Cliff didn't like guessing games. He wanted to chastise Ron for making him jump through hoops. He stepped out in the hallway, so the nurses wouldn't hear him get angry.

"Who is Cole's girlfriend meeting for lunch?" Cliff asked in a subdued tone, only because it was the quickest way to get the answer. He didn't have the mental energy to get angry with Ron now. It'd be easy to take Julia's situation out on him.

"The pool guy," Ron answered in a snarky voice.

"No way!"

That revelation jolted Cliff into detective mode.

"They're having lunch at a salad place, in Downers Grove," Ron added.

Downers Grove was a suburb thirty minutes out of town. Seemed like a strange place to meet for lunch.

Not if they're having an affair and they don't want anyone to know about it.

"Are you still out of sight?" Cliff asked.

"I am. I'd love to hear what they're saying. Ms. Reynolds would recognize me. The pool guy's never seen me. Maybe I can go inside and find a place where I can hear them talking, but she can't see me."

"Don't risk it. Don't get made. I'd like to be able to ask her about the lunch. In a roundabout way, without her knowing we know she met with him. If she denies it, then we've caught her in a lie."

Cliff hung up, just as Julia's doctor came back down the hall toward her room. He had to consciously make the mental shift. In a way, he felt like a clown at a circus, juggling several balls at once. He followed him inside.

Dr. Moody went through almost the same routine. His facial expression was as cold as the wall of a cave.

"I don't see anything that concerns me," he said. "Oxygen levels are holding. We're going to try taking her off the ventilator entirely."

Cliff thought he saw a smile come from the doctor's lips. Probably not. The nurse was already at work removing the tube from Julia's windpipe. Cliff winced when he saw it.

"That's one question answered," Dr. Moody said a few minutes later after Julia had been off the vent for several minutes. "It looks like she's going to be able to breathe on her own."

Cliff felt elation fill every part of his body.

"That also means her brain is functioning enough to tell herself to breathe," Dr. Moody said.

"That's good news."

He patted Cliff on the shoulder. "It won't be long now. We should start to see signs of her waking up."

"I can't wait."

"When she first comes to, don't be surprised if she begins to shake uncontrollably. She'll be disoriented. And anxious. That's a side effect from the drugs. As long as she doesn't go into a seizure, we won't have to put her back on the ventilator."

"And if she does have a seizure?" Cliff asked. "What will you do then?"

"We'll have to put her back into a coma. Let's hope that doesn't happen."

"I'm praying."

Cliff's phone rang again. Ron was calling. Cliff didn't want to answer, but was curious.

"The girlfriend left. I'm following her."

"Okay. Only call me if you have something important," Cliff said sternly. "The doctor is trying to wake Julia up."

"Oh... I'm sorry. You should've said something. Good luck."

Over the next few hours, the doctor came in with more frequency. Cliff could feel increased optimism among him and the staff.

Ron never called back.

"She's completely off the anesthesia now," Dr. Curtis said.

Dr. Moody hadn't been in for several hours.

Around 5:30 in the evening, Cliff's phone buzzed.

Who could that be?

The Lieutenant.

Cliff was out in the hall at the time stretching his legs and pacing. "Hello, sir. How are you?"

"Not so good. There's been another murder," he blurted.

"Who?"

"Harold Potter was found shot to death in his home."

The shock hit Cliff like he'd been jolted with a defibrillator. A nurse pushed one down the hallway a few minutes ago which is probably why he thought of it. Before Cliff could have a chance to ask the Lieutenant more details, Julia's doctor came down the hall at a fast pace.

Practically running.

"I've got to go!" Cliff said. "I'll call you back."

Cliff hung up on the Lieutenant. Then followed the doctor inside.

Julia was sitting up in the bed. Her eyes were open. Even the hurt eye was open slightly more than a squint.

"Hello Cliff," she said in a raspy voice.

His heart began to do a dance in his chest.

He couldn't believe it.

Which one could he not believe?

Julia was awake or Harold Potter was murdered?

Neither one.

18

If there were such a thing as a cloud nine, Cliff flew past it so fast on his way to cloud ten or eleven, he didn't have a chance to take in the scenery.

The joy he felt was unspeakable.

Julia was awake. She even knew his name. Her throat was clearly hoarse from having the tube down her throat. Except for the bruising on her face, she looked perfectly normal. Not like someone who'd been in a medically induced coma for the last seven days, fighting for her life.

She even ran her hand through her hair like she was concerned about how she looked.

"Julia. My name is Dr. Moody. How are you feeling?"

She reached out her hand and he shook it.

"I'm a little tired," she said. "But I feel okay. Where am I?"

"You're at University Hospital. You were injured."

Julia looked over at Cliff with a puzzled look on her face. Cliff was standing off to the side of the room. He couldn't get to her because the nurses were on one side of her hospital bed and the doctor on the other.

"How many fingers am I holding up?" Dr. Moody asked her.

"Four," she answered.

"Follow my fingers."

He moved them from side to side and then up and down. She followed them with her one eye.

"I'm going to look in your eyes," he said. "Try and relax."

He shone a light into each of them. At least the best he could with the damaged eye. Julia winced when he touched it.

Dr. Moody looked over at the machines, nodded his head, then pulled out the chart, and made some notes.

"What's the last thing you remember?" he asked.

Julia's eyes wandered around the room like she was thinking. Then she looked at me as if I could help her remember.

"Is today Saturday?" she asked.

"No. It's Sunday," Dr. Moody said.

"I came home from work on Saturday. Last night. Cliff and I went to dinner. I think."

Dr. Moody questioned her further.

Based on her answers, it seemed like the last thing Julia remembered was from a week before the attack. That Saturday night, Cliff and Julia had a dinner date. Just the two of them. They were going to go to a movie but were too tired.

She remembered most of those details.

Nothing about the game. Or the attack. Or the pregnancy.

"I don't really remember anything else," Julia said.

"That's okay. That's to be expected."

The doctor ran her through a battery of generic questions. What year is it? Who is the President of the United States? What color were his eyes? How old was she? Where was she born? What's her date of birth? Where does she work? When was she married?

She answered them all perfectly.

"Was I in a car wreck or something?" she asked.

"You suffered a blow to your head," Dr. Moody said. "You had a concussion. That's why you can't remember."

"Oh. Okay."

"Can I speak with you outside for a moment?" Dr. Moody said to Cliff.

"Of course."

Cliff walked over and kissed Julia on the forehead after Dr. Moody vacated the spot next to her.

"I'll be right back," he said, lovingly.

She seemed fine with it.

Once Cliff was out in the hall, Dr. Moody explained what he was observing. "Your wife is doing great. Beyond my wildest expectations."

"That's such a relief."

"It's nothing short of a miracle. I've never seen anyone recover so fast after being in a coma for that long."

"I knew she would."

Cliff felt a pang of guilt when he said it. He'd had plenty of moments of doubt. He mentally slapped it back down. He needed to cut himself some slack. For the most part, he'd been optimistic.

Dr. Moody continued. "Everything looks normal. Her vitals are good. EEG is normal. She's made an amazing recovery."

"She doesn't remember anything about the attack," Cliff said in a worried tone. "Or the week leading up to it."

"That's to be expected. Her short-term memory has been affected, but not her long-term recall. Over time, the memories might come back. They might not."

"You're not concerned about it?"

"Don't you wish you didn't remember the attack?"

He had a good point.

"It's the body's defense mechanism," he explained. "She's blocking those memories. Or maybe she sustained some temporary or permanent damage to that part of her brain in the attack. The brain is a complicated organ. We don't fully understand how it works. Once the swelling is completely gone, we'll have a better idea what she remembers. I expect her memory to come back to her in pieces. A little at a time."

"I'm just glad she's doing as well as she is."

He nodded.

"We're going to run more tests. As long as her cognitive functions are normal, I'm not concerned about it. Over the next few days, she may experience headaches. Difficulty sleeping. Those kinds of things. Those will pass. If they persist for a long time, we'll look at her again."

What was a long time to a doctor?

He decided not to ask.

"What about her eye?" Cliff asked.

"An ophthalmologist looked at it and he thinks it'll heal just fine. She doesn't need surgery. Julia may have some blurriness for a few weeks. Especially riding in a car at night. She might see some glare. But all in all, she should be good."

"What about the pregnancy? She doesn't remember losing the baby. Should I tell her?"

"That's up to you. You might consider waiting until she's past the trauma. We don't want her to have a setback. An emotional trauma could send her into a depression. It won't damage her brain any further, but it might slow the healing."

"I would think she'd want to know."

"You can make that decision. All I'm suggesting is that you wait a few days or weeks. Or wait and see if she brings it up. She could wake up one day and remember it on her own."

"I'll think about it. Thank you for all you've done."

"We're going to take Julia down to run some tests."

"When can she go home?"

"Let's play it by ear. We're going to get her up and see if she can walk on her own. Then test her motor skills. Let's see how she does with those. But I'd say sooner rather than later. She's really doing well."

"I think our prayers did it."

Dr. Moody let out a sound that could only be construed as agreement. Then he took off down the hall.

Cliff brushed some tears out of his eyes before he went back into Julia's room. As soon as she saw him, she reached out her hand and he was by her side within seconds.

He kissed her cheeks and took her hand in his.

"I'm so glad to see you," he said.

"What happened to your foot?" she asked. Cliff was still in a boot.

"We were in an accident," Cliff said. "I bruised my foot."

"Oh... I don't remember it. Was it when we went to dinner? Were we in a car wreck?"

"Don't worry about that now. We can talk about it later."

Julia put her hand to her forehead like she was straining to try to remember something.

"Becca and Sam invited us over to their house to watch the Bears game, next Sunday," Julia said. "Do you want to go? She's having a bunch of people over."

"We can talk about that later."

A nurse interrupted their conversation. She unhooked Julia from all the devices except her IV drip.

"Julia, we're going to go run some tests," the nurse explained. "We'll get some x-rays and an MRI and get a more extensive EEG."

"What are the tests for?"

"We want to look at your brain."

"I hope it's still there," Julia quipped.

We laughed.

"I was thinking about getting a brain transplant once," Cliff said. "Then I changed my mind."

That caused Julia to laugh out loud although she immediately regretted it. She grimaced in pain and reached for her head.

"That's funny," Julia said.

"Your husband is a keeper," the nurse said. "He hasn't left your side in a week."

"I've been here for a week?" she asked.

Cliff nodded.

"Why don't I remember?"

"I'll explain everything later," Cliff said.

"Love you," she said to Cliff as they wheeled her bed out of the room.

"He is a keeper," Cliff heard Julia say to the nurse as they disappeared down the hall. "But you shouldn't tell him. He'll get a big head. Although, it'll be hard for his to get bigger than mine feels right now."

How was Julia joking around so quickly?

Cliff suddenly felt exhausted. He hadn't left the hospital. Even to go home. A friend brought him clothes and toiletries. He'd been camped out at the hospital the entire time. He couldn't wait to get her home and for everything to go back to normal. As soon as they were out of sight, he went back into her room and slumped down in one of the chairs.

Then he remembered something he had to do.

He voiced a prayer thanking God. When he said amen, something else came to his mind causing all the stress and tension to return.

The Lieutenant.

Did he really hang up on his boss?

Did his boss really say that Harold Potter was dead?

Cliff looked at his phone. The Lieutenant had called back three times. He'd be mad. At least until Cliff told him the news about Julia. Then he'd understand. Hopefully, he wouldn't take Cliff off the case. As happy as he'd be for Cliff, the murder investigation was his priority. Cliff clearly wasn't giving his full attention to the investigation.

Investigations, plural. Two murders. They had to be connected.

Potter's murder certainly complicated things. It muddied up his already fragmented theories. Who would want both Potter and Cole dead? He could think of a few people.

It did probably eliminate Potter as Cole's murderer. The man was suspicious. Cliff had always felt like Potter knew more than he was letting on. Now he wasn't sure what to make of it. He clearly didn't kill himself.

It seemed strange that he was having coffee and saw the girl-friend and pool guy swimming naked, texted Cole to tell him, and then wasn't curious enough to watch what happened.

Maybe he saw the murder take place.

Why didn't he say something?

He might've been afraid for his life.

As it turned out, he should've been.

Cliff called the Lieutenant back. He started by apologizing and explaining why he'd hung up on him. After a couple of minutes of update, the Lieutenant was clearly ready to move on to the investigation. He was still at Potter's house. As was Ron.

"Tell me what's going on with Potter," Cliff said.

"He was shot in his home."

"Time of death?"

"This morning. Between seven and nine."

Cliff tried to process the possible suspects. He knew Dr. Blackburn was at his office around 8:30. So was the girlfriend. He still didn't know why she went to see Blackburn. She then went to meet with the pool guy at a restaurant. The thought occurred to Cliff that maybe all three were involved in the deaths.

He didn't have time to process that conspiratorial thought.

Excitement rose up inside of him when he suddenly remembered something. Ron was at the subdivision at that time. Cliff wondered if he saw anything. If he had, the Lieutenant probably would've mentioned it by now.

As if on cue the Lieutenant said, "Ron was outside the subdivision. He tailed Dr. Blackburn. He didn't see anyone come in or out during that time."

"That means the killer was likely someone in the subdivision," Cliff mused.

"Most likely."

Cliff wondered if the security cameras would show anything or if they'd been tampered with again. He made a mental note to ask Ron to check into it.

"It looks like Potter was shot with the same gun used to shoot Dillinger," the Lieutenant concluded. "A .22 caliber. At close range. No exit wound. Probably a subsonic round."

"It has all the earmarks of a mob hit. Except, how would a hit man get inside the subdivision without being seen?"

"There's more. We found a mallet. Hidden in the garage. It looks like it has minuscule traces of blood on it."

Cliff felt his eyebrows raise halfway up his forehead.

"That may have been the blunt object used to hit Cole in the head," Cliff said.

"Exactly."

"That ties Harold Potter to Cole's murder."

"I think they're already tied together."

"Unless the mallet was planted," Cliff said. "I don't like it when things are too easy. Why would Potter hit Cole over the head with a mallet and then keep it in his garage?"

"It's clearly been cleaned off. He probably thought that was enough."

A theory started to form in Cliff's head.

The mob paid Potter to lure Cole back to the house with the text about the girlfriend. Cole came back. Somebody was waiting by the pool. He confronted Cole. Struck him with the mallet. Carried him to his bed and shot him. Then made the five-million-dollar bet. Potter was a loose end. He was talking to everyone. The press. The police. So the mob killed Potter and planted the mallet.

He considered sharing the theory with the Lieutenant but decided not to. Not until he had more information.

"I need to find out who made that five-million-dollar bet," Cliff said instead. "If I find that person, I think we'll find the killer or killers."

"I agree," the Lieutenant said.

Cliff wondered if Julia would remember the name of the company Rizzo gave him. He doubted it, since she didn't even remember the attack or knew that the Bears had already played the game.

"This is typical mob behavior. Get rid of witnesses," the Lieutenant said, voicing Cliff's theory. "They came back and killed Potter and planted the mallet in his garage."

Cliff had already rejected that theory. How would they get into the subdivision without Ron seeing them?

"Maybe," Cliff said. "But I've also got three suspicious neighbors. With motive and opportunity. Who discovered the body?"

"Dr. Blackburn."

"He seems to be in the center of everything. How did he find Potter's dead body inside of Potter's house?"

That didn't make sense. Blackburn didn't seem like the type to make a social call.

"Apparently, they were having a POA meeting today," the Lieutenant answered. "To discuss the security company. Potter is the President of the POA. He didn't show up at the meeting, even though he was the one who called it. Dr. Blackburn and one of the other residents went to check on him. They knocked on the door. He didn't answer. They looked in the windows and got suspicious. They called the police."

"If they didn't see anything, why would they call the police?"

"I guess the whole neighborhood is spooked. Who can blame them? They've had two murders within one week. Their security system was tampered with. I imagine some for-sale signs will be going up soon."

"I suppose."

"The police arrived and went around back and looked in the sliding glass doors which were slightly open. They entered and found the body."

Cliff rubbed his eyes. Cole's sliding glass doors were open. Could be a coincidence.

"Do you think you can handle this, Cliff?" the Lieutenant asked.

"Yes. The doctor said Julia's doing great. She might even be able to go home in a few days. I should be free now to pursue the leads and conduct the interviews. Have Ron call me. I'll start working on an interview list."

"He was going to call you already, but he didn't want to bother you."

Harold Potter's death would be something important enough for Ron to call him.

"I'm sorry I hung up on you," Cliff said. "You called right as they were waking Julia up."

"Don't worry about it. I'm glad she's okay. You know I've always liked her better than you."

"I know. I don't blame you. I like her better than I like you as well."

"Seriously. Give her my love."

"I will. That'll mean a lot to her."

"And get this case solved. I've got people crawling all over my backside."

"I will. Have Ron call me. Potter's murder puts a new twist on things."

Ron called as soon as they hung up. Before Cliff could put together his list. So he came up with it off the top of his head.

"You need to interview Potter's ex-wife," Cliff said. "When I talked to him, he was going through a nasty divorce."

Cliff could hear Ron writing in the background.

"Cole's girlfriend for sure," Cliff said. "And Dr. Blackburn. And the pool guy."

"Also Mr. Mayfield," Ron added. "He won't talk, but we should at least get him on the record as being uncooperative."

"Call Rizzo again and see if he's had any luck finding out the name of the corporation who made that bet," Cliff said.

"I already called him. That was on Friday. He hasn't called me back. I assume he doesn't know."

"Okay. Set up the interviews as soon as possible. Especially Dr. Blackburn. I really want to talk to him."

"Will do."

"How's Julia?" Ron asked.

"She's good. Thanks for asking. I think everything's going to be fine."

"Good to hear."

They hung up.

About twenty minutes later, the nurse wheeled Julia back into the room.

"Aren't you a sight for sore eyes?" Julia quipped with a wide grin on her face as she saw him. She touched her swollen eye as she said it.

Cliff laughed heartily, releasing a lot of the tension in his shoulders and neck.

"It's good to have my Julia back."

19

The next morning

Dr. Moody said Julia could go home.

His exact words were, "I'm probably committing medical malpractice by letting a patient go home the day after she comes out of a coma, but I can't find a medical reason to keep her."

Julia was still dealing with cracked ribs, which were painful. And a dull headache. Her eye was halfway open or halfway closed. Depending on if you were a glass half full or half empty kind of person.

Dr. Moody sent her home with pain medicine to take as needed. Knowing Julia, she wouldn't take it. She'd rather tough it out.

When Cliff and Julia walked into their home for the first time in over a week, Cliff felt like a huge weight had been lifted off his shoulders. While he still had the burden of the Cole Dillinger case constantly on his mind, Julia had been his biggest worry. Now that she was home and on the road to recovery, he could see that the light at the end of the tunnel was not an oncoming train. Or the gateway into heaven.

His wife would live a long life according to the doctor and without any long-term side effects. Unbeknownst to Julia, the biggest obstacles she'd have to overcome were emotional.

How would she react to losing the baby?

The doctor's advice was to put it off as long as possible. Until her physical injuries were healed, and they were back to their old routine. Cliff had even considered not telling her. As cruel as that seemed, telling her seemed crueler.

"What you don't know, won't hurt you." That's what his mom used to say growing up.

It might be a moot point if Julia's memory came back. She still didn't remember anything from the previous two weeks. That'd likely take time according to the doctor.

From the moment they walked in the door, Cliff tried to pamper Julia. She'd have nothing of it. It started in the garage. She insisted on walking in on her own power and carrying her own bag which was nothing more than a grocery sack with the clothes she was wearing the night they were injured.

She almost got angry with him when he said he was taking the day off so he could take care of her. "You go to work. Get out of my hair for a while." She smiled so he'd know she was kidding.

"Seriously. I could use some time to get my nest back in shape."

Julia loved taking care of the house. Things there probably did need her attention.

Cliff also really needed to get back to work. Julia was right. It'd be good for both of them to get back to normal as soon as possible.

Once Julia was settled, she shooed him away. He went into his home office and made a phone call and lined up an interview with Harold Potter's ex-wife, Gloria Potter. After that, he got in a hot shower, shaved, and put on a suit and tie.

His doctor said he had to wear the boot for one more week, but he didn't put it back on. If Julia was going to be a trooper, so would he.

Cliff looked at his watch. Today was Cole Dillinger's funeral. It wouldn't start for a few more hours. That meant interviews with key witnesses and suspects today were out of the question. All the neighbors would be at the service. As would the Bears players and coaches.

Trying to ask anyone questions at a funeral was tacky at best, a reprimandable offense at worst. After discussing it with Ron and the Lieutenant, it was decided that they would go to the funeral and Cliff would go to the office and organize his desk and make some notes in the murder book. Then go meet Harold Potter's ex-wife, Gloria Potter, at two.

Cliff arrived at the attorney's office early. The law firm was on the fourteenth floor of one of the most coveted addresses in Chicago and was one of Chicago's most prestigious. From the looks of the lobby, Gloria Potter was paying a small fortune in attorney fees. Probably in the $1250.00 an hour range.

To his knowledge, Mrs. Potter's attorney was a divorce lawyer. Not a criminal attorney. That told Cliff that he wasn't concerned about her criminal culpability. Cliff had already basically ruled her out as a suspect. If he learned something in the interview that raised suspicions, he'd put her back in the crosshairs. For now, he was on a fishing expedition.

What could she tell him about Harold Potter? The man was an enigma. A strange bird. Was he a killer? Cliff wasn't sure yet. He didn't fit the profile. Although killers came in all shapes and sizes. What Cliff did know was that Harold Potter had inserted himself into the middle of the mess. Now he was dead because of it. Either because he was responsible for Cole's death, or knew who was.

When looking for dirt or skeletons in the closet, who better to ask than an ex-wife?

Cliff was led back to a large and modern conference room with stunning views of Lake Michigan. He was made to wait for a good fifteen minutes past the appointment time. A typical lawyer tactic to try and gain the upper hand. Let Cliff know they controlled everything. Including the time of the meeting.

Gloria Potter entered the conference room like she owned the place. Some people commanded a room. Others tried. Gloria was trying too hard.

She wore a red business suit and a multicolored scarf. Her blonde, almost ivory shiny hair, came to just above her shoulders and was flipped under. She probably paid a week of Cliff's salary to maintain it. Gloria Potter was attractive because of the presentation, not a natural beauty like Julia.

First impressions were that Gloria was like a mannequin in a department store. She was attractive but only because a designer knew how to make her look better than she was.

He would give her one thing. The lady was a walking jewelry store. She should've had a bodyguard with her. Valuable gold, sapphires, and diamonds adorned several parts of her body like Christmas tree ornaments.

Alfred Cheetham, her attorney, made the introductions in his custom-tailored suit with designer cufflinks. Cliff fought back a smile. 'Cheat 'em' was a good name for an attorney. Cliff didn't like attorneys. They were a necessary evil in the world, and he understood the reason for their existence in the legal system, but he didn't have to like them.

Cliff stood to his feet, nonetheless in deference, and then had to fight back a grimace when he stood up too fast. His ribs were still sore. He also should've worn his boot. The long walk from the parking garage to the fourteenth floor left his foot throbbing.

The doctor had warned him. He couldn't damage his foot any further, but the boot would help with the pain. Right now, he was struggling to keep the intensity of the suffering from showing on his face or in his demeanor.

Cliff reached out his hand and shook theirs across the table so he wouldn't have to walk to the other side.

After they sat down Cliff said, "My name is Detective Cliff Ford. I'm investigating your husband's murder."

"Ex-husband," Gloria Potter said, snootily.

"I was under the impression that the divorce wasn't final yet," Cliff said.

Gloria exaggerated a couple of blinks with extremely long and fake eyelashes with more eyeliner than frosting on a birthday cake.

"Harold is dead," she said sharply. "That means we're no longer married. That makes him my ex."

So she's one of those.

"Sounds like you're happy he's dead," Cliff chirped, with a hint of mockery behind the words.

"You don't have to answer that," Cheetham said. "Detective, you're badgering the witness already."

So he's one of those.

"My apologies," Cliff said insincerely. "She just doesn't look the part of a grieving widow."

"I'm not grieving," she said, unsympathetically.

"Have you met someone else?" Cliff asked, unable to help himself.

"I'm not sure that's relevant," Cheetham said.

"With all due respect, I'm the one who will determine if it's relevant or not," Cliff said.

Cliff shouldn't have taken the bait, but he wasn't in the mood for her attitude. Playing nice with them would get him nowhere anyway. He might as well make it adversarial. Thirty to forty percent of all murders were committed by spouses. Fifty percent of those had a third party involved.

That made the question relevant, even though in his short time with Mrs. Potter, he confirmed his initial impressions were right. She didn't murder her husband. He'd bet his house on it.

He still owed it to his investigation to dip his toe into the rabbit hole. Just in case. After all, he should be with Julia at the moment. Instead, he was in this fancy office with a woman who thought she was better than he was. That didn't sit well with him. If he had to be uncomfortable, he might as well make her uncomfortable as well.

"Detective, let's not get off on the wrong foot here," Cheetham said, almost apologetically. "Ms. Rossi is meeting with you voluntarily. We want to help you with your investigation any way we can."

Cliff assumed Rossi was her maiden name.

"I appreciate that," Cliff said, matching his congenial tone.

The exchange, though awkward, got Cliff the desired result. She was on the defensive and he had established the upper hand.

"How long were the two of you married, Mrs. Potter?"

He saw her sizzling on the inside.

"My name is Gloria Rossi!"

She turned to her attorney. "Can you tell the detective to call me by my correct name?"

Her attorney glared at Cliff.

"I'm sorry," Cliff said.

He wasn't. He did it on purpose to get under skin a little further. It seemed to be working. People let their guards down when a detective was either nice to them or when they were agitated with him. If they trusted him, they often felt comfortable sharing too much. If they hated him, they often blurted out secrets in anger.

Cliff chose the latter approach. He would enjoy bringing Gloria down a notch if the opportunity arose.

"How long were you and Mr. Potter married?"

"Twelve years."

"Any kids?"

"No. Thank God."

"Were you married before?"

"Yes."

"Kids from your previous marriage?"

"Yes."

Cliff asked a few more general questions and things moved along quickly. Then he got right to it.

"You stood to gain financially by Mr. Potter's timely death, didn't you Ms. Rossi?"

"I don't like what you're insinuating."

"I'm not insinuating anything. I'm asking a question."

"I don't like the inference behind the word, timely. I did not want Harold dead. I just wanted him out of my life, forever."

Cliff could've taken the bait on that statement and made inferences but resisted.

"What I mean is that you save a lot of money by not having to go through a messy divorce. Especially, since the divorce is not final. Because of that, you receive all of Mr. Potter's assets. Had the divorce been final before his death, the assets would go into probate and be distributed according to a will to his heirs. Is that not correct?"

"No, it's not."

"Please explain."

"Harold and I had a prenup. He didn't get any of my money."

"I understand that Mr. Potter owned a software firm."

"I own the firm."

"Isn't he the President?"

"I'm the CEO and the Chairman of the Board. It was my daddy's company. I inherited it when he passed away several years ago. My daddy made Harold sign a prenup that said he got none of the company if we divorced."

"So what would he have gotten for his twelve years?"

"Nothing. I mean. I offered to give him the house. Of course, it has a mortgage on it. I don't think he could make the payments. He'd probably lose it."

That would explain why Potter was trying to sell his story to the tabloids for a million dollars. His gravy train was about to end. The thought also occurred to Cliff that Gloria had the wherewithal to hire someone to take care of her problem. He'd look into her father and see if he had any Italian mob connections.

Maybe he had ruled her out too soon.

Gloria wasn't done. She clearly welcomed the opportunity to rant.

"I paid for every morsel of food that man put in his mouth for twelve years," she said pointing her finger at Cliff for emphasis. "I wasn't about to keep paying for it after we were divorced."

"Did Mr. Potter want the divorce?"

"Of course not. Why would he?"

Cliff could see why their marriage didn't work. It only made him think about how lucky he was to have Julia. An intense desire came over him to get the questions over with and get home to her. But he had a job to do, so Cliff continued asking questions for another half an hour. He got more than he expected out of her.

Two things. Both important.

Harold Potter had financial problems. Serious problems. He was about to be as broke as a squirrel with a couple of nuts. Cliff learned something else that was gleaned from the last line of questioning.

"Did Mr. Potter have computer skills?" Cliff asked.

Gloria laughed.

"Not at all."

"He ran a software design company."

"I ran the company. He wouldn't know code if it bit him on the backside.""

"He was the President."

"That was in name only. Actually, he was fired months ago. As soon as I filed for divorce, I canned him. When he worked for me, his main job was to play golf with clients. He didn't even do that very well. He was a miserable golfer and he cheated."

She probably held her power over his head the whole time.

"Would he know enough to hack into the security system of the POA?"

"The only hacking he ever did was swinging at a golf ball."

Gloria smirked at her joke.

Cliff was disappointed. Driving over to the attorney's office, Cliff thought of the possibility that maybe Potter was the one who erased the security tapes. Potter made it sound like he was a software engineer. Apparently, he had no skills at all.

Cliff started to wrap things up when Gloria added an important detail.

"Harold wouldn't need to hack into the POA security system," she said, reviving his interest.

"Why's that?" Cliff asked.

"He's the President of the POA. He has the password to it."

Cliff could barely keep from showing his excitement.

"With that password, would it be possible for him to go into the system and erase archived footage?" Cliff asked.

"Absolutely."

"Would Mr. Potter know how to do that?"

"I suppose. A high school kid in a computer class could do it. Harold was an idiot, but he could figure it out."

Cliff threw out a number of rapid-fire questions.

"Does your husband own a gun?"

"Not that I know of."

"Has he ever fired a gun?"

"Not in my presence."

"Have you ever known him to be a violent man?"

"I used to have to kill the spiders in the house."

"Do you know of anyone who would want to kill Mr. Potter?"

"No."

"Did he have any ties to the mafia?"

She laughed.

"He'd be afraid if he saw a mafia type in a diner."

"Do you own any weapons?"

"No."

"Thank you, Ms. Rossi. You've been very helpful."

And he meant it.

Another piece of the puzzle might be falling into place. Harold Potter was at the center of every clue. The text to Cole. The mallet in his garage. Access to erase security tapes. Cliff wasn't sure how all the pieces fit together. He just knew from experience that they eventually would.

Cliff was nice to Gloria and her attorney as he was leaving. She had been extremely helpful. More than she probably realized.

She seemed satisfied with the meeting as well. As though she took some satisfaction in knowing she'd thrown her ex-husband under the bus.

On the drive home, Cliff called Ron and told him what he'd learned.

"I've got several things as well," Ron said. "I spoke to Cole's attorney before the funeral."

"I thought we weren't going to talk to anyone at the funeral. It's not a good look."

"He came up to me with the information."

"What kind of information?"

"Harold Potter was blackmailing Cole Dillinger. He wanted a million bucks. If he didn't get it, he was going to tell everyone about the affair with Mrs. Blackburn and the incident with Mayfield."

Cliff struggled to keep the car steady. That was huge news. Even bigger than his.

That made sense, considering what Cliff had just learned from his ex-wife. Potter was desperate for money. He'd become accustomed to a certain lifestyle, and it was about to be ripped out from under him.

"What else?"

"Ballistics confirmed that the gun that killed Potter is the same gun that killed Cole."

"That narrows things down. We likely have one murderer. Mrs. Potter said that her husband didn't own a gun. She'd never seen him shoot one. And that he was scared of his own shadow."

"Interesting. I wish we had the murder weapon."

"Me too. Anything else?"

"Yes. Rizzo called me back. The name of the Finnish corporation is Dursley Enterprises."

"You've been busy."

It was a lot of information for Cliff to process all at once.

What did it all mean though?

20

Julia was ecstatic to be home. Even though, in her mind, she'd only been gone for one day. Two weeks of her life were missing, and she still couldn't get used to it.

What happened to me?

Cliff was vague. So was the doctor. They said she was injured but didn't say how. Was it in a car wreck? Did she fall? How did Cliff get hurt as well?

Cliff said he'd answer her questions. Maybe tonight. Julia didn't plan on bringing it up. She wanted to make tonight special for her husband. The nurses said that Cliff never left her bedside. He was there twenty-four hours a day. Hadn't even gone home.

How did he get any work done?

She intended to repay him and knew exactly how to do so.

I'm going to cook him a special dinner and then make love to him. That'll make him happy.

Julia went into the kitchen and looked for something to cook him for dinner. When she opened the refrigerator door, she almost gagged. She slammed the door shut before it stunk up the whole house.

Holding her breath as much as possible, she somehow managed to clean out all the spoiled and rotten food. Dumped the majority of it in the trash. By the time she was done, the refrigerator was mostly empty. She had nothing to cook him for dinner.

They'd have to order take-out.

She started working on a grocery list. The doctor said she couldn't drive until her eye was better. That stunk as much as the refrigerator. She didn't want Cliff to have to chauffeur her around. At the same time, she understood. She couldn't see well enough to put on makeup much less drive.

After she finished with the list, she became bored.

"What have I missed over the last two weeks?" she said out loud. Julia liked to talk to herself when she was alone.

Even though Cliff said he'd explain things, curiosity was pulsing through her veins with each heartbeat.

"I think I'll turn on the television and see what I missed. Maybe the news will shed some light on what Cliff is working on."

He told her he was working on a big case but didn't give her any details. She found the remote and turned on the television.

"Who died?" she muttered under her breath.

A funeral was on the local channel preempting normal programming. She flipped around and found it on all the channels. Even national cable news.

"It must be somebody important. Maybe the mayor or somebody."

She almost dropped the remote when she heard the news reporter say the name.

Cole Dillinger.

What? The quarterback.

"What in the world happened to him?"

She sat down on the couch in front of the TV and stared at it with her mouth agape. The lady broadcaster said he was murdered.

When?

Is Cliff investigating the case?

Julia watched the funeral for nearly an hour. There were several touching eulogies. A lot of tears. Thousands of people lined the streets of Chicago. The procession took nearly an hour to get to the cemetery.

A real tragedy, the commentators said more than once.

"No wonder Cliff was so anxious to get back to work."

"I've got to know what happened."

Julia couldn't stand it when she didn't know something. She went to her computer and powered it up. The headlines were everywhere.

Cole Dillinger was murdered on the day of the game. The Bears lost to the Giants. Their undefeated season was ruined. Rioting in the streets of Chicago had gone on for four nights.

"Was I injured in the riots?" she asked, wishing someone was around to answer her questions.

She couldn't remember. The news reports said hundreds were.

"Did Cliff get hurt trying to protect me?"

"I bet he did."

Her heart warmed. "My knight in shining armor."

"Chicago Police have yet to name a suspect," she read the headline on the computer screen.

Cliff must be under enormous pressure.

She suddenly felt bad.

"What can I do to make it up to him?"

Julia looked at the clock on the wall. He wouldn't be home for several hours. She logged off the computer and walked into the bathroom and looked at herself in the mirror.

"Ewww. I look hideous."

She hadn't had a shower in a week. Just sponge baths at the hospital. Of course, she didn't even remember those. She'd been in a coma the whole time.

Julia peeled off her clothes. She got in the shower and let the sprays pummel her body for ten minutes. Then washed her hair three times. It felt like she had hospital gunk matted in it.

After the shower, Julia ran a tub of hot water with suds in it. She soaked for nearly an hour. As if the shower hadn't gotten it all. By the time she was done, she felt like a prune.

She stood in front of the mirror again and assessed her progress.

"Cliff is not going to want to make love to this."

Her whole side was purple and blue. Her left eye looked like she'd gone twelve rounds with a prize fighter.

"I look like the elephant man."

Her face was still swollen and multi-colored. There wasn't enough make-up in her bathroom, to cover it all up.

"I'll turn the lights off."

It won't work.

Her side hurt too much. She also suddenly felt exhausted. Like she'd run a half marathon.

Tears began to well up in her eyes. She wanted tonight to be special. It won't be. She had no food to cook him, and she looked like death warmed over.

What could she do to keep herself busy until he got home? She needed to do something or she'd sink into a depression. She tried on some clothes, but her nicer outfits were too snug. Not that they were too big. She'd lost five or six pounds at the hospital. It's just that they pressed against her bruises.

Sweatpants and an oversized night shirt were the only things that felt comfortable.

"What's this?" she said.

Something in the bottom of the trash can in the bathroom caught her eye.

"Is this what I think it is?"

It looked like a pregnancy test. It showed a positive result.

Julia gasped.

Then stared at it for a good minute. Not able to believe it.

"Is this mine?"

"Of course, it is. It's in my bathroom!"

"I'm pregnant!" she squealed.

Does Cliff know?

He didn't say anything. He must not know. Was she keeping it from him? Was she going to tell him that night? But got hurt before she could?

A joy came over her like she'd never felt before. She was going to be a mother.

Julia heard a sound.

A door shut.

"Julia. Surprise. I'm home," she heard Cliff say.

Boy, is he going to be surprised.

Tonight was going to be special after all.

* * *

When Julia heard Cliff's voice, it felt like a trapeze act had broken out in her chest. She hid the positive pregnancy test in the drawer and practically ran into the kitchen/living room area where he had just placed his keys on the island.

She took a flying leap into his arms and immediately regretted it. They both cried out in pain at the same time.

"Honey. I'm glad to see you, too," he groaned. "But my ribs are still sore."

"I know. I'm sorry. I got too excited. My ribs hurt, too."

She tried to kiss him profusely, but the side of her face was too sore, and Cliff was barely holding her upright on his one good foot. He gently set her feet on the ground and then bent over with his hands on his knees. Trying to catch his breath and will the pain to go away.

She took his hand and led him over to the couch where they both sat down.

"How was your day?" she asked.

The pained expression was still on his face. "Good. I made some progress on my case."

"I'm so glad."

"How are you doing?" Cliff asked, looking her over from the top of her head to her toes like a doctor assessing a patient, or a buyer looking to purchase a used car.

She didn't look or feel very good. Even with all of her efforts. She looked like a housewife who'd been out of the workplace so long she didn't care how she looked for her husband when he came home from work.

To his credit, Cliff didn't let it show.

"I'm well," Julia lied. "I got a lot done."

She wasn't going to tell him the truth. She was exhausted. At least a dozen places on her body were crying out in pain. So much so that she might have to take a pain pill.

"I cleaned out the refrigerator," Julia beamed proudly. "It stunk to high heaven."

She contorted her face for effect.

"I'm sorry. I should've thought of that. Actually, I did. But I didn't want to leave you alone at the hospital."

"That's sweet."

"Are you hungry?" he asked.

She wasn't really, but assumed Cliff was. She didn't want to ruin the evening by saying she wasn't hungry.

"Let's have Chinese food delivered," he said.

That almost made her gag again. Some of the food in the fridge was leftover Chinese.

But she didn't say anything.

The food arrived and Julia ate more than she thought she would. They gorged on steamed dumplings, egg rolls, vegetable chicken on rice, and shrimp Lo Mein. Sharing a little of each.

If making love was going to be hard before, a stomach full of fried MSG was going to make it next to impossible.

She had to try.

"I thought maybe we could do stuff tonight," Julie said, using their word for sex. "I figure it's been a while for you."

"I'm not sure I can."

Her feelings were suddenly hurt.

"Is it because I'm so ugly?" she said with a pouty lip.

By the look on his face, Cliff immediately realized his mistake and tried to correct it.

"No, honey. It's not you. You're beautiful. And I love you. I want more than anything to be close to you."

He stroked her head and kissed her forehead. Then kissed her hurt eye. Then lightly touched her lips with his.

"It's just that... making love to you would be torture."

She playfully slapped him on the shoulder pretending she was offended. She knew what he meant.

He tried to laugh, but she could tell it hurt his ribs. She knew better than to let a laugh escape her mouth. The pain was almost unbearable. Her throat was still sore, and a thousand times that day, she had resisted the urge to cough knowing she'd aggravate the cracked ribs.

"That didn't come out right," Cliff said, backtracking. "I'd love to make love to you. It's just that, my foot is still bruised, my ribs are sore, and this last week has been the most stressful of my life. I'm exhausted. But I will if you really want to."

She was relieved he didn't want to.

Cliff snuggled closer.

"You smell good," he said, taking a large whiff of her hair.

Then he kissed her more deeply. The mood was romantic, but she had a hard time reciprocating. Her mouth felt like a Chinese buffet. What she really wanted to do was get up and brush her teeth and gargle with mouthwash for an hour.

Then kiss him.

He must've sensed her reservations because he pulled back.

I'm ruining things.

Tonight wasn't going as planned.

"Is anything wrong?" he asked.

"I feel like I have Chinese food breath or something."

"I don't mind. I do too."

Then the conversation turned serious.

"Tell me about your big case," Julia said.

Cliff hesitated.

"I know about Cole Dillinger's murder," she blurted out, taking the initiative. For whatever reason, Cliff was reluctant to talk about it. He was trying to protect her from something. She was trying to make it easier for him to tell her in a roundabout way.

Cliff's eyes widened like he was surprised she knew about Cole's murder.

Julia wished her eyes could widen. Her left eye felt like it'd had ten injections of Botox in it. The skin around it was frozen in place.

"How do you know about that?" Cliff asked.

"I have my sources."

He faked a glare of annoyance at her.

"I saw his funeral on TV."

Cliff looked over at the dark screen against the wall opposite the couch where they were sitting.

"Oh," he said with resignation. Like he hadn't thought about the fact that Julia would be curious and turn it on. She rarely did. She could count on one hand the number of times she'd turned on the television when Cliff wasn't there.

"Is that your big case?" she asked.

He nodded.

"That's huge. I can't believe Cole Dillinger is dead. I can only imagine the pressure you're under. Do you have any suspects?"

Cliff laughed. "I've got more suspects than I can pray over."

"Tell me about it."

He proceeded to tell her everything. The energy in the room suddenly picked up. For her as well. She didn't feel as tired. Cliff loved talking to her about his cases. She liked to think she helped him on occasion.

The case sounded complicated almost immediately. It clearly wasn't a straightforward murder investigation. It was filled with twists and turns. Julia tried to keep it all straight in her head which was still in a little bit of a fog because of the powerful drugs that knocked her out for a week.

The suspects were obvious.

The jealous husband whose wife was having an affair with Cole. That part of the story had a familiarity to it. Cliff said she was there when they questioned them which suddenly made sense even though it didn't jog any memories or ring any bells.

The pool guy and girlfriend were suspicious. They had motive and opportunity. Julia discovered the blood by the pool. Cliff thanked her for that, even though she had no memory of it.

Harold Potter was the obvious suspect. Julia knew not to always gravitate toward the obvious. Things weren't always as they seemed. Still, he texted Cole which was strange in and of itself. A mallet was found in his garage. With blood on it. Potter had financial problems. Access to the security cameras.

She met Potter as well according to Cliff. She had a picture of him in her mind but didn't know how accurate it was.

"Potter was killed by the same gun used to kill Cole," Cliff said, with excitement in his voice. "Ballistics confirmed it."

"That's interesting."

"That doesn't make sense," he added. "How does someone kill Potter with his own gun?"

"That's a good question."

"I know! And I forgot to tell you about the bet."

"What bet?"

"A five-million-dollar bet was placed on the Giants to win the game against the Bears."

She didn't understand the significance. Cliff must've sensed it because he explained.

"The bet was placed a few minutes after Cole died."

"Oh." Julia felt her mouth gape open when she realized what it meant. "Whoever made the bet knew Cole was dead and that the Bears would never cover the spread."

"Bingo."

"Who made the bet?"

"A Finnish corporation. Dursley Enterprises."

Julia suddenly remembered something. She plowed through the brain fog to piece together the information before she blurted it out.

"Harry Potter," she said, crossing her arms in front of her chest.

"What about Harry Potter?"

"A Muggle."

"What in the world are you talking about?"

Cliff looked at her like she'd lost her mind.

"Harold Potter made the bet."

Cliff's mouth widened so far, she could've fit three egg rolls in it. It couldn't go any wider.

"How do you know?" he asked, skeptically.

"The Dursley family are the only known living relatives of Harry Potter."

To her surprise, Cliff's mouth could widen further.

"The Dursleys are a Muggle family," Julia explained.

"Who are the Muggles and why do you keep talking about them?"

She waved her hand dismissively.

"It's not important. What is important is that the Dursley family are in the Harry Potter books and movies."

"How do you know all this?"

"While I was in the hospital… after I woke up, you were gone somewhere. I don't know where. The TV in the room was on. A Harry Potter movie was playing. I don't remember which one. But I do remember the Dursley family. They were characters in the movie."

She paused for effect.

"Harold Potter owns that Finnish corporation. I'd bet my life on it."

Cliff's mouth returned to some semblance of normalcy.

"Look it up," she said. "I bet I'm right."

Cliff did look it up. He took out his phone and searched for Dursley family and Harry Potter movies.

He found it immediately.

"You're right. Harold Potter had to be the one who made the bet. He was the one who murdered Cole. Potter tried to extort a million dollars out of him. He refused to pay. Potter lured him to the house with the text. Hit him over the head with the mallet, then shot him."

"One of the other neighbors has to be involved, too," Julia said.

"Why's that?"

"Like you said, Harold Potter didn't kill himself with his own gun. He had to have help. Somebody wanted to get rid of Potter so he couldn't talk."

"The one-million-dollar question is who?"

Julia didn't know. What she did know was now was not the time to bring up the pregnancy.

"Let's go over all the details of the case again."

21

The next morning

The easiest thing for Cliff to do would be to declare the murder of Cole Dillinger solved. That'd make a lot of important people happy. The Lieutenant. The Commissioner. The Mayor. The Governor. Hundreds of thousands of Chicago Bears fans across the world.

Who could blame Cliff for taking the road of least resistance?

A beyond reasonable doubt case could be made that Harold Potter was the murderer. The mallet was found in his garage. According to the lab report, it had minuscule traces of Cole Dillinger's blood and Potter's fingerprints all over it. There's no doubt it's the blunt object used to knock Cole unconscious.

By his own admission, Potter sent the text to lure Cole home. He also made the bet through a shell company he set up in Finland. Then erased the security tapes after leading Cliff on what might be several wild goose chases.

That'd be enough to convict.

Game over, to use a sports analogy. Slam the murder book shut and take a victory lap.

Of course, Harold Potter was dead. Who was going to say he didn't do it? The file would be closed, and no one would ever open it again.

Except, Cliff wasn't wired that way. He rarely took the easy way out. A case wasn't solved until he was satisfied it really was.

He had a loose end. The gun. Harold Potter might've hit Cole over the head with the mallet. Might have even shot him with a .22 caliber gun. But he didn't kill himself with that same gun.

That's for sure.

Could he have killed himself with the gun? Yes. But gun residue wasn't found on his hands. The weapon was nowhere near the body. Not even on the premises.

So, who killed Harold Potter?

Sounded like a question for a mystery novel.

The case got murkier when Cliff had Ron run the ballistics fingerprints on the bullets found in Cole and in Potter through the database of solved and unsolved cases.

He got a hit.

Ten of them actually.

The gun used to kill Cole Dillinger and Harold Potter had been used in at least ten different murders in Chicago. All the cases had mob connections.

A monkey wrench that would even flummox a monkey.

Mob murders were the worst. Any number of people could have done it. The Chicago mob, in particular, went back decades. They had an impenetrable layer around them that took months of undercover work to infiltrate.

Cliff would probably have to call in the FBI if he got more evidence of mob involvement. They might even take the lead and he'd be relegated to the role of errand boy.

If he declared the case closed, he could avoid all that.

Not going to happen.

Cliff didn't roll over that easily. Although, he should probably take the Lieutenant up on the offer of indefinite leave and go home and be with his wife.

She'd be furious.

Besides, now that Julia was better, Cliff had a new resolve to work this case. He wasn't even afraid of the mob connection. Gloria Potter was back on the list of suspects to investigate. She certainly had motive.

Potter could also have been framed. The mallet could've been planted in his garage. The Finnish corporation might've been cleverly named to draw attention to Harold Potter.

The whole thing seemed too tidy and neat. Cliff didn't like it when an investigation was leading him around by the nose. Like another person, the murderer was telling him what to think.

He also had three neighbors who lied to him. The pool guy and Kate Reynolds said they weren't having an affair. Potter said he saw them with his own eyes. Ron saw them together in a diner outside the city of Chicago.

Dr. Blackburn said he went to his office that Sunday morning. Ron confirmed on the security camera that he didn't.

Mr. Mayfield hadn't said anything on the record but certainly had motive and his refusal to answer questions was suspicious. It never set well in the pit of Cliff's stomach when witnesses lied to him or lawyered up.

But where would any one of the neighbors get a gun used to murder ten people in Chicago? A gun linked to the mob. Gloria Potter was the only one who might have a mob connection. And that was shaky at best.

It seemed nearly impossible even though it wasn't.

The Lieutenant called Cliff and Ron into his office to discuss it. They huddled up early that morning to come up with a game plan. As much as the Lieutenant wanted to put this case behind him, and was under tremendous pressure to do so, he agreed with Cliff. There were too many loose ends.

So, it was decided. Ron would go through the ten mob murders to look for a connection. He'd also start a full-scale investigation on Gloria Potter and her father. Cliff would interview the pool guy and Kate Reynolds. Then go pay Dr. Blackburn a visit.

Justin Jackson and Kate Reynolds were called, and a time was set for that afternoon. Dr. Blackburn was with patients and would have to call him back.

Cliff wanted the pool guy and girlfriend to come in at the same time, so they'd see each other. He'd put them in interview rooms A and B. Right next to each other. He wanted to make them nervous. They'd wonder what the other was saying.

He had a few hours to wait, so he called Julia for the second time that morning to see how she was doing.

"I'm fine," was how she answered the phone. "You don't have to call me every half hour."

"Don't exaggerate," Cliff said. "It's been nearly forty minutes since I called you."

"Go solve your case. I'll call you if I need anything."

Julia did seem to be doing surprisingly well. When Cliff woke that morning, she was already out of bed. Downstairs. Drinking coffee and eating cereal. Since she didn't have milk, she filled the bowl with soda.

After she fixed him one of the surprisingly good concoctions and a cup of java, she went on the computer to figure out how to have groceries delivered.

Cliff was dragging that morning from the pain pill they'd both taken the night before. That's why he had slept late. The pill seemed to have the opposite effect on Julia. She had her usual energy. She even had a glow about her. She was bustling around the house like nothing had happened over the last few weeks.

It told Cliff he made the right decision not telling her about the baby. Let her recover first.

"I'm meeting with the pool guy and Cole's girlfriend this afternoon," Cliff said to her.

"Good. That'll take your mind off me. Don't you dare call me in the middle of the interview."

Sassy Julia was back like she hadn't lost a step.

210

He started to quip something back but resisted. Annoying her wasn't going to keep her in a good mood.

"Ask the girlfriend how the security system got turned off?" Julia said out of the blue.

"Why?" Cliff asked.

"The pool guy said he arrived at seven and turned off the security system. Cole's girlfriend, Kate, said she got up and took a shower and heard a knock on the door. She went to answer it. The pool guy was standing there. Wouldn't the alarm go off when she opened the door?"

"I can't believe you remember all these details."

Cliff had gone over them with her the night before. When he was telling her about his case. When he was avoiding the urge to tell her about the baby.

"You're the one who should've been a detective," Cliff replied.

"No thank you. I don't have the patience for it. I'd walk in the interview room, grab her by the collar, slam her against the wall, and demand answers."

"I feel like doing that sometimes."

"Don't. I don't want you to spend the night in jail. I have big plans for you tonight. "

"Oh, you do, huh!"

"Yes sir. Got to go. You're only allowed to call me one more time today."

Cliff hung up and redialed her number.

She giggled when she answered.

"I can't believe you wasted your one phone call. What if you get arrested? You won't be able to call me to bail you out."

"Doesn't count. I forgot to say I love you when we hung up."

"Okay. I'll let it pass this time. I love you, too."

She hung up before he had a chance to formally say it. He thought about calling her back, but she wouldn't think it was funny. Better to quit while he was ahead.

Cliff pocketed his phone and went back to his desk to think of questions to ask Kate Reynolds and Justin Jackson. The security system question was at the top of the list.

He wouldn't throw either of them against the wall and demand answers, but it was time to take the gloves off.

* * *

Julia's spirits were soaring. Her body felt good. The pain pill was still working. Maybe it was the elation she felt from being pregnant. Her heart was filled with unspeakable joy.

"I'm pregnant!" she kept saying over and over again.

She could hardly believe it.

Cliff and Julia had talked about children extensively before they got married. They both wanted two kids. A boy and a girl. While they couldn't control that part, they could control the timing.

With their two careers, they put having kids on the backburner. Six months ago, they decided it was time. They weren't trying to get pregnant; they just weren't trying not to.

As the months passed, Julia became concerned and wondered if there was a problem. Her gynecologist allayed those concerns.

"These things take time," she had said. "It doesn't always happen right away. Give it a year. After that, we'll run some tests."

She couldn't wait to tell her doctor, who also worked with her girls at the shelter. She'd be so excited. Julia called the office to set a prenatal appointment. The date was set for two weeks from Wednesday.

How exciting!

What a relief to know that she could get pregnant.

She went back to her things-to-do-list after crossing that one off. Julia figured out how to order groceries online and have them delivered. After filling out an order and paying for it with a credit card, the computer said they'd be there later that day. In time for her to make Cliff a wonderful romantic dinner.

Things had to be perfect when she told him about the baby.

Julia intended to conserve her energy for the afternoon and evening and cook Cliff a wonderful meal, but she couldn't sit still. She went into the spare bedroom that was nothing more than a junk gatherer. Where they threw things if they didn't know what to do with them.

That was going to be the nursery.

Julia began cleaning it out. She tried to remind herself to go slow, but she had boundless energy. The joy was driving her. She made three piles. One for stuff to throw away. Another for things to go to charity. A third for things she wanted to keep but were in the way and needed to go in the attic.

All the furniture pieces except a rocker and chest of drawers needed to go. With her sore ribs and back, Julia struggled to lift them, but eventually managed. By the time she was done, the room was basically empty, but ready for the baby's furniture.

Julia was exhausted and needed to sit down. It didn't take long until she was bored again. She went into Cliff's office and got several blank pieces of copy paper and a pencil. Then went to the kitchen and sat on a stool by the island. She drew a rectangle in the middle of one of the pieces of paper to simulate the nursery.

"This is where I'll put the baby's bed," she said. "Over here is probably better, but it's right under the heat and air conditioning vent. I don't want that blowing on our baby."

She drew a picture of a crib in the rectangle. On a separate piece of paper, she started a list of things she needed for the crib.

Mobile. Sheet. Mattress pad. Blanket. Stuffed animals.

"Over here will be the changing table," she said. Then drew it.

Diapers, baby powder, and wipes were all added to the list.

"I'll get a lot of these things at the baby shower," she deduced.

Then let out a squeal.

"I'm having a baby shower!"

She considered starting a list of people to invite but resisted the urge. That was still months away. So was the need to set up the nursery, but Cliff would agree. They should start shopping for furniture right away.

They also needed to paint the room.

"We can't do that until we know if it's a boy or a girl."

On a separate piece of paper, she made a list of things to paint on the wall. Julia was somewhat artistic and could paint things like trees, butterflies, and birds.

"The curtains definitely need changing to make it look more like a kid's room."

When she was done with that, Julia went back to the den and sat down on the couch. There she started a list of baby names. Just boy names. If it was a girl, her name would be Margarita Jell Ford. Rita for short. After her sister. Jell was her mother's middle name.

That's the first time Julia felt sadness that morning. Rita was killed a few years before. Julia let herself feel the grief for about a minute, then tamped it down.

"Nothing is going to ruin this day. Rita would be happy for me."

Julia thought about calling her sister, Anna, who lived in New York, but decided to wait. She'd call her after she told Cliff. He deserved to be the first to know.

She looked back down at her list of names. Cliff would not be able to resist turning Jell into a nickname. Jelly belly. Jelly bear. Jelly roll.

It warmed her heart to think about it.

"I better hope it's a boy. If it's a girl, Cliff will pay more attention to her then he does to me!"

Julia knew that wasn't true. Not totally. Cliff had enough room in his heart for both of them. He was going to be an amazing father.

Giving Cliff a boy, though, would be a dream come true for him. Someone to play catch with. Go to games with. Of course, if it was a girl, she'd expect Cliff to do all of that with her as well.

"Our life is not going to be the same."

Julia intended to take time off work. She wanted to be a stay-at-home mom and not go back to work until the kids were in school.

Then realized she was getting ahead of herself. She couldn't help it. Her mind was racing a mile a minute.

Her phone rang interrupting her thoughts. It'd been an hour. Cliff was probably calling her again. The phone was in the other room. She ran to answer it, ignoring her body that was crying out in pain from the sudden movement.

It wasn't Cliff.

"Mrs. Ford?" the lady on the other end of the line asked.

"Yes. This is Julia."

"My name is Carolyn Davis. I'm a nurse at Doctor Moody's office. He wanted me to check on you and see how you're doing."

"That's nice of him. I'm doing very well, thank you."

"How is your pain tolerance?"

"I took one pain pill last night to help me sleep. I haven't needed one today."

"Are you having any headaches?"

Julia searched her body for one. She'd been so busy she hadn't really thought about it. Her head did hurt slightly.

"A little bit of one. Nothing bad."

"Have you had any nausea?"

"No. Not at all."

That made her wonder when she'd start feeling morning sickness.

"How's your appetite?" the lady asked.

"I ate too much Chinese food last night. So I'd say it's good."

The nurse chuckled.

Julia walked back into the den and sat down on the couch.

"Any cramping or bloating?" she asked.

"No, Ma'am."

"Any bleeding?"

"No."

Julia thought that was an odd question.

"Should I expect any?" Julia asked.

"It's not unusual after a miscarriage."

Julia felt like someone had just hit her on the side of her head with a two by four.

"What? I... I don't understand."

"You should go back to having regular cycles within a few weeks. If you don't then you should see your regular doctor."

Julia's hand was shaking so hard she could barely keep the phone to her ear.

"Wait a minute. Are you saying that I had a miscarriage?"

She could hardly get the words out of her mouth.

The nurse hesitated.

Tears began to roll down Julia's cheeks.

The silence told her everything she needed to know. It must've happened in the hospital. After the attack. No wonder she didn't feel morning sickness.

"When did I lose—my baby?" Her voice cracked as she said it. She was practically sobbing now.

The nurse hesitated again.

"I'm sorry," the nurse said apologetically. "I thought you knew."

"I didn't know."

Does Cliff know?

"I'm very sorry for your loss. You were early in the pregnancy. Only six weeks. The doctor will be glad to hear you're doing better. If you need us at all, please call the office," the nurse said.

"I will."

Julia hung up the phone. Stunned.

She put her hand on her stomach.

"Cliff doesn't know. He would've said something if he did."

"I can't tell him, now. He'll be devastated."

22

Kate Reynolds wasn't what Cliff had pictured in his mind. Ron did the first interview, so he'd never actually met her. She was model beautiful, as he had envisioned, but he expected her to be stuck up, aloof, and dismissive. Instead, he found a timid and insecure young woman, not comfortable in her own skin.

That came as a shock, considering how perfect and beautiful her skin was. He saw that in Julia sometimes. His wife was gorgeous, yet she still saw every imperfection in the mirror, regardless of how many times Cliff told her how beautiful she was.

Kate had the world telling her she was beautiful. Even paying to take her picture or look at her on a runway. Yet, she was shy. Like she needed a shot of self-esteem.

Cliff would have to change his plan of attack on the fly. Originally, he thought he'd come at her hard. With accusations. Jump on any inconsistency. If she admitted to the affair, he'd hit her with threats of imprisonment. Obstruction of justice, since she'd already told Ron they weren't having an affair.

Even accuse her of murder, if he saw an opening to justify it.

Those scorched earth tactics wouldn't work on the unassuming young woman sitting in front of him. She'd go into a shell and withdraw at the first sign of adversity. She'd clam up. He'd never get anything out of her with that approach.

A good cop/bad cop technique would also work, but Ron was busy pursuing the mob thread.

They went through the normal introductions. Kate remained seated when he entered the room. Not out of disrespect. More out of the insecurity. Not sure how to act.

Cliff's first impression was that she wouldn't have been more nervous if she had a ticking bomb attached to her. She was fidgeting. Wringing her hands. Constantly moving them. She'd set her elbows on the table, then move them so her hands were on her lap. She'd reach for a drink. Set it down. Then reach for another one.

She had a nervous twitch in one eye.

This woman stood in front of dozens of people taking her picture. In this element, she was like the proverbial fish out of water. She'd probably never been in trouble before.

Cliff poured his own drink to try and make the atmosphere seem as casual as possible.

"Is there anything else I can get you, Ms. Reynolds? Soda? Coffee? Tea?"

"No. I'm fine with water."

"May I call you Kate?"

"You may."

"How about you, counselor? Can I get you anything?"

"I'm good."

The attorney didn't seem the least bit engaged. Like he wasn't expecting any fireworks and would rather be somewhere else. After all, as far as the attorney knew, she was the grieving significant other. The questioning was a formality in his mind.

She probably hadn't told him about the affair with the pool guy.

"I'm very sorry for your loss, Ms. Reynolds," Cliff said, in a gentle tone. "I can assure you that I'm doing everything I can to find Cole's murderer."

"Thank you. I wake up sometimes thinking it's all a dream and that he's in bed beside me. Then I open my eyes and realize I'm living a nightmare."

It seemed like tears might well up in her eyes, but they didn't.

Cliff couldn't help but notice them. Kate's eyes were stunningly beautiful. She wore the perfect amount of makeup. Subtle. Elegant. Classy. Unlike Gloria Potter who wanted you to see her coming from a mile away and needed an ice pick to get it off every night.

"Do you have any idea why anyone would want to kill Cole?" Cliff asked, giving her a softball question to start out.

Kate shook her head no.

The first line of questions were straightforward. "Do you remember seeing anyone suspicious in the neighborhood? Any strange people hanging around the house? Was Cole acting differently in the days leading up to his murder? Had his demeanor changed in any way? Did you overhear him arguing with anyone? Did any workers come to the house who hadn't been there before?"

She answered no to all of those questions. Her attorney kept his stoic demeanor and didn't say anything.

"What about the neighbors?" Cliff asked. "Would any of them have a reason to kill Cole?"

Kate took a sip of water. Her hand was still noticeably shaking. She saw that Cliff noticed.

"I'm sorry," she said. "I'm nervous."

"It's okay. Try to relax."

She took in a deep breath. Cliff matched it. He was nervous for her.

"You asked about the neighbors. I don't think so. They all seem so nice. Except for that Mr. Mayfield."

"He's the one flying the Giants flag on the fence," Cliff remarked.

Kate rolled her eyes.

"Yes. That's the one. He and Cole had a fight. I think. A few months ago. I don't know the details. Cliff was pretty mad at him."

"Did Cole see the Giants flag flying on the fence?"

"No. But I told him about it. He said to ignore it. The guy was being a jerk."

"Did Cole ever say that Mr. Mayfield threatened to kill him?"

"No. I think he would've told me if he was afraid of him."

Mayfield was still a suspect to pursue.

Things were about to get more intense.

"Do you know Dr. Leon Blackburn?"

She didn't flinch.

"Yes. He lives across the street from us. From Cole. From where Cole used to live."

Before he could ask the next question, she asked, "Is there somebody behind that mirror?"

She pointed to the wall that had an observation room on the other side of it and a two-way mirror taking up the entire wall. Cliff had been behind it many times, observing an interrogation.

"Yes, there is," Cliff answered. "We have an expert in body language watching this interview. She can tell when a person is lying based on the tone of their voice, their inflections, and their mannerisms."

Her attorney sat up slightly. Kate's eyes got as big as the coaster she had her water sitting on.

No one was there, but Kate didn't know that. Her attorney probably suspected Cliff was bluffing. She did get more noticeably nervous after he said it, if that was even possible. Which was the reaction he was hoping for.

"If you tell the truth, then you have nothing to worry about," Cliff said, sincerely.

"That's why we're here," her attorney finally interjected something. "To tell the truth."

"Can you repeat the question?" Kate asked, clearly flustered.

"Do you know Dr. Leon Blackburn?"

"Yes. I know him," she answered.

"How do you know him?"

"I've seen him around the neighborhood."

"Have you ever met with him privately?"

"No!" she said emphatically.

Cliff's heart skipped a beat. He had her in a lie. Now was the time to pounce. He had pictures of her leaving Dr. Blackburn's office which he was ready to spring on her. Any sympathy for her was out the window if she lied to him.

Before he could bring the hammer down, she said, "I had an appointment with him once."

He felt the excitement inside of him drop down a notch. Like he'd missed a hole in one at the miniature golf course by inches.

"What kind of appointment?" Cliff asked.

"He's a plastic surgeon. I don't know if you knew that or not."

Cliff nodded.

"He thought I could use some work."

That seemed absurd to Cliff, but it wasn't appropriate to say so.

"Where did you meet?" Cliff asked.

"At his office."

"When?"

"This past Sunday."

Cliff purposefully twisted his lips to the side in confusion. "The day before Cole's funeral? That seems odd that you'd go to a physician's consultation to get plastic surgery the day before you buried a loved one."

"I didn't want to. The appointment was set several months ago. He's a very busy man. I understand it's hard to even get an appointment."

She suddenly got defensive, like she was anticipating what Cliff was thinking.

"Meeting with him wasn't my idea," she added. "A lot of my friends are having work done. So I thought I'd check it out. What could it hurt?"

"What happened at the appointment?"

"Nothing. I was kind of uncomfortable. We were alone. I thought some of his staff would be there. It was not during normal hours. You know. On a Sunday and all. I didn't like it."

"Why did you meet on a Sunday?"

"That was his idea."

"Did he say or do anything inappropriate?"

"Not really. I mean, it seemed like he wanted to. But I let him know that I wasn't interested."

"Did he back off?"

"Yes. Everything was professional after that. He told me all these things I should do to my face and breasts. You know, to improve my looks. I'm not going to do them. My agency wouldn't let me anyway. They want a more natural look. They'd fire me on the spot if I had my breasts augmented."

Kate sighed.

"What happened next?"

"I told Dr. Blackburn I'd think about it and left."

"Where did you go?"

Her eyes turned up and to the left. This was the critical juncture. Would she admit to meeting the pool guy?

"I think. . . I went home."

"Are you sure?"

"No. Actually. I made a stop. I met Justin Jackson at a restaurant in Downers Grove."

"Why did you meet Mr. Jackson?" Cliff asked.

"Cole left a check for him at the house. You know. For his pool work. Before he was murdered. Justin asked if I could bring it to him."

"Why didn't you just mail it?"

"I. . . uh was going that way."

"I'm going to show you a text, sent to Cole the morning he was murdered."

Cliff gave a copy to Kate and to her attorney.

She noticeably gasped when she saw it.

"Who sent this?" she said angrily.

"Is it true?" Cliff asked.

"No! It's not true. I was not in the pool with Justin naked! I was engaged to Cole."

She seemed genuinely outraged.

"I didn't know you were engaged," Cliff said. "I thought you were just dating."

"About two weeks ago, Cole asked me to marry him and I said yes."

"Did he give you a ring?"

"Yes."

Tears welled up in her eyes.

"Why aren't you wearing it?"

Her attorney pulled a handkerchief out of his pocket and handed it to her.

"I am," she said.

She flashed the diamond on her right index finger.

"I didn't feel right wearing it on my ring finger. Not anymore. I mean. We're never going to be married. Right?"

She seemed distressed. Probably was if she was engaged to Cole and having an affair. The guilt must be racking her insides like a Middle Ages torture machine.

"Why would someone send Cole that text?" Cliff asked.

"I don't know. I would never cheat on Cole. Not with Justin."

She must've suddenly realized how that sounded and added, "I would never cheat on him with anyone."

"Would Cole ever cheat on you?"

Cliff debated on whether to tell her about Mrs. Blackburn. He decided to wait until after he confronted her husband.

"I don't know," she said honestly. "I mean. Cole was a good-looking guy. Girls threw themselves at him all the time. As far as I know, he never cheated on me. Did he?"

Cliff didn't answer. Instead, he changed the subject. He didn't like answering questions from witnesses anyway. He wanted to be the one asking the questions.

So, he shot them out of his mouth like a rapid-fire machine gun. Which was his most effective style. "Do you own a gun? Does Justin own a gun? Did you and Justin conspire to kill Cole?"

"No! No! No!"

She was emphatic.

"Is my client a suspect?" her attorney asked.

The tension in the room had reached a boiling point.

"This text, if true, gives your client a motive for murder," Cliff said.

"The text is a lie!" Kate blurted.

"You would say that even if it was true, wouldn't you?"

That's as belligerent as Cliff was willing to get at this point.

"I didn't kill Cole. I was not and am not having an affair with Justin. I swear."

"What if Mr. Jackson said you were involved romantically? Would you say he was lying too?"

"Did he say that? If he did, he's lying!"

Kate had a backbone after all. She was fuming mad.

Cliff sat there for a moment, letting the insinuated accusation hang over the room.

"Do you have any other questions?" her attorney asked.

"Yes. But wait here please. I'm not ready to dismiss you. I'll be back shortly. I need to talk to Mr. Jackson."

Cliff interviewed Justin for a good thirty minutes. His story matched hers. Of course, they'd had plenty of time to make sure it did.

Julia had given him the one inconsistency in the pool guy's story. He had decided to bring it up to the pool guy first.

"Mr. Jackson, when I first met you, the day of Cole's murder, you said that you arrived at the house at seven."

"That's correct."

"You said that you turned off the alarm."

"That's right."

"Ms. Reynolds said you knocked on the door and she answered it in her bathrobe."

"Yeah. So?"

"You left that part out."

"It didn't seem important."

"Why didn't the alarm go off when she opened the door?"

"I don't remember, man. I just remember turning it off."

Cliff grilled him for ten more minutes. The guy was either an idiot or a bad liar. Or both.

Cliff went back in the room to talk to Kate Reynolds.

"You said that you took a shower, and right afterwards, Mr. Jackson knocked on your front door."

"Yes," she said.

"How did you hear him knocking all the way in the bedroom?"

"He might've rang the doorbell. I don't remember."

"What did you do?"

"I answered the door."

"Why didn't the security alarm go off?"

"It did. I mean, it didn't sound the siren. It makes a beeping sound, and you have one minute to enter the code to shut it off."

"Were you the one who entered the code and turned off the alarm?"

"I think Justin did."

"Does he know the security code?"

"I assume so. Yes. He comes and goes all the time when we aren't there."

"So he turned it off?"

"I believe so, yes."

Cliff wondered if she was smart enough to come up with that on her own in the spur of the moment. He ended the interviews and let both Kate and Justin leave. Making sure it was at the exact same time.

A plan had formed in his mind. To follow Kate. If they were involved in an affair, they'd leave the interrogation and meet somewhere. He followed them out of the parking lot and tailed her. Careful not to be seen.

She drove several miles. They reached a T in the road, turned right, then went on a long stretch of highway. After a couple of miles, she made a sudden turn into a park. It had a children's playground and a walking trail.

It also had a second entrance. Cliff was able to pull in there without being seen.

Moments later, the pool guy pulled in and parked next to her.

Cliff was able to get out of his car and walk around the restroom facility and get within earshot of them without being seen.

He could hear a heated discussion.

"Did you tell them we were having an affair?" Kate said angrily.

"No. I swear. Why would I do that?"

"Somebody sent a text to Cole saying we were swimming naked in the pool."

"Who would do that?" Justin asked.

"I bet it's that Potter guy. You know. The guy who lives next door. Up on the hill. He's such a creep. He's always watching me sunbathing from his window."

"He's dead, you know."

She gasped. "I didn't know that."

"Somebody murdered him. I heard it on the news."

"No way. I didn't hear that. I don't watch the news."

That meant she didn't kill Potter. Cliff had already figured as much.

"I can't believe that weasel would tell Cole that we were having an affair when we aren't," Kate said, sending a shockwave through Cliff.

"I don't know. I hope this doesn't get out. My girlfriend would be furious."

"My agency doesn't like scandals."

"The detective was trying to trick you." Justin said. "I didn't tell him we were having an affair. He was trying to get you to admit something that wasn't true."

"I told him the truth. That we're just friends."

"That's what I told him. I barely know you."

"We probably shouldn't meet like this," Kate said. "They might be following us."

Cliff skulked back in the shadows.

"We didn't do anything wrong," Justin said.

"I know. I guess I'm being paranoid."

Kate's arms were crossed in front of her. It was a cold and windy day.

"I'm sorry about Cole," Justin said. "He was a nice guy. He was always good to me. I guess I won't be doing any more work at the house."

"I miss him. I'll probably go back to New York."

Cliff could hear in her voice that she was fighting back tears.

Kate stuck out her hand to shake his.

"It's been nice knowing you. I probably won't ever see you again."

He shook it. "I guess not. Good luck."

Hardly a goodbye between two lovers.

They got in their cars and drove away.

Kate Reynolds was a model, not an actress. If that was an act, she deserved an Oscar.

Cliff didn't think it was. They were both telling the truth. Harold Potter was the one who lied.

Why?

23

Later that night

When Cliff got home from work, he noticed a change in Julia's demeanor. She tried to put on a happy face, but he could see right through it. The doctor had warned that she'd have her ups and downs. Cliff attributed it to her doing too much too soon.

A wonderful dinner was on the table. Julia obviously put a lot of effort into it. She'd also cleaned out the spare bedroom which took considerable effort. He still wasn't sure how she managed to move the boxes and furniture, given the nature of her sore ribs, back, and headache which she admitted was now raging.

He felt bad for her and wished he'd been home to help her. The night of the attack, they talked about turning the room into a nursery for the baby. Julia had been beyond excited that night. She knew where she wanted to put the crib. The changing table. The rocker. The chest of drawers. She described walls painted with trees, birds, butterflies, and rainbows.

They even talked about baby names. Nothing specific when it came to boys, but if the baby was a girl, they'd name her Margarita, after her sister, Rita.

Perhaps somewhere in the dark resources of Julia's mind, she remembered that conversation and something inside was telling her to clean out the room. She wouldn't know why, but maybe someday he'd tell her. Years from now. After they already had two or more kids.

Telling her right now would be too much for her to handle. He needed to get his wife healthy. He couldn't put her through another trauma. The room reminded Cliff of how fast those dreams were dashed and he was feeling the loss. He'd just have to carry it for both of them.

In an attempt to lighten the mood, Cliff told Julia about his interviews with Kate Reynolds and Justin Jackson. Funny how a murder investigation could inject some energy into dinner. It'd always been that way. Julia loved talking about Cliff's work. Even more than her own. She said it made her feel close to him.

He got a benefit as well. She usually had some gem of an idea that helped him in the investigation. He needed that now, considering how unbelievably complicated the Cole Dillinger murders were to solve. Complicated by all the personal distractions over the last ten days.

"I think we can exclude them as suspects," Cliff said.

"Any chance they knew you were there?" Julia asked, with her usual perceptiveness and ability to look beyond the obvious.

"It's always possible. But I don't think so. It didn't seem like an act."

"It's good to eliminate suspects, right?"

"Absolutely."

"Let's see who we have left. Mr. Mayfield, the neighbor. Gloria Potter, the ex-wife. Dr. Blackburn, the jealous husband. The Chicago mob. That doesn't narrow it down much. Who are you going to interview next?"

"Dr. Blackburn. He's suspect number one."

"When are you interrogating him?"

"Tomorrow morning. Ten o'clock. At his house."

They didn't stay on the subject that long. While Cliff saw a temporary uptick in Julia's mood, talking about the case had dampened his.

How in the world was he going to figure out who killed Cole if it wasn't Harold Potter?

If Potter did kill Cole, then who in the world killed him?

* * *

The next morning

"Can I go with you to interrogate Blackburn?" Julia asked.

He didn't mind taking her. He just wasn't sure it was a good idea. "Are you sure you want to go out? Are you feeling up to it?"

She came over and practically draped her arms around his neck. "I don't want to be home alone all day. With nothing to do. I want to be with you."

The night before, Julia had been the same way. Clingy. On the verge of tears. She didn't want to let him out of her sight. They had to be touching. He even went to sleep holding her. His shirt was damp from her tears.

This morning, she was the same way. A sharp contrast to yesterday morning when she was cheery and ready to take on the world.

"What about your eye?" Cliff asked.

"I'll stay in the car if you don't want anybody to see me."

"That's not what I meant."

Julia's eye had turned pussy. With the ointment the doctor had given her, it actually was kind of gross to look at.

"I'll wear the patch," she said.

The doctor had given it to her to wear in the sunlight. To protect the eye from too much glare. The night before, in an attempt at humor, Julia came out of the bathroom wearing a nightgown and the patch.

She started talking like a pirate.

"Let's fool around, matey" she said playfully. "Aaar. I'll pretend to be a pirate."

That didn't work. It did provide a brief respite to the downer they'd both been feeling all evening, but neither of them could make fooling around happen. The best they could do was cuddle as the dark cloud continued to hang over the room.

Thinking about the interaction did bring a smile to Cliff's face.

"I know what we can do," Julia said, with a smile on her face for the first time that morning. "Bring a big lamp. You know the kind they use to interrogate witnesses. We'll shine it in Dr. Blackburn's eyes, and I'll ask the questions. Wearing the patch. That'll scare him into a confession."

"I think you should get in his face, not wearing the patch. That's even scarier."

Cliff immediately regretted the joke. Julia was already touchy about how the injuries made her look.

She stuck out her tongue at him, letting him know she wasn't hurt much to his relief.

"Can I go?" she asked. Almost like a kid asking to go to the candy store.

"Why not? And you can come in. I want to know what you think about Dr. Blackburn. You might catch something important that I don't see."

Julia practically skipped away to get changed. He was glad she was going. Otherwise, he'd be worrying about her the whole time and have a hard time focusing on the task at hand.

Maybe going to the interview was just what she needed. He knew that whatever Julia was going through was only temporary. She'd snap out of it. The sooner the better. She was right. Sitting around the house brooding wasn't going to get her out of the funk.

He also meant it when he said she'd be a big help. Cliff had a feeling that the interview with Dr. Blackburn was important. Like a break in the case was coming soon. It was an instinct he had that the Lieutenant said couldn't be taught. A sixth sense about cases.

This one seemed on the verge of being broken wide open. Considering he really had nothing on Dr. Blackburn, he had no idea where the optimism was coming from.

Dr. Blackburn said he went to his office the morning of the murder. The security cameras didn't confirm it. Harold Potter said he saw Cole and Dr. Blackburn arguing on the street. But Potter lied about the girlfriend in the pool naked with the pool guy. Even lied to Cole when he sent him a text to lure him back to the house. Potter was probably lying about the doctor and the confrontation with Cole in the middle of the street.

But why did the doctor lie about going to the office the morning of Cole's murder? That's what he was going to find out.

Cliff joined Julia in the bedroom, and they got dressed together. He voiced those concerns to her. She didn't know what to make of it. Not that he expected her to, he just wanted her to be thinking about the same question he grappled with.

The interview was not for another hour, and they had time, so they stopped off at the *Hipsters Coffee Café*. That's the coffee shop where they first met. Cliff ordered his usual smoothie. Chilled coffee. One frozen banana. Almond milk. Rolled oats. A heaping spoonful of peanut butter. With chocolate sprinkles on top. And an extra shot of caffeine.

Julia ordered her usual, a Vanilla Latte, no foam, with a double shot of caffeine as well.

It'd take the funk they were in a few hours to break through all that caffeine. If it even could. Cliff had a feeling the fireworks at Dr. Blackburn's would provide even more adrenaline. Halfway through his drink, Cliff felt like he'd stuck his hand in a light socket.

Julia was wearing her pirate's patch. Clearly uncomfortable. As self-conscious as a drunken sailor at a Sunday morning church service.

"People are staring at me," she said nervously.

"They're always staring at you."

"This time for a different reason. I look like I'm about to rob everyone of their money."

She actually didn't look bad. Julia was wearing black slacks and a winter sweater. Her beautiful black hair covered most of the bruising on the left side of her face.

"Most people will assume you just went to the eye doctor," Cliff said.

"The only thing missing is a peg leg and a hook on my arm," she said tersely.

"Let's make sure we don't argue about anything."

"Why?" she asked in a confused tone. "We don't usually argue."

Cliff lifted his smoothie in the air. "We won't be able to see aye to aye," he said in a pirate's voice.

For whatever reason, that struck Julia as funny. She suddenly couldn't stop laughing. She'd giggle. Put her hand to her mouth to stop it. Start to take a drink of her vanilla latte, then start giggling again. A few seconds later, she'd burst out laughing again.

People around them were noticing. It made Cliff self-conscious.

"I can't look at you," she said, turning her head. "You'll make me laugh."

"What do pirates fear the most?" Cliff asked.

"I'm not playing your game," she said, turning her nose up in the air and looking away.

"A sunken chest and no booty."

She burst out laughing. Much harder than the joke warranted. He thought it was helping her so he kept it up.

"What's a pirate's favorite subject?

"Stop it!"

"Aaart."

She started giggling again.

"What's a pirate's favorite fish?"

"Shut up."

"Swordfish."

"Why is a pirate good at playing the flute? Because he spends a lot of time on the high Cs."

She put one hand in the air to get him to stop. The other was over her mouth trying to keep her from losing it altogether.

"Why couldn't the pirate play cards?"

She glared at him. "Why?"

"He was sitting on the deck."

"Are you done yet?"

"I could go on all day."

"Please don't."

"Come on. Those were funny."

"Don't quit your day job."

"Knock knock."

She ignored him. "Did you make these up on the spot?"

"They just came to me."

"Why am I not surprised?"

Cliff had a unique ability to remember jokes. He brought them out whenever he could. Julia remembered dates. She was like a walking encyclopedia.

"Between my jokes and your pirate's patch, Dr. Blackburn doesn't have a chance."

That made them both start laughing again.

"Let's get out of here, before they throw us out," Cliff said.

That was just the release they both needed.

* * *

10:02 a.m.

Cliff and Julia were inside the Blackburn's house, sitting in the den, in the same seating arrangement they had the first time they interviewed the couple. Cliff wondered if Julia remembered. By the look on her face, he didn't think so. She had let out a sound of amazement when they drove up to the house.

"How many people live here?" she asked with her mouth opened in awe.

"Two. As far as I know."

"Why do they need this much room?"

"I think they buy something like this because they can. Not because they need it."

She was even more impressed once they got inside. Her one visible eye was glossed over.

Neither Dr. or Mrs. Blackburn mentioned the patch on her eye.

"Thanks for meeting with us," Cliff said. "I'd like to clear up some inconsistencies in your story, Dr. Blackburn."

He sat up straight and glared.

Cliff liked to lead with something shocking like that when possible. It put the suspect on the defensive immediately. If they're guilty, it makes them afraid that they made a mistake. Even if they aren't guilty, it makes them nervous. Cliff preferred that the witnesses and suspects felt intimidated.

"Do you know Kate Reynolds?" Cliff asked.

"Yes," he answered. "Barely."

Mrs. Blackburn was the one who glared this time. Cliff remembered the vitriol she had for Cole's girlfriend the last time they were there. He knew the question would get a rise out of her as well.

"Have you ever met with her privately?" Cliff asked.

Dr. Blackburn changed positions on the couch. A noticeable sign of nervousness.

"I wouldn't say privately."

"What would you say?"

"I met with her at my office."

"I didn't know you met with her," Mrs. Blackburn said.

If looks could kill, he'd be arresting Mrs. Blackburn for murder. She was looking at him like a pit bull ready to attack an intruder. Dr. Blackburn looked away from his wife clearly to avoid making eye contact with her.

"When?" Cliff asked.

"Last Sunday morning."

Mrs. Blackburn let out a sound of disgust.

"Were you alone with her?"

"Yes."

His wife was about to become unglued. If Cliff and Julia hadn't been there, she probably would have.

"Your office is closed during that time. Is that correct?" Cliff asked, keeping up the pressure to maintain the tension in the room.

"Yes. She wanted to meet when the office was closed. A lot of my high-profile clients don't like to meet with me during normal office hours."

"What was the nature of your meeting?"

"It was her idea." He did look at his wife when he said it as if that might somehow appease her. "She wanted to meet with me. She wanted to have some work done. Some plastic surgery. On her nose, I believe."

Mrs. Blackburn was seething. Her arms were crossed. Her jaw clenched. Her lips pursed together tighter than a freezer door.

She obviously hated Kate. Cliff wondered if Dr. Blackburn had picked up on it. Why would his wife have such strong feelings for someone they supposedly barely knew?

His statement also created an inconsistency. Kate Reynolds said the meeting was Dr. Blackburn's idea. If Cliff had to choose, he'd believe Kate over the doctor any day of the week. The doctor was probably lying to downplay it in front of his wife, so Cliff didn't think much of the white lie.

He also didn't want to lose his momentum by getting sidetracked with a he said/she said that could never be proved one way or the other.

"Did you ever do any work for her?" Cliff asked.

"No. I didn't think she needed any. We only met for a few minutes."

Kate said the doctor was insistent that she needed work. Again a minor inconsistency, but it did tell Cliff that Dr. Blackburn was willing to lie if it served his purposes.

"What did you do then?" Cliff asked.

"I worked on paperwork and then came home."

"That's right. The first time I interviewed you, the day of the murder, you said that you always go into work on Sunday mornings to do paperwork. It's quiet during that time. You said that you went in to work that day. Is that correct?"

"I believe so."

"You believe you did, or you're sure you did?"

"I did."

"Where do you park when you go to work on Sundays?"

"In the back parking lot."

"The medical complex across the street has security cameras. Are you aware of that fact?"

Dr. Blackburn started to squirm again but caught himself.

"How would I know if they have security cameras?"

"They do. We looked at those tapes. I didn't see your car. Why is that?"

"Maybe you had the wrong time."

"I looked at it from eight in the morning until noon."

Technically, Ron viewed the tapes, but Dr. Blackburn didn't need to know that.

"Perhaps you had the wrong day," he said.

"It's time stamped."

"Then the cameras were doctored. Like the ones in the subdivision."

"About that. You're on the POA board, aren't you Dr. Blackburn?"

"Yes."

"Do you know the password to the security system?"

"I suppose. I think we all have access to that information."

"So anyone on the board for the POA, could've erased those security tapes."

"I guess that's possible."

"Including you."

"I don't think I'd even know how to do it."

Cliff would get back to that.

"Dr. Blackburn, you told me that you own several guns. Rifles and a handgun."

"Is that correct?"

"Yes. What type of handgun?"

"I have a Rohrbaugh R9 Stealth Elite and a Glock."

"Wow. I'm impressed. That Rohrbaugh is an expensive gun."

Cliff already knew what guns he had registered. He was interested in what he didn't have registered. It was a shot in the dark, but worth the effort.

"Do you own a .22 caliber handgun?" Cliff asked.

Dr. Blackburn began to squirm noticeably for a third time. The questions were clearly flustering him for some reason.

"I don't know."

"Could we go look?"

"Do you have a warrant?"

"Do I need one? If I do, I can have a policeman at your house in about five minutes, to take you into protective custody. Then I can get the warrant and do the search. Is that how you'd like for this to go down?"

"May I be excused for a minute?" he asked.

"Okay."

Cliff would give him two minutes and then come looking for him.

"What happened to your eye, dear?" Mrs. Blackburn said after her husband left the room.

Cliff was surprised it hadn't come up before now.

"I scraped my eye putting in a contact," Julia said. "The doctor makes me wear the patch when I'm outside."

Cliff was amazed at Julia's ability to think on her feet, although the explanation didn't make sense. The bruises on her face were still visible.

"The patch matches my shoes, though," Julia quipped.

"That's the most important thing, isn't it? We women have to match."

Dr. Blackburn suddenly appeared.

Holding a gun.

Cliff bolted to his feet. His gun was out of his holster in seconds.

Mrs. Blackburn let out a scream.

"Drop the gun! Now!" Cliff shouted.

Dr. Blackburn's eyes widened when he saw Cliff's gun..

"Do you want to die?" Cliff said.

Cliff's finger was on the trigger, watching for even the slightest twitch.

24

Dr. Blackburn wasn't holding the gun in a firing position, so Cliff relaxed his finger on the trigger slightly. Still, he didn't like it when suspects suddenly entered a room with a weapon in their hands.

"Put the gun down on the floor," Cliff ordered. "Slowly."

Dr. Blackburn was clearly shaken. He bent over gently and did as Cliff said.

"Now back away from the gun."

Dr. Blackburn took several steps backward.

Cliff saw movement out of the corner of his eye. He didn't look to see what it was until Blackburn was safely away from the gun and no longer a threat.

Julia was the source of the movement. She stood from the love seat and walked over and sat next to Mrs. Blackburn whose hands were clutching tissues in front of her.

Tears streamed down her cheeks.

"Why did you kill Cole?" Julia asked her in a quiet voice. "You loved him."

Mrs. Blackburn didn't answer. Her head was down, and she stared at her hands. Cliff stood there with his mouth agape.

"Was it because Cole asked Kate to marry him, and she said yes?" Julia asked.

Cliff thought he saw a nod of the head but couldn't be sure.

"You thought he should be with you, didn't you?" Julia asked barely above a whisper.

Cliff wanted to give his full attention to Julia's questions, but he needed to secure the gun. He took out a handkerchief and gently lifted it off the floor and wrapped it in it. Then walked around the coffee table and sat back down in his front row seat to watch the action unfolding before his eyes on the couch.

"He broke up with me," Mrs. Blackburn said quietly, between sobs.

"When?" Julia asked.

The two of them were oblivious to everyone else in the room. When neither of them were talking, it was so quiet you could hear a needle drop in a haystack.

"Two weeks before he died," she said, trying to catch her breath which was labored from the crying.

"That's when he got engaged to Kate."

"Yes!" she blurted out and began to cry uncontrollably.

It took her a few seconds to regain her composure.

"I begged him not to do it," she said, looking Julia in the eye, like they were best friends talking about a high school breakup. "He didn't love Kate. He loved me."

Dr. Blackburn stood off to the side with a look of shock on his face. His mouth was opened so wide a swarm of flies could fly into it.

"Cole was the love of my life."

Dr. Blackburn's confusion suddenly turned to anger as his eyes narrowed and his fists were tightened. He took two steps toward the couch.

Cliff still had the gun in his hand. He had thought about holstering it, but kept it out, just in case.

"You were having an affair with Cole Dillinger!" Dr. Blackburn shouted from his position which was now directly behind the couch.

Mrs. Blackburn's sobs suddenly dissipated as anger filled her face as fast as a roaring lion's who'd been poked with a stick.

"Don't you tell me I don't know about your little Sunday morning trysts," she retorted.

A stare down ensued. They both glared at each other with the intensity of two prizefighters in a ring.

Dr. Blackburn blinked first and feigned ignorance. Like he didn't know what she was talking about.

"Don't give me that look," Mrs. Blackburn said, with as much anger as she could muster. "That's right," she said. "I know you don't go into your office on Sunday. Do you think I'm stupid? I know you have sex with your clients. You go meet your little floozies."

He didn't deny it. Kate Reynolds had also confirmed it. Dr. Blackburn had made a pass at her when he had her alone at his office. He didn't force himself on her, but Cliff got the impression he would've pursued it if she'd shown the least bit of interest.

A woman's scorn was on full display.

"It's okay for you to step out on me, but I can't have my own fun! No thank you mister. What's good for the goose is good for the gander."

Cliff stood up in case anything turned physical.

Mrs. Blackburn turned back around and crossed her arms and plopped down against the back of the couch. Her bottom lip was out so far, if it kept going, she'd need plastic surgery to fix it.

Dr. Blackburn walked away from the couch when he saw Cliff take an aggressive stance still holding the gun. He was no longer behind Julia and his wife and he took a seat in one of the side chairs. He slumped in it more than sat down.

Cliff holstered his gun and sat down. As much as this was compelling theater, he wanted to get to the good stuff. What happened to Cole Dillinger? He was anticipating a full confession.

"Tell us what happened," Julia said, in a gentle and nonjudgmental voice.

Please don't clam up now.

Then Cliff realized something.

"Before you say anything," Cliff said, "I have to tell you that you have the right to remain silent. Anything you say can and will be used against you in the court of law. Do you understand these rights that I've read to you Mrs. Blackburn?"

Better to cover all his bases up front.

She nodded her head that she understood.

"You probably should get an attorney," Dr. Blackburn said angrily. "You should know I'm not paying for it. You lying b—"

He caught himself for he spoke the disparaging word.

"I don't care about an attorney," she said angrily. "I want you to hear this. I loved Cole. We were soul mates. He pleased me in a way you never could."

"Then why did you kill him?" Dr. Blackburn asked.

That was a good question. Cliff was glad they were arguing. It saved him from having to ask. Mrs. Blackburn seemed willing to tell all just to hurt her husband regardless of the legal consequences. Cliff didn't care. He read her her rights. Anything she said would be used against her in the court of law. Even if she regretted it later.

"I should've killed you instead," she said. "I thought about it many times. I could've done it, you know? While you were sleeping. Then Cole and I could be together."

"How long were you fooling around on me?" Dr. Blackburn asked, keeping the rhetoric at a fever pitch.

Cliff was willing to let them spar back and forth. He was gleaning valuable information.

"Six months!" she said, with vitriol dripping out of both sides of her mouth. "Yeah. That's right. Cole and I have been lovers for a long time. I loved him and he loved me."

"You're so pathetic," Dr. Blackburn said. "I never should've married you."

"I loathe the day I met you!"

Cliff needed to step in. This wasn't moving the confession along.

"What happened the morning you shot Cole?" Cliff asked.

Mrs. Blackburn gave her husband one last glare.

"I saw Cole drive up that morning," she said, lowering the tone to a reasonable level. "He wasn't supposed to be home. You know. He had the game and all."

Large black lines were streaming down her face. She looked like a football player who wore black under his eyes to shield the sun.

"I saw Cole talking to Leon out in the street. I got dressed and went over there. Cole was looking for Kate. I don't know why. He was angry."

Mrs. Blackburn still held a tissue in her hands. She tried to wipe her face. It only smeared the black.

"Cole said Kate was cheating on him. With some guy named Justin. I tried to calm him down. He wouldn't listen to me. It's like I was invisible. It made me mad."

She took a deep breath.

Cliff realized he wasn't breathing normally either, so he took one himself.

Julia caught his eye and nodded as if to give him reassurance.

Mrs. Blackburn continued. Her tone was quieter, but the words had the same intensity.

"I pleaded with him. He wouldn't listen. I told him I'd leave my husband. That we could be together. That Kate wasn't good enough for him. I don't know what he ever saw in her. She was a skinny little you know what."

The tears returned.

"Take your time," Julia said.

Cliff didn't want her to take her time. He wanted her to get to the part where she shot Cole. A case was building against her. It'd be ironclad if she confessed to shooting him. She hadn't actually done so yet.

"Cole got angry at me. He started yelling. Then he got mean. He told me that he didn't love me. That he loved Kate, and that we'd never be together."

Cliff could see the pain in her eyes.

"I begged him. He pushed me away. I asked him why he would want to be with Kate if she was cheating on him. He said it didn't matter. We'd never be together. That made me angry, and I left."

Things didn't make sense to Cliff. Was Mrs. Blackburn the one who hit Cole over the head with the mallet? How did she get it out of Potter's garage? Was it their mallet? Did she plant it in Potter's garage?

"So Cole was alive when you left his house?" Julia asked.

"Yes."

Keep going.

She did. "I came back to my house. I knew that Leon had guns in the safe. I grabbed the first one I could find. That one."

She pointed at the one Cliff had in his hands. The one in the handkerchief.

"I went back to Cole's house. He was in his bed sleeping."

Mrs. Blackburn took a huge breath in then let it out in a slow sigh.

Cliff was waiting with bated breath.

"I shot him in the back."

He had it! The confession. Julia heard it. A third party who could confirm it in a court of law by affidavit.

Julia held Mrs. Blackburn's hands now. Clearly not thinking about courts and cases and jail. Her first response was compassion for this woman who was in tremendous pain. That's what he loved about his wife.

"What did you do next?" Julia asked, still barely above a whisper. Cliff wished she'd talk a little louder.

"I ran home and put the gun back in the safe. I thought when you came over that day, that you'd ask Leon if he had a gun, and you'd find it."

Dr. Blackburn glared at her.

Cliff's face probably showed his confusion. Who hit Cole over the head with the mallet?

She dropped the next bombshell.

246

"Harold Potter showed up in my backyard! He said he saw me leave Cole's house carrying a gun. He said he'd tell the police if I didn't pay him money."

That sounded like something Harold Potter would do. It occurred to Cliff that none of this would've happened if Potter hadn't sent Cole that text.

"He was blackmailing me. He wanted a million dollars to keep his mouth shut. Otherwise, he'd go to the police. I told him that the police were going to find the gun. He told me to get rid of it. I couldn't. Leon would notice it was gone and then he'd know I killed Cole. And they would arrest me."

Cliff wanted to interrupt and ask a question, but figured it'd be better to let her keep spilling her guts.

"Potter said he could help me. It was his idea to make it look like Leon killed Cole. He said he'd make up a story about Cole and Leon arguing on the street. He'd delete the video camera footage so no one would be able to see Leon leaving. He was so sure he could fix everything."

It suddenly made sense. Potter lured Cole back with the fake text. He hit Cole over the head with the mallet and then moved him inside and onto the bed. Potter didn't want to kill Cole, just incapacitate him so he couldn't play in the game. He left the house and made the bet. He thought he had all his bases covered. He hadn't counted on Mrs. Blackburn coming to the house and shooting Cole.

When he saw her leave the house carrying a gun, he saw a chance to blackmail her and turn the attention away from him. He followed her to her house and confronted her.

"Is that why you killed Harold Potter?" Julia asked.

Julia was so brilliant at putting the pieces together.

Mrs. Blackburn nodded.

Cliff just solved two murders without hardly saying a word thanks to Julia.

"I didn't know how to get Potter a million dollars. I sure didn't have it. I could take it from one of Leon's accounts, but he'd find it.

I told Potter I'd get it anyway. I kept putting him off. He threatened me. He said he was going to turn me in. So I took the gun and shot him. When the police found the gun, they'd think Leon killed both of them."

That was what Cliff thought at first. Cliff still had questions about the gun. The connection to the mob murders.

"This gun isn't registered," Cliff said to Dr. Blackburn. "Where did you get it?"

Dr. Blackburn's shoulders sagged.

"I suppose I really shouldn't answer that. I know I was breaking the law by not registering it."

The doctor had a defeated look on his face. Was he involved in something more sinister?

He looked like his spirit had been crushed. As if he'd been hit by an SUV speeding down the freeway going the wrong way.

"I did some work for a woman," he explained. "Her husband paid me in cash. He was very appreciative of my work. The gun was in the bag of cash. I asked him about it. He said it was a gift."

Another piece of the puzzle fell into place. Cliff had heard of that. The mob getting rid of murder weapons by giving them to ordinary citizens. So they couldn't be traced back to them.

"I figured the gun was dirty," Dr. Blackburn conceded. "The man was shady. He looked like he was right out of the *Godfather* movie. I brought the gun home and put it in my safe and haven't touched it since."

That explained the subsonic rounds. They were probably already in the gun. Cliff guessed that if he looked at it, he'd find two rounds missing.

Cliff had heard enough. He stood to his feet.

"Mrs. Blackburn," Cliff said, "You're under arrest for the murders of Cole Dillinger and Harold Potter."

She nodded like she expected it.

"I'm sorry," she said. She probably meant it.

Cliff pulled out a pair of handcuffs. "Please stand to your feet," he said to her.

She did without hesitation.

He cuffed her hands in front of her. Julia consoled her by rubbing her hand on her shoulder.

Cliff wasn't sure yet what he was going to do with Dr. Blackburn. He could arrest him for having an unregistered firearm. Also, for lying about going to his office. At this point, he didn't see the point in hauling him out of there in handcuffs. It didn't seem worth ruining a man's career and reputation over the minor charges that he could plead down to misdemeanors with a good attorney.

The Lieutenant could make that call.

Cliff called the Lieutenant to give him the news. He was coming right over. The place would be swarming with activity within minutes.

Cliff also made a phone call to Starr Olson. The reporter who'd tipped him off that Potter was trying to sell a salacious story to the media. That tip led him to Potter. In a roundabout way, it also led him to Mrs. Blackburn. He might not have known about her affair with Cole if Starr hadn't told him about Potter.

He made her a promise. To give her a heads up when he was about to make an arrest.

She answered on the first ring.

Cliff stepped outside, but still in view of what was happening inside.

"Starr, this is Cliff Ford."

"I know who it is. You're on my caller ID. Even in my favorites list. Although, I'm thinking about dropping you. You were supposed to give me some information on Cole Dillinger's murder. I'm waiting."

"The wait is over. That's why I'm calling. I'm making an arrest today."

"Who is it?"

"I can't tell you that. But I can tell you to be at the station in about twenty minutes for the perp walk. You'll be able to put two and two together. You also might want to send someone out to Cole's subdivision. You'll be the first one there."

"Which house?"

"Look for all the police cars. Hurry though. I'm sure the word will get out soon."

"Thank you. You're the best."

"Thanks for the tip. It really helped."

Cliff did hope to get Mrs. Blackburn out of there before the press arrived. No one had likely tipped them off yet, but word would get out fast. The press followed the police scanners.

The Lieutenant was the first to arrive. Cliff explained everything to him. Police cruisers arrived shortly thereafter.

Cliff led Mrs. Blackburn out of the house and put her in the back of his car. The replacement vehicle for the one destroyed in the riots. Julia got in the passenger side. Nothing was said on the drive to the station. Cliff heard light sobbing coming from the back.

Starr Olson was outside the station when they arrived. Cliff caught her eye. She winked at him. Their little secret.

Good for her. She got her scoop.

He took Mrs. Blackburn to booking. The Lieutenant and Ron said they'd handle everything at the scene.

When he was done, Cliff and Julia went home.

Cliff made a phone call to the Lieutenant.

"Can I take you up on that extended leave?" Cliff asked.

"You can. You deserve it."

"One month."

"How about two weeks."

"What happened to *indefinite* leave?"

"That is indefinite. I said about two weeks. Take fifteen days if you like."

"I'll see you in three weeks."

Cliff hung up the phone and went to his computer. Julia went to the bedroom to change. She came into his office a few minutes later in much more comfortable attire and without the patch.

"What are you doing honey?" she asked.

"I just booked us two round trip airline tickets."

"To where?"

"To Jamaica. Our plane leaves in the morning. We're going for ten days."

"Why Jamaica?" she asked.

"It's the only place I could think of where you could wear your patch and fit in."

25

Union Rescue Mission
Six months later

Cliff confirmed that Angus was indeed a real person and not an angel.

He and Julia spent a lot of time with him over the past few months. Julia and Angus hit it off right away. Cliff told her how Angus had saved their lives.

The mission fed lunch to the homeless every Saturday. Cliff and Julia volunteered for the serving line every chance they got. Even attended services occasionally. Angus was a passionate and fiery preacher. Cliff enjoyed listening to him.

They were in front of the mission now where a table was set up. Cliff scooped out ladles of piping hot stew to the steady stream of people and Julia handed out pieces of bread.

The spot where they stood was less than thirty feet from where Julia was attacked that fateful night. Several hundred feet from where Cliff's unmarked car was overturned and burned and where he suffered most of his injuries.

Julia still didn't remember any of it. Like the doctor said, Cliff wished he didn't either.

Cliff never mentioned the loss of the baby to Julia. He thought about telling her a thousand times. None of them seemed like the right time. When she was happy, he didn't want to spoil things. If she was having a hard day, he didn't want to make it worse.

Eventually, he made peace with it. She was better off not knowing.

Cliff heard Angus's booming voice somewhere off in the distance. The giant of a man was everywhere. Talking to the homeless. Making sure the food didn't run out. Inviting people to church. Witnessing to anyone who'd listen.

As the line began to thin, Angus came up and stood next to Julia. He wrapped his big arm around her and asked, "When are you going to leave this joker for me?"

"Women live six years longer than men," Julia replied. "Angus, you'll be my first choice when Cliff kicks the bucket."

"I'm standing right here," Cliff said. "I can hear every word you say."

"So," Angus replied. "This conversation doesn't concern you."

"It's about me! About my death. Which apparently, the two of you are looking forward to."

"I'm not looking forward to it," Angus said. "It's just good to plan for my retirement years."

Cliff rolled his eyes at him. Julia kept her head down to hide the smirk on her face.

"I'm not getting my hopes up," Angus said with his patented smile. "You'll probably outlive me."

He gave Julia another hug and a kiss on the forehead.

"Don't make me come over there, Angus," Cliff said.

Angus let out a deep laugh. "That I'd like to see," he said. "You'd better bring a small army with you."

"I'm not sure a small army would be enough."

Angus put his hands on Cliff's shoulders and said, "Thanks for the help today, buddy."

"You're welcome."

Then he was off doing his thing again.

"What do you want to do now?" Cliff asked Julia.

"Let's help clean up. Then I want to go to a furniture store. I'd like to pick up something."

"That sounds good."

They helped put the food away and Cliff took down the table. They found Angus and said their goodbyes.

"Where to?" Cliff asked once they were in the car and leaving the downtown area.

"*Everything Home,*" Julia said.

The place was a giant warehouse. They'd gotten furniture there before. It took twenty minutes to get there.

"What in particular are you looking for?" Cliff asked, after they parked and entered the building.

Julia ignored him and walked with a purpose toward the far back right of the store. She stopped when she got to the area with baby furniture.

Cliff's heart almost jumped out of his chest.

"We need to pick out a crib for the baby," she said, with a glowing smile on her face.

"Does this mean what I think it means?" he asked excitedly.

"Yes. I'm pregnant!"

Julia squealed like a baby. Cliff was squealing on the inside.

He picked her up and twirled her around. Then set her back down. Gingerly.

"I probably shouldn't do that. I don't want to hurt the baby," he said.

She slapped him on the shoulder.

"You can't hurt the baby. God made it so the baby is well pro-tected in my womb."

For some reason, that whole exchange sounded familiar.

Before he could say something, Julia planted a huge kiss right on his lips. Oblivious to all the other customers in the area.

"How did you get pregnant?" Cliff asked.

Julia twisted her lips to the side.

"I thought you knew how babies were made," she quipped.

"I mean. When? When did you get pregnant?"

"Probably when we went on that weekend getaway to Wisconsin. Six weeks ago."

Cliff had a sudden case of déjà vu.

They did have this exact conversation before.

Not The End

Thank you for purchasing this novel from best-selling author, Terry Toler. As an additional thank you, Terry wants to give you a free gift.

Sign up for:
Updates
New Releases
Announcements
At terrytoler.com

We'll send you *The Book Club*, free of charge. A fun Cliff Ford Mystery adventure.

READ MORE BOOKS FROM TERRY TOLER

Jamie Austen Thrillers

Read all the Jamie Austen Thrillers. They must be good.
They've been number one on Amazon in ten different countries.
Click on the link below.

THE JAMIE AUSTEN THRILLERS (12 book series)
Kindle Edition (amazon.com)

https://amzn.to/3vmPUy7

Cliff Hangers Mystery Series

Who wants to read a good mystery? We've got you covered! Read the Cliff Hangers where homicide detective, Cliff Ford, solves crimes in Chicago, with help from his wife Julia. These books have everything Terry Toler is known for. Page turning suspense, a hint of romance, and an ending you won't see coming.

The Cliff Hangers Mystery Series (4 book series)
Kindle Edition (amazon.com)

https://amzn.to/36WX3go

About Terry

Terry Toler is an Amazon international # 1 best-selling and award-winning author. He writes clean fiction with a message and life-changing nonfiction. He's a public speaker, entrepreneur, and has authored more than forty books.

Sign up for his newsletter where you'll get free stuff, exclusive content, and news of releases and promotions. He can be followed at terrytoler.com.

If you like his books, please take a few minutes to leave a review on Amazon. We really appreciate it. It helps draw more readers to his books. Thanks!

www.ingramcontent.com/pod-product-compliance
Lightning Source LLC
Chambersburg PA
CBHW050404260626
47156CB00003B/867